THE END
OF THIS DAY'S
BUSINESS

THE END
OF THIS DAY'S
BUSINESS

KATHARINE BURDEKIN

AFTERWORD BY DAPHNE PATAI

THE FEMINIST PRESS
at The City University of New York
New York

Published 1989 by The Feminist Press at The City University of New York, 311 East 94 Street, New York, N.Y. 10128

Distributed by The Talman Company, 150 Fifth Avenue, New York, N.Y. 10011

93 92 91 90 89 6 5 4 3 2 1

Library of Congress Cataloging-in-Publication Data

Burdekin, Katharine, 1896–1963.
  The end of this day's business / Katharine Burdekin ; afterword by
Daphne Patai.
    p.   cm.
  ISBN 1-55861-016-2 : $24.95. — ISBN 1-55861-009-X (pbk.) : $8.95
  I. Title.
PR6003.U45E5   1989
823'.912—dc20
                                                            89-34897
                                                            CIP

Cover design by Gilda Hannah
Text design by Paula Martinac

Printed in the United States of America on acid-free paper by
McNaughton & Gunn, Inc.

This publication is made possible, in part, by public funds from the
New York State Council on the Arts.

THE END
OF THIS DAY'S
BUSINESS

I

ON MAY DAY IN THE YEAR 6250, Old Style, a man called Neil, sometimes Big Neil, or, to distinguish him from other Neils, Neil Carlason, was splitting up logs for winter firewood in a little front yard or garden just outside the town of Salisbury. The house behind him was that which he shared with four other men, but none of them were there this very sparkling, white and blue and green May morning. They were not working, as it was a holiday. They had gone off to Salisbury to swim in the Men's Pool, or play a game, or just lounge about and talk to other men, to have in the evening a drink of wine or beer, perhaps to help light the big bonfires that were ready on the playing field, to dance about, sing, shout and fight. Neil thought he might perhaps go to Salisbury in the evening when it began to get dark, but even of that he was not sure. No May Day, the day the men celebrated as the beginning of summer with childish merriment and often extremes of masculine violence, had ever before found Neil so queer, so dull, so unhappy. Perhaps he had been hoping at odd times in this last year, when his incomprehensible vague discontent had occupied the top of his mind, that next May Day would set him up, cure him forever of his strange glooms. He had hoped that he would feel, as usual, thrilled and excited at the thought of the evening with the leaping flames of

1

the bonfires, and all the singing and shouting and improvised wrestling matches, and jumping valiantly right through the flames as the younger men did (and nobody was braver at that than Neil, or minded the risk of burned feet less) and perhaps getting into a real serious bloody fight. And always there was the chance of a new and temporarily very delightful love affair, for though the women took, of course, no part at all in the May Day celebrations, regarding it with Olympian superiority as an unimportant, noisy, violent and purely male affair, yet some of them who wanted perhaps to look at the many handsome men and boys who gathered there, or perhaps to cast their eyes over some particular man, did come to the edge of the playing field and stroll about, talking to each other in low voices, or laughing now and then, their quiet assured movements and soft voices contrasting naturally and deliciously with the wild movement and deep roaring voices of the throngs of men.

But even this thought of the women did not lighten Neil's heavy heart, nor make him feel any less strange and dull. He was a successful man in love. From the age of sixteen, when, counted as a man, he had gone to work, and to live in a house with men, he had only received one rebuff. At first shyly, then more boldly, he had pressed his claims to women's attention, which had been nearly always well received. Neither was it always they who tired of him first. Success made him fickle; several times he had, with less and less nervousness each time, indicated to a woman that he was now in love with someone else. The first time, being very inexperienced, he had been rather frightened, though older men had told him that it didn't matter, that women did not mind, or take it in any way amiss that a man should be tired of one and take on another. So Neil became quite used to the way his lovers took these changes. First came a rather intent look, then a small smile and a shrug of slim delicate little shoulders, the very shoulders which Neil had found so super-feminine and adorable a short while before. But what lay behind the intent look, Neil never knew. No man knew what women thought. They talked to each other, never to men or boys. But now, since last night, or was it for a year, or was it, thought Neil, flogging his poor, dull, weak brain which had never really learned to think, was it really since he had been about nineteen, that his phenomenal sexual success (and that it was phenomenal he knew from the continual jealousy of other men) had ceased to be that pride and joy he had felt it as a youth? He had enjoyed it always; he thought he would not ever be able to help enjoying it, as he had enjoyed the gradual development of his physique, magnificent among a race of tall, strong men, as he had enjoyed the violent games, the wrestling, the feats of strength, and the single-stick combats when one could chip a man's head and see the blood run down, or the straightforward savage fist battles when one could, *if* one could, crack a man's skull with one terrific ponderous blow. Neil had done that. Afterwards he was both sorry and elated. He was a marked man, dangerous, a little too strong. But no one, for that reason, refused to fight him if insults had passed. Such conduct would be unmanly in the extreme, and a man might as well be dead as a coward.

Neil picked up his largest wedge, settled it in the top of the short log he wanted to split with a couple of heavy short-armed taps, then heaved up his huge hammer and brought it down with all his force. The log rent with a loud noise and fell apart. Neil had driven the sharp wedge clean through it. But his prowess only seemed to increase his discontent. He tossed the hammer aside with a sulky frown, and sitting down on an unsplit log he tried by pressing his palms on his forehead to think harder and to more purpose.

What really was the matter with him? He had gone out last night, May Eve, and up on to the old lumps and humps and banks of an ancient place, the ruin of an old, old town, far older than the oldest part of Salisbury, that had been called, so his mother's sister had told him, when as a very small boy he had first rolled down its green banks, Old Sarum. The day remained in his mind. He had been very happy. And some association of happiness and the queer old place remained always with him, so that last night when, amazingly, he couldn't sleep at all, he had got up and dressed and gone up in the moonlight to Old Sarum, and there he had thrown himself face downwards on the short sweet down-grass, and had astonishingly wept. He had cried his heart out, and when he came to think of the reason, he could find none. He had not cried since he was a boy, and then his tears, as he remembered them, had been nearly always tears of rage, except on those very rare occasions when his Mother, whom he in common with all males adored in a half-terrified way, had been seriously annoyed with him. Ah, he could remember crying *then,* as if the sun had gone and the earth was dark forever. But the joy, when she had forgiven him, and was tender, and the sun shone again, that seemed to make up for those bitter childish lamentations. This shadow, since he could not discover what caused it, seemed as if it never might lift. For he was not ill. People hardly ever were ill, and then as a rule only as the result of an accident. He was not old. Sometimes he had thought it would be rather terrible to be old, and weak, and stiff. Unable to rival men in sports, or beat them in fights, or attract women. For of course women didn't care about old, worn-out men, naturally. But Neil was only twenty-four. Last night he had been twenty-three, and this May Day morning he was twenty-four. He had at least thirty more years of the fullest vigor. And even after that his decline would be very gradual, and it would be another twenty before he was like old Andreas, who was past work and didn't care any longer for May Day bonfires, and spent all his time sleeping or pottering about in his little garden, or talking, or at any rate listening, to Neil's eccentric but famous aunt, the same who had first taken him up to Old Sarum.

Then he liked his work. It was all out of doors and laborious, something that used his strength. As a boy, when he had been confronted with the variety of jobs open to men, unskilled or semi-skilled, for of course a man had to do what his strong muscles and weak mind and masculine nature fitted him for, he had rejected the indoors factory jobs as stuffy, working on ships or in docks because he didn't want to leave Salisbury and rarely be able to see his Mother, tree-felling in the forests for the same reason, as he would have to go away to Savernake or somewhere, and had decided to be a laborer in the big gardens where the vegetable stuff and fruit were grown. The women who ran the gardens were silent and just, they admired his strength and willingness to use it; he was indeed rather a pet among the under-gardeners.

Then his Mother was still alive, and was not very often away, like his eccentric aunt, Grania, who was an artist and might be anywhere in the world at any moment. His mother was an engineer in the Salisbury power station, and so she couldn't go away so much. And she was always the same, tender to him, and delighted when he won prizes in the sports. Neil felt her to be proud of her son, proud of his manly vigor and beauty, and his popularity.

So there was nothing in his present life to account for his discontent, and when he looked back at his childhood it seemed exactly like any other boy's, and just as happy. To the age of eight he had lived with his Mother, playing with other very small boys in the Nursery while she was at work. At eight, as boys did, he had gone to a day-school. Carla, his sister, two years older, had already been two years at her girls' boarding school, and when she came back from her first term she was rather haughty and wouldn't play with him, much. But he didn't mind. There were plenty of boys in the Nursery. And plenty of boys at the day-school. Then at fourteen, as boys had to, he left his Mother and lived with other fourteen to sixteen year olds in a boarding school, where he must learn to live a man's life. For he would never live with women again. Men never lived with women, only boys and very young girls. The women lived in their houses, perhaps two or three together, or one alone by herself if she had young children, and the men lived in groups of five or six. Some old men lived by themselves. Andreas did. But the young men, never. They would feel cold and lonely by themselves, miss the quarrelling and the violent fun, both. Then he had become a man (but with no sort of ceremony or initiation, such as the girls went through at seventeen, in the utterly mysterious and forbidden hearts of the Women's Houses), and had begun to work, and to live with men, and to make love to women. Not ever to girls, because that was not allowed. If a young woman had a little narrow metal circlet keeping her long hair off her face then she *was* a woman, through her initiation. But if she had none she was a girl, sacred and quite out of reach. It was hardly possible to be attracted to girls, so cold and forbidding an atmosphere surrounded them. But women were different. They were not always cold, though they were always reserved. Women were in some ways less frightening than the girls, but in some ways more so. More assured, quieter, more proud and certain of themselves. But nicer, anyway, thought Neil. Women, Grania, and all the ones I have loved have been nicer to me than Carla ever was as a girl. He hardly thought of his Mother as a woman. Not in this connection. She was just his Mother.

Thus he wandered through his life and saw it as a very ordinary, happy boy's and man's life, indeed hardly to be improved upon unless he had been a famous athlete or dancer. They were the favored among men, while they kept their youth and suppleness. But they were worse off than ordinary men when they grew old, because they had been so admired and applauded, and they missed it, and sometimes fell into deep miseries, and even had been known to kill themselves. There was another thought for Neil. He pressed his hands still harder on his forehead. It was not only old athletes or old dancers who killed themselves. There had been men, not that he knew any, but he had heard of them, who were weak, for some reason, puny, ugly, unattractive, and could neither hold up their end with men, nor have any women to love them, who gradually sank deeper and deeper into despondency, and so to suicide. And men crippled in accidents were of course allowed to kill themselves by custom and convention, and everything was made easy for them. But what had cripples, weak men, or old athletes to do with Neil? He had a *man's life* and would have it for many many years yet. Or, he thought, with a horrible start of fear and woe, he would *not* have it. For what could be the end of such fits of dreadful, miserable weeping as he had experienced last night in the moonlight on Old Sarum, and his gloom of today, which was even worse because he felt no inclination to express it, but, in the end, suicide? If he had stopped enjoying a man's life, what other life was there for him? Would death be better? But he could not think of death. It meant leaving so much, things he really did enjoy, must enjoy. Or, he thought, terribly bewildered now, have I never really enjoyed *any* of it? Even women? Even those marvelous moments of power and *rightness* when a man fulfilled his purpose, and became, for a brief time, a sweet time, one with, equal to a woman? If he could not, if his gloom finally robbed him of that enjoyment, then he was lost. For of course there must be women, and there must be men, God had willed it, and that they should be quite different, and lead entirely different lives, because the women were the Mothers, and in all but physical strength, naturally superior. There was nothing to worry about in that. A dog might as well worry because it was not a cat, as a man that he was not a woman.

But, Neil thought, how can I bear any more wakings up like this morning? He had come home from Old Sarum sleepy and somehow peaceful after his outburst, and had undressed and gone to bed, sure that now all would be well. All had not been well. He had waked to a wretchedness unparalleled in his experience except for the homesickness of the first few days in his boarding school, after he had left his Mother. Yes, it had been even worse than that. And when Magnus and the others asked him what he meant to do with the early part of his May Day, he had said in fierce sullenness that he meant to split logs and told them to go away and leave him alone. Now he was alone, and no better.

He began to notice himself, a thing he was not accustomed to do. He took his hands away from his forehead, and looked at his hairy, muscular right arm. It was a useful member. It had done much work. It had killed a man. It had embraced women. It was handsome, in a male way. But quite suddenly he felt as if he didn't really like it, nor his pillars of legs, in the baggy modest breeches men wore, nor his great hands with their blunt-ended fingers. He revolted against his own flesh, and the sensation was terrible. Shyly, with a glance round first, for men were naturally modest, and would not bare more than their arms, legs and heads in a public place, he opened his shirt and glanced at his muscular male chest. He hated it. But if he hated his body, then he hated himself, for it was part of himself. Neil hated Neil. If anyone else hated Neil, Neil would beat him, that is, if he showed his hatred insultingly, but if Neil hated Neil, what could be done? And what *was* Neil, that he had suddenly begun to hate himself? This could not be grasped. He began again drearily to consider what would become of him, and from that he switched back to what *had* become of him. Was it possible, he wondered, for a man to be unhappy somewhere very deep inside, and for it suddenly to come up to the top? That must be nonsense, surely. A man thought things, and did things; the deeds followed from thoughts and the thoughts from other thoughts, quite plain in the head. Could there be any *other* think-place—in the stomach, perhaps? On Old Sarum, last night, his waves of grief had seemed to start in his stomach and roll up to his mouth and eyes, to come out in great sobs and groans and pouring tears. But perhaps there were more waves behind those waves, started in his stomach, long years ago. But that must be nonsense. A man thought things, and did things. But then again, behind his going up to Old Sarum there had been no plain thought. Behind his sullenness with the other men this morning there had been no plain thought. There evidently were times when a man did things without knowing why.

He passed his hand over his dark close-cropped hair, and then stroked his short black beard. He began to wonder what it would be like to have long hair like a woman. It would be a terrible nuisance in fights and wrestling. But at ordinary times would it feel nice, or only tickly and uncomfortable? Of course he could remember what it felt like to have no beard. And he could remember his joy when it first began to come through, because all men had beards, and if his beard was coming he would soon be a man, and live with men, not boys. Some men had very weak, scanty beards, sources of mockery. Neil's was strong and close. But as he stroked it he liked it no better than his arms and legs and chest. It was part of Neil, that Neil hated. He began again to think of women's long hair. Girls plaited it sometimes, or tied it back, but women never did, unless their work demanded it. They twisted the side pieces, the locks that might fall over their faces, in and out of their circlets, and left all the rest loose. Fair or red or dark, or gray or quite white—the long loose hair of women, flowing over their shoulders, sometimes down below their waists. Perhaps that was one reason why women all had that peculiarly proud, almost tipped-back carriage of the head and shoulders, because the hair, the heavy hair, pulled the head back. If I had long hair, thought Neil, should I have that proud look to my head? Or would the little weight of my beard pull my head forward again, so that I should still carry my head like a man? He didn't know what he was thinking, really. His thoughts swirled about in a muddy whirlpool. He felt something was there, important, he did not know what. Hair, beards, women, Neil—*something*.

A woman's voice cut his meditation cleanly like a sharp cold knife. He looked around. There she was, at the gate of the little garden, looking at him, smiling. Not one of Neil's former lovers. A woman who had not been very long in the town. She knew Neil's sister, Carla. Neil hastily, with fumbling fingers, fastened up the breast of his shirt. He rose and went to the gate. He was wondering whether this woman, her name was Bernadine, would be attracted to him. He wondered that about every young woman who ever spoke to him. He couldn't help it. So many of them were. But now, as this woman, this Bernadine, looked up at him with the frankest appraisement and, he was sure, admiration, he felt both miserable and shy. He used to like to meet that appraising, admiring look. It was natural, and a compliment to him personally. But suddenly he thought of people looking over animals, to see if they were worth buying. And besides that, if he hated Neil, and he *did*, he didn't like anyone to look at Neil like that. Not at his great chest and shoulders and his stalwart arms and legs, no, not even at his dark hair and beard, not even at his very blue eyes. He found it shameful. He hung his head, looked at his feet, and muttered something about its being a nice May Day.

Bernadine, a small woman, very fair, with large gray eyes, looked at him with very faint surprise.

"Aren't you going to Salisbury, Big Neil?"

"I don't know," Neil murmured almost inaudibly.

"But you will this evening? To jump through the bonfires and make a jolly noise with the others?"

But Neil said again, though her voice was kind, warm, and inviting: "I don't know."

"What's the matter, Neil?" she asked him, after a pause.

Women were not emotional except in a purely physical sense; they very rarely expressed surprise or grief or anxiety in their tones of voice or the look on their faces. But Neil did hear a faint tremor of solicitude, of anxiety. Or he thought he did. He looked at Bernadine, and as if he were seeing a woman for the very first time he took in every detail of her dress and appearance. Her circlet, and the fair hair flowing through it, under and over, out and over her shoulders. The soft white shirt she was wearing, which left the hollow of her neck bare, and her short, tight-fitting summer jacket, and her dark trousers, fitting tight to her delicate, slim little figure (so different from the loose breeches which enclosed Neil's mighty frame), and her bare ankles and her soft shoes of embroidered leather. From head to foot she was feminine, attractive, what Neil expected a woman to be. But he seemed bewildered. And so he said again, in a low voice, unhappily: "I don't know, Bernadine."

She shrugged her shoulders, that controlled gesture Neil had seen many times before, meaning that it didn't matter much what a man said or thought or even what he did. She said: "Well, perhaps you *will* go to Salisbury this evening, after all." She waved her hand to him carelessly, and went on down the road. Neil looked after her. He wondered whether he would go. Delights rose up in his mind, but their poignancy, their fever, was still cooled, dulled by his trouble. If he did go, if he did meet Bernadine—what then? What *after that?* All the same he thought he would go to Salisbury. But not till the evening. And meanwhile—somehow he found his mind had been made up for him during the conversation with the woman—he would go off and spend the day with old Andreas. Work in his garden, or just sit about and talk, and sleep. He needed some extra sleep.

He put away his log-splitting tools, and was soon off, walking at a tremendous pace over a short cut to the Devizes Road. Andreas lived on this road, about three miles out of Salisbury. Neil wondered, as he went, whether his aunt, Grania, might be there. She was in Salisbury, he knew, for he had met her in the street outside the Women's House no longer ago than last night. Before that she had been away for some time. In Russia. Neil thought, she will be there. She always goes to see Andreas when she comes back. With perceptions quickened by his trouble, a sort of astonishing enlightening of the mind, he realized he was going to see Andreas more because he hoped that Grania would be there, than because he really wanted Andreas. Not that he didn't like the old man. He did. He found something peculiarly peaceful and refreshing about his company. I like him better, thought Neil, with another enlightening of his mind, than any other man. In fact he's the *only* man I do *always* like.

But having discovered this, he left off thinking about Andreas. Grania, his mother's sister, was, Neil had decided when he was old enough to judge such things, the ugliest, most unattractive woman probably in the world. To begin with, she was far too big for a woman. She was as large as quite a lot of men. She was muscular and heavily-built. Her hands were like a laborer's, great square-ended things. Her face was perhaps handsome, but not womanly. Only her eyes, thought Neil, are very beautiful. A lovely blue. (They were exactly the same color as his own, but he thought them darker. They looked darker, for not being set above a forest of black facial hair.) But this extreme ugliness and unfemininity of his famous artist-aunt did not worry Neil at all. She had always been sweet to him. He remembered her putting him to bed, bringing him little presents, taking him out for walks, playing such games as women did play with very little boys, telling him stories, doing everything a mother's sister could do—that is, when she was there. Often, for long periods, she was not there. But how he had loved to see her again! How he had leaped, screamed and shouted. And he remembered how once when Carla had been taunting him with her girlish superiority, and making him feel, momentarily, of course, that to be a boy was indeed a punishment, an unlucky fate, instead of just a natural happening, how Grania, who was sitting in the Nursery staring into the wood-fire behind the safety bars, had suddenly turned round and with the most biting sarcasm, a severe mental flogging, had reduced even the proud young Carla to tears. "Why!" thought Neil, striding ever quicker and quicker along the Devizes Road, "I *like* Grania better than Mother! I do. I always have. I love Mother, of course, but I *like Grania better.*"

This was such an astonishing thought, that one could like any woman better than one's Mother, that Neil stopped dead in his pace to consider it. Loving and liking, liking and loving. One loves one's Mother. One loves women differently. One *likes* Andreas and Grania. But no one else. No, really, not all the time. One can always quarrel with any of the other men, over women or something. But not with Andreas. And of course one can't quarrel with women, but one can, easily, get to want not to see certain ones any more. To avoid them. But not Grania, of course.

He went on again, quickly, to get to Andreas' cottage, and see at any rate one of the people he liked. He did not find it at all sad or extraordinary that out of all the men and women he knew it was only possible to like two. He felt it, on the contrary, as a great and elating discovery that he did like two, in a permanent unshakable way. His unhappiness seemed to stand away from him. He went on almost gaily, humming a little tune, swinging his stick.

When he got to the cottage he felt happier than ever, for there were both Andreas and Grania in a corner of the garden, arguing about some plant or other Andreas was holding in his old veined hand. Neil walked softly up behind them. That they should be arguing pleased him. Andreas was the sole man of his acquaintance who would dare to argue with a woman about anything, and probably he only dared because Grania, the eccentric, liked talking to a man with whom she obviously could not be still in love, and presumably liked him to argue as well as talk. Neil listened. The subject of controversy was the plant, of which neither of them could remember the name: Grania said it needed sun, Andreas said it needed shade and coolness. As Neil eavesdropped he thought how extraordinary it was that he should have, as the two people he liked, a woman who would argue with a man, and a man who would argue with a woman.

Grania said: "Well, you obstinate old man, put it in that shady place and ruin it. It's not my plant."

Andreas weakened a little.

"If you're really *sure,* Grania, that it is what *you* think it is, and not what *I* think it is, perhaps—"

"I am sure, I know it wants sun."

Andreas consolidated again.

"No," he said, "I shall put it in the shady part. We shall see who's right."

Neil followed, happily. Grania swung round, and Andreas, who was kneeling, looked up startled.

"Why, Neil!" said Grania, looking pleased. "I didn't expect to see you here today."

She kissed him on both cheeks. Neil had a feeling of homecoming, as if he had had a long walk over the downs in the snow on a dark winter's day and had come back to a fire and a chair and a lighted room. "I shall tell *her,*" he thought, "and she will tell me what it is, and when I know what it is it will go away and I shan't ever have it any more."

But he was not going to say anything in front of Andreas. He looked at Grania, therefore, in silence, and with something of the concentrated interest he had brought to bear on Bernadine. She was dressed more or less the same, of course, but with what a difference! Her trousers were covered with paint-stains, clay-stains, every kind of stain. Her long, ugly, lumpy, masculine thighs would have been better, Neil thought, with an inner blush for his immodesty in even thinking of a woman dressed as a man—but *really better,* he still thought, in men's loose breeches. And her shoulders too would have fitted a man's coat better than that old orange woman's jacket—but then he came to her face and stopped criticizing. He knew, suddenly—everything today came to him in sudden flashes like lightning—why she was so *likeable.* It was because her face expressed so much more than other women's. She was controlled, of course. All women were. He had never seen her lose her temper, or laugh when she didn't mean to laugh, or heard her say anything she didn't mean to say. But her face, large and too coarse-featured for womanliness, had not that cold, remote, secret look of other and far more beautiful faces he had seen. She was reserved; Neil knew nothing of what she really thought, any more than he knew what his Mother and his sister really thought, but she did not *look* reserved. Her face and her eyes were always changing in small, subtle ways. He became aware that she was laughing at him.

"Well, man, you do stare! Do you think going to Russia and being half-frozen all winter has improved me?"

"Nothing could improve you," said Neil solemnly, without the smallest intention of offense.

Grania took none. "That is a fact," she said.

"But why, Neil, are you here, instead of junketing in Salisbury with your friends? You didn't come just to see your famous ill-favored aunt, did you?"

"I believe I did," said Neil. "At first I thought I was coming just to see Andreas," he awarded him an affectionate but very slightly contemptuous sideways nod, "but then I really think I hoped you would be here too. And you are."

"But," Grania persisted, looking at him more gravely, "what do you want coming out here today for? Don't you generally swim or have sports and games in Salisbury on May Day morning and afternoon?"

"I always have up to today. The other men went, and I stayed behind to split logs. Then I got tired of splitting logs and thinking—"

"What?" said Grania.

Andreas, still on his knees, said: "That man's always thinking. He thinks quite a lot. One of these days he'll think too much."

"Well, *you* won't die of that, old Andreas," Grania said. "Plant your wizened little whatever-it-is in the shade and later we'll see it die by inches. Neil, come and sit with me on the veranda."

They went on to the veranda, and when they were seated Grania said at once: "Now what's the matter, Neil?"

But now Neil found it hard to tell. He hesitated, coughed and got red. At last he began: "Do you remember the first day you ever took me to Old Sarum?"

"I don't think I do. I've taken you there lots of times. You used to like rolling down the banks so much."

"Well, I don't care about rolling down the banks now, of course, but you—or something—or perhaps you, made me like the place very much. I like it better than any other place. So last night when I couldn't sleep I went out there and stayed there a long time. It was moonlight. The grass was dark-looking and the bare chalk patches very pale. White, nearly."

"Well, and what did you do?"

"I had the most terrible crying fit," said Neil, and his voice sounded less ashamed than bewildered.

"Oh," said Grania. Her voice really expressed nothing at all. "And what did you do then?"

"I felt better, and I went home to bed and slept very well, and woke up in the morning thinking I'd be all right, I mean I *had* thought when I went to sleep I should be all right, but I *wasn't*. I felt just as unhappy or more so, only I didn't want to cry. What I want to know is, can a person be miserable *inside* for a long time and not know it, and it all come bursting up?"

"Yes," said Grania.

"Or," Neil went on slowly, "can a man be miserable for a long time, or a little time, *without* any reason?"

"No."

"But I can't *find* any reason. There isn't one. Everything is perfectly all right. And yet, Grania, I feel that if this was to *go on*, for a great number of years, I should—shouldn't be able to bear it. *You know.* Men do kill themselves sometimes."

Grania moved slightly in her chair.

"We won't let it get to that, Neil."

"Can you tell me what it is?" asked Neil, casting himself gratefully on the wisdom and power of all women, as personified by his Mother's sister.

"Tell me what you think about when you're not crying but just feeling miserable."

"I—I hardly know. It seems to be—this sounds absurd, I know—but I seem to hate myself, my arms and legs and even my beard, and I have no pleasure in thinking of the things I can do with myself, wrestling, or winning carry-the-sack, or fighting, or making love, nothing I can do with myself pleases me to think of. At least it does—and a woman called Bernadine came to the gate and talked to me—and I did like thinking—of her—and yet I *didn't.*"

"Was that this morning?"

"Yes. Grania, you know the way women look at men, if they like them, that is."

"Like I look at Andreas, you mean?"

"No, *no!* No woman ever looks at a man as you look at Andreas, except related people. That's so strange in you. Perhaps why I can tell—and I believe I couldn't tell Mother. And certainly not Carla. I should be afraid, with them. But I mean, things I used to enjoy, the way they look at me, I *do not like now.*"

"But, Neil, if they're attracted to you, surely it's very natural," said Grania, looking at him intently.

Neil thought, under that penetrating stare, "She *will* know what it is, if I can make it a bit clearer. She's coming to know." He pressed his palms to his forehead in a tremendous effort to think clearly, and then express his thought.

"Grania," he said slowly, hesitatingly, "*they*—it may be they that make me hate myself—or it may be me hating myself that makes me not like—to be ashamed, unproud—they, it seems as if I, *me, Neil,* were so much live *meat.*"

Grania relaxed. She took his hand and stroked it as she had done sometimes when he had been small, and distressed. She said nothing. Neil was first relieved, then again anxious.

"Is it—do you know what it is?"

"I think so. Neil, your hands are very like mine, aren't they?

Only yours are right for your sex, and mine are wrong. Now Carla has much nicer hands. But neither of us, Carla or I, has a crooked little finger like *that*," she said, hooking her straight little finger under Neil's crooked one.

"Andreas has one like that," said Neil absently, hardly listening, "but Grania, *what is it?* Shall I ever be better?"

"No, child. The embryo of the dignity of a human being cannot be aborted."

"I don't understand. I am a human being, but how does that help me? What shall I do, then? Go on—and on, and in the end?"

Grania gave him back his hand.

"I can't tell you the end, Neil. It might be that. But you shan't—" she stopped. Her face was expressionless; so was her body. Neil knew he was forgotten. He began to feel frightened, she was so still. His fear grew, but he sat quiet. He did not know it, but what frightened him was the psychic disturbance of a titanic conflict that was going on in Grania's mind. It was the last of a long series; whatever won this one was the final victor, for there would be no more battles.

At last she relaxed. Whatever had been going on was now finished. Something was victorious. Something was dead. She did an extraordinary thing. She took off her circlet, untwisting the bands of hair, and put it on her knee. Her dark hair, as dark as Neil's, fell forward over her cheeks, giving her a wild, brooding look. Neil was amazed and frightened. He felt himself in the presence of vast forces, their nature unknown and perhaps malevolent. He did not feel Grania herself malevolent, but he was terrified of something he had stirred up. And never before had he seen a woman without her circlet.

Grania said: "See the little light thing, and that little bit of spring there to make it comfortable. Just a little thing to show when a girl becomes a woman, and then it's convenient, of course, to keep one's hair back. To think that all the uniforms, and the orders, the medals and stars and ribbons, and the vestments, and the crowns, should come just to that one little trivial circle of metal. And all the weapons, the least of which could scatter it to shining dust. But then crowns were only for one or two, and vestments not for all, nor medals and stars, nor even uniforms, but *this*," she swung it on one finger, "is for every adult of half the whole human race. There is its power. My head feels cold without it."

She put it on again, pulling the hair over and through it with the dexterity of custom. Neil was relieved to see it back on her head. Seeing a woman without her circlet made him feel prickly and uncomfortable and rather frightened, the same sort of sensation as he got if he heard a group of women laughing together in their quiet controlled fashion. As to Grania's words, they conveyed nothing at all to him.

"I don't understand," he said. "Why did you take off your circlet?"

She turned on him a fierce mocking stare, which didn't abash him, because often when he was a boy she had looked at him like that, and it never meant that she was angry.

"Ah, *why*, Big Neil? *Little* Neil, *tiny* Neil. Why, why, why? Yes, there'll be a lot of whying and howing over what's to come. But before we start on that, you listen, you great lump of live meat. I'm not your Mother's sister."

"Not Mother's sister? Who—why—"

"I am *Carla*'s sister. But I'm not your *Mother*'s sister. I happen to be your Mother herself. You're my son, not hers, and little Carla is not your sister, but your cousin."

"You—my Mother?" said Neil, in blank amazement. "I don't believe it."

"You dare say I'm lying, man?"

"No, no. But—but—*she* must be my Mother. Not you. You're Grania. She *is* my Mother. Why, you can't expect me suddenly not to be her son, after all these years. She *is* my Mother."

"I see the difficulty," said Grania, taking his hand again. "I know that emotionally you never can accept me as your Mother. I don't want you to, either. I don't want you to be afraid of me, as you are of Carla. But you must accept it *with your mind*. Look at those two hands."

Neil looked at them, at his right, and Grania's left. His was much bigger, but except for the crooked little finger the two hands were amazingly alike in shape.

"You see, don't you, Neil? And our hair is very dark, but Carla's is a sort of light brown. Carla's eyes are gray, but ours are blue, and a very nice blue though we say it ourselves."

"Yours are darker than mine, I think."

"No," said the artist. "They're exactly the same color. Yours look lighter because you have that black beard and mustache, and heavier eyebrows."

Neil pondered heavily, trying to accept, with his mind, this astonishing news.

"Why didn't you bring me up?" he asked.

"Well, there was a reason I didn't understand until very much later. But there were other, more superficial reasons, which I did understand. I was very disappointed you were a boy, my poor little Neil. Then I have a restless, roving disposition and I didn't think it would be good for a boy to bring him up first in one country and then in another until he was fourteen and old enough to go to school. It wouldn't have mattered so much for a girl, who goes to school at eight anyhow. Then Carla was settled here and rather wanted to bring up a boy as she had a girl already. So when you were a year old I handed you over to her. You had a happy childhood, didn't you, young Neil?"

"Yes. But then— I think I would have been as happy if you had been my Mother, all the time, I mean. Not just now, when I can't understand it at all. Why couldn't you have *been* my Mother and let Mother—*Carla*—" Neil pronounced the name with some difficulty—"bring me up, as my aunt?"

"It doesn't do. There must be no divided allegiance. If a woman does for any reason give her son over to another woman, the second must be thought of, by the boy, as his Mother. That's not only custom and convention, it's a legal rule. With girls it doesn't apply."

"I am beginning to *think* it," said Neil.

"And do you mind?"

"No. Could I—do you think—tell you something that's rather queer and shocking? I should like to tell you, *now*."

"Tell me."

"I *like* you better than Mother. I always have, I think. But I only discovered it today."

Grania kissed his ear, gently, like a rabbit's nibble.

"You've discovered a lot today, man, haven't you?"

"Yes. So I like to *think* you my Mother, but I'm afraid I never shall feel it. I can't call you anything but Grania."

"Call me Jezebel or the Virgin Mary, I don't mind."

"Those are rather funny sounding names. I don't want to call you anything but Grania, as I always have."

Neil thought some more, and then came out with a most unusual shocking and immodest question. He did blush a little as he put it, but put it all the same.

"Who is my father?"

"Neil! I am amazed at you."

Neil looked shyly up at her, but she was not looking remote, or cold, or stern, as she well might have been. If she were amazed, it was with a delighted surprise.

"Can't you guess?" she said.

Neil looked down again at his hand.

"Andreas?"

"Yes. That man down there is your father."

"You were sort of telling me just now, when you were comparing our hands, the first time. I wasn't really taking it in then."

"Yes. I was sort of telling you. I think you might have thought something before, about your and Andreas' fingers."

"But why should I? It isn't *my Mother* that's always up here talking to Andreas;" complicated modest emotions made Neil turn away his head. "I can't tell you what I feel," he went on, in a low, rather hurried voice, "but as things seem to be, I like you and Andreas to be my think-Mother and my think-father. No one could ever *feel* a father, anyway."

"Are you sure no one ever could?"

"How could they? Why, no one ever knows. But I *feel Andreas*, himself, and I like him to be my father. Does *he* know?"

"I told him years ago."

"But if he knew such a very—very unusual thing as that, who, for certain, his child was, why didn't he tell other men? Why didn't he tell me?"

"I told him not to. Andreas is a bit of a superman. He can keep things to himself if he wants to. But he's not so super as *you*, Neil."

"Am I?"

"Yes," said Grania seriously. "Quite a remarkable man. Indeed, child, you don't know how remarkable."

"But then why do I hate myself and be ashamed? As if I were a little weedy man that couldn't live a man's life?"

"It's the shame that makes you great, my son. It's not the envious physical shame of the little weedy man, it's a spiritual human shame, a genuine half-conscious stirring of your human soul. But if you hadn't been big and strong and popular with women it might *not* have been that. You haven't had to contend with *my* difficulties in sorting out motives."

Neil shook his head to show he understood none of this. "Will you take away my shame and let me be an ordinary man?" he implored. "So that I can be happy again, and enjoy things?"

"I can't make you happy, Neil. I can't make you an ordinary man. I can't make myself an ordinary woman. We are not going to be happy. But we *are* going to be—good. Be and do."

"Is there something to *do?*" asked Neil, rejoiced at the prospect of action.

"Not with your muscles, I'm afraid. It means thinking and thinking, and trying to understand terribly difficult things. Women's things."

Neil groaned.

"I shall never be able to do that. Men can't."

"*This* man has got to. We shall be in it together. Does that make it any better?"

"Yes," said Neil, after a pause. "It makes it, whatever it is, wonderful. But is it possible for a woman and a man to do any *thinking* together? It seems extraordinary, even if you are my Mother. You'll soon throw me out of it, and get another woman to help you," he added despondently.

Grania laughed, a short grim laugh.

"No woman in the world would help me. Now listen, Neil. I'm not going to say any more today. You've got plenty to think about to keep off your glooms and shame-feelings. We're just going to behave ordinarily for the rest of this May Day, you and Andreas and I. And in the evening we'll all go down to see the bonfires."

At the sound of "you and Andreas and I" and the thought of

going down to see the bonfires in such company Neil felt a strange thrill of pleasure. It would be quite different from any May Night he had ever spent before. But he said doubtfully: "I don't think Andreas will go, unless you make him. He doesn't like seeing other men do all the things he can't do now."

"He'll like to go with me and you," said Grania. "Andreas! Come up here, will you?"

Andreas came stiffly stumping up the wooden veranda steps. Neil wondered how old he was. He had never asked him, not being particularly interested. He seemed to be about seventy-five. Years and years older than Grania, who was, he knew, about forty-eight. Why had she been so attracted by a man of fifty? Andreas never could have been very much to look at. He was rather small and lightly built and had a snubbish sort of nose. Neil felt love, something more than liking, come into him. It was something to do with Andreas' very white beard, such a contrast to his own, and to Grania's dark hair which had not yet even begun to go gray. He wanted, he felt, to protect Andreas, to stand between him and the cold wind, or snow, or anything that might make him uncomfortable. He wanted to put his own warmth and solidity and youth between Andreas and the world. He did not feel anything of this kind for Grania. She was far beyond the need of his protection.

Grania said: "Andreas, will you come with me and our son to Salisbury this evening to see the bonfires and watch the young men and boys plunging about?"

Andreas opened his eyes very wide. "What did you tell *him* for?" he asked, jerking a rather contemptuous thumb at Neil. "There now! I keep it to myself all these years, and never boast to other men that *I* know who my son is, and then you go and tell *him!* Well!"

"It was nice for him to know," Grania said mildly. "He is pleased about it. About me, too. Only he can't grasp it of course."

"Oh, I say nothing about *that*," said Andreas hastily. "That's not my affair at all, whether he knows you're his Mother or thinks you're only his aunt. That's women's business and naturally I don't meddle. But I don't see why the great silly oaf should share *my* secret. Now he'll go spilling it all over the place. Besides, it's not very decent or modest that he should *know*. People can guess as much as they like. But knowing is different. It's all right for me to know, but not for him."

"You're too conventional, Andreas."

"Things are as they are. And quite rightly so. Now we shall have Neil going racing round all over the place telling people I'm his father and that *you told him*. It'll be absolutely scandalous."

"Neil's not going to tell anyone. Either about that, or anything else. Are you, Neil?" Grania asked him, with a cool, clear, warning glance.

"No. Never. No one. Andreas, you really needn't mind so much. It'll make no difference. I like you just as much. I think I like you more."

"I do mind," Andreas grumbled. "And I don't give a potato for your liking, anyhow. It's nothing to me whether you like me or not. I've got my own life, and I prefer to live it undisturbed."

Grania suddenly uttered a loud hoot of unwomanly laughter.

"You hypocritical old man," she said. "You pretend you're so conventional and modest and never even think anything a man shouldn't, and yet you dare to stand there mumbling and criticizing and making Neil feel uncomfortable, because *I've* decided he *was* to be told who his father was. Do you think I mayn't have some reason you don't know anything about?"

Andreas was somewhat abashed. "Well, it's your fault, Grania. You've been seeing me all these years and you never stop me arguing about anything, and naturally I've got into a habit of it. I can't stop now. But I'll try if you like," he added earnestly.

"No, no. But can't you see that you don't *really* mind? You're just rather jealous, because now Neil's just as favored among men as you are. You want to be the only one."

"Neil's not so favored, anyway. *He* hasn't got a woman to come and talk to him just *for* talking. If you talk to *him* that doesn't mean anything. You're his Mother. But you and I aren't related at all. Who'd ever want to go and talk to him, I'd like to know?"

"Neil, will you clout your father gently on the head? I'll give you permission."

"He can't clout me, not even with your permission. I'm an old man, too old to be clouted."

"Then shake him by the hand, Neil. Give him such a grip that he'll be paralyzed for a week."

Neil took his father's hand and appeared to grip it fairly hard. He smiled rather shyly but with beaming affection at Andreas.

"Now, Andreas, isn't Neil a nice son to have?"

"He's pretty well. But then, what use are sons? If it had been a daughter, now! There'd have been something to think about on wet days." Andreas, very red in the face from embarrassment and pleasure, for in spite of his feeling of jealousy he was pleased really that Neil should know, turned round to go back to the garden.

"Here, you haven't said whether you'll go to Salisbury with us," Grania said.

"Yes, if you'll leave plenty of time and not walk too fast."

"It'll be a nice little family party," said Grania sardonically.

Andreas shook his head resignedly.

"Of course it's all wrong, but I suppose you know what you're doing."

"I do, old man. You can be easy about that."

"Anyway," he conceded, "you must do what you like. And whatever is said, or whatever scandals and troubles arise, they will be *all your fault!*"

"They will, Andreas."

Andreas shook his head again, to show that he was doubtful and disapproving, but did not intend to argue any more. Presently they heard him singing in an old bodiless tenor voice, but sweetly and in tune.

"He is happy," Grania said.

"He is always happy," Neil replied, a little enviously. "Everyone looks up to him, because of you. *He* doesn't go about being gloomy and shameful. I think Andreas has had a lovely life."

"You shall have a lovely death, darling," said Grania, but lightly, so that Neil only laughed.

In the evening as they all walked down into Salisbury, slowly, to accommodate Andreas' old limbs, Neil was conscious of an entirely new kind of happiness and excitement and pride. He had slept most of the afternoon and felt physically refreshed, but his pride had little to do with the huge reserve of power he had in his

back and his legs and arms as he strolled along the road with
Andreas and Grania. There seemed to be a reserve of power which
was gradually filling up in his *mind;* as if there had always been a
place for it, a dry pool, with the springs above it cut off and
diverted. The knowledge that the old man stumping along by his
side was his father had undammed something, but it was not just
that by itself. He felt, without thinking about it, a warm *human*
sympathy flowing from Grania to him, to Andreas, from Andreas
to Grania, round and round like the beating of a heart. So that
though he could neither *feel* Andreas his father (because one
couldn't feel fathers), nor feel Grania his Mother, because a man
could not suddenly change his Mother, yet as he walked between
his known progenitors, towering physically above them, he felt
himself the small precious core, the very kernel of a proud and
valuable whole. Not one word of which could he have expressed,
only, as surges of this new exciting pride came over him, he now
wanted to knock Andreas head over heels into the ditch, just to
remind him of their kinship, and now wanted to hug him, and now
wanted to take Grania's arm on one side and Andreas' arm on the
other, and draw them by physical pressure *through himself,* somehow, into closer contact with each other. And now wanted to kneel
in the road and kiss Grania's hands or feet, to express his overflow-
ing gratitude for this new pride she had given him. For he felt that
for the first time in his life he had a pride and a pleasure that had
nothing to do with his muscles, his physical courage, his work, his
outward position among men, or his sexual successes. Now perhaps Neil need not always hate Neil, for Neil had acquired something new, and far beyond the range of other and lesser men. So,
though Grania's presence controlled him and he gave no expression to his joy beyond an occasional bass humming, he walked
rather drunkenly, now lurching into his father and now into
Grania. Andreas grew a little peevish when he had been bumped
for the fifth time.

"You're as bad to walk with as a puppy, that's always getting
under one's feet," he said, giving his son an irritated push that
made no more impression on Neil than if he'd been a tree. "Get
over, can't you?"

"Then he reels into me," said Grania, drawing away a little. "Why can't you walk straight? You can't be drunk *yet*. We had nothing but small ale for dinner."

"I am so happy," Neil said apologetically. "It's got into my legs."

"Then go the other side of Grania," Andreas said, unappeased. "Or go behind and be happy by yourself."

"No, no. I like to walk between you."

"And must you always do what you like?" asked Andreas sarcastically.

"Of course he must on May Day, Andreas." Grania's deep soft voice had a chuckle on it. "That's Men's day. Young men's day. So be quiet, you old grizzled, grumpy dog."

"Young men," said Andreas, addressing the air, "are nothing but walking sacks of conceit, so blown up that if you did but stick a pin into one he'd burst. Now you, Grania, didn't like me when I was a young man."

"I didn't know you, you ancient. But I should think you were fairly poisonous, certainly."

"Not that the young men of my day weren't a good deal better, more manly certainly, than young men are now."

"Well, if Neil isn't manly in one sense, and he is not, I believe, we know whose fault it is, anyway."

"Yours," said Andreas instantly. "With your spoiling him, encouraging him to think, and telling him things he shouldn't know. Of course he'll be ruined. Neil, *will you not* barge like that!"

Grania came between them.

"Oh, well," Andreas said, moving away from her, "let him come in the middle if he likes. The whole thing, you and me and him, walking to Salisbury like this, in almost broad daylight on May Day, with hundreds of people about, is so scandalous that it doesn't really matter if one of us looks prematurely drunk."

"It's getting dusk, Andreas," Grania comforted him, now back on the other side of Neil. "It'll be dark before we get there."

"And I shall be weary," said Andreas, changing his ground of attack, "it's all right dragging me along *in* to this silly May Day business, but who'll drag me back about midnight?"

"You needn't go back, Andreas," Neil said eagerly. "You can come and sleep at our house. Some of the men are certain to be out all night."

"Yes, and I know who some of the men will be. I don't care for sleeping at the house of total strangers with no one there I know."

"I shall be there," said Neil, after a pause, during which he took a sudden, startling resolution.

"Indeed?" said Andreas, with polite incredulity.

"Neil, Neil," murmured Grania into his ear on the other side, "don't try to go too fast, my dear. If you try things and fail you'll be worse off than before."

Neil was awed by this manifestation of the supernatural wisdom of women, which made them always able to read a man's secret thoughts, but he did not waver.

"I *shall* be there, Andreas," he said resolutely. "If you get tired you can go straight on up to the house and lie on my bed. It's the room on the right as you go in at the door."

"Yes, yes. I shall have a nice sleep, no doubt, and I'll see you in the morning, at breakfast time."

"You damned obstinate old man!" Neil shouted in his ear, for as misgivings began to pour into his mind he got angry, "I shall be there *before* the morning I tell you! Nearly all of the night."

"I'm not deaf," said Andreas, putting his hand over his ear, "thank you very much for the offer of a bed and I'll see you—"

"Men, stop quarrelling," Grania said quietly.

They stopped. Neil stopped talking altogether, but Andreas kept up an indistinguishable muttering in his beard. Grania's mouth twitched a very little. Gradually, without an articulate word being said by anyone, harmony was once more restored. And so this very peculiar family party came through the fine, cool early darkness to the Salisbury Playing Field.

Once there, it split up. Andreas' and Neil's guilty feelings became too strong for them. They dared not stay any longer with a woman. They vanished into the roaring restless swirl of men and boys, which every now and then cast out flotsam in the shape of one man, or a little group of men, or a couple of youths. These drifted up, by accident as it were, to the feet of the women who strolled, quietly talking among themselves, on the outer edge of the field, under dark tall trees. The bonfires were some of them lit, and there was enough red flame-light for people to recognize each other. There were no girls there at all. May Night was by convention barred to them. No one walking under the trees was without a circlet, and no one would walk there tonight unless she felt at least vaguely amorously inclined. But Grania was not even vaguely amorously inclined; she did not want to talk to any of the women she knew, and she did not expect to see either Andreas or Neil again that night, yet she stayed there, on the margin, between the noisy physical tumult of the men and the quietness, the cold, spiritual strength and pride of the women, not walking, not talking, a strange and solitary figure, too tall and not tall enough, too strong and not strong enough, too proud, and not proud enough, symbolizing in her position the place, or no-place, or every-place she had in the world.

The women thought: "Grania's back. Eccentric as ever, of course. How extraordinarily big and ugly she is. Genius has its pains."

The men, those who saw her standing there, thought: "Grania's back. How extraordinarily big and ugly she is. Would any man?—not me. And yet if she *wanted* one, would it be? It would be rather strange. But no. They say her work's known all over Europe. But—"

Grania was not thinking of herself, nor now of Andreas and Neil. Her mind was on a journey, away from the red flames and flickering shadows, the noise and the movement, away from Salisbury, up the Avon valley, out into the dark silence of Salisbury Plain, to Stonehenge. No house was allowed to be built within two miles of it, on any side. Since far far back, in the Christian era, no more stones had ever been allowed to fall. It was now, not as it had been in the beginning, but as it had been for much more than four thousand years.

"Why," thought Grania, "have we, the women, always taken such care of Stonehenge? It is not *ours*. No woman's brain directed the laboring, straining men who put up those stones. It was all *theirs*, and the women only bore the men who were to do it. Yet we have cared for it, and kept it, and left it in loneliness so that its pride should never be smirched by the nearness of little impermanent creations. That's not *reasonable*, to care for Stonehenge. That's not feminine or sensible, to have that great masculine monument always there to prick our natural pride. It's an emotion, a streak of male unreason, in generations upon generations of the women of England, that they would not let Stonehenge fall down. And if they, the others, can have emotion, can have unreason, about England's greatest Old Monument, and if the Wiltshire women can have that peculiar flaming and utterly groundless and silly pride that Stonehenge stands upon Salisbury Plain, while it might have stood in Wales, or anywhere, why shouldn't women, in due time, become a little unreasonable, a little emotional about *other* things than Stonehenge, and then this tyranny, steel-cold and purely reasonable, can be weakened and finally cast down. And all the men know *who built Stonehenge!* Not only me telling Neil, *as I shall do*, but every mother to tell her little son when she first takes him there. Not, 'Oh, people in a time long, long ago', but '*Men* made that, little Neil. Men, without mechanical power. But with the power of their minds and muscles and *wills* they raised those stones to the glory of God.' And watch the will, the spirit, grow in the boy as he looks up at those stones. The tremendous force and concentration of male emotion, the *essence* of male emotion there is in Stonehenge, the pure unreasonableness, and massive dignified stupidity of the outward form and inward spirit of Stonehenge would create a will even in *these* weaklings—*if they knew.*"

Her mind rushed to that still, gigantic circle out there in the darkness, with the little wind that here blew the bonfires to a roar out there flowing almost silently past the stones and away over the plain. She lingered by each quiet but subtly dangerous giant, in spirit, touching each one, loving each one, homesick for them, as she had sometimes been in Russia or Germany or more distant lands.

"I must go there tomorrow," she thought, "and lie there all day long till sunset. Stonehenge. Even the name has power—one sees it sometimes, fiery on darkness, going to sleep. Stonehenge was the Beginning. Sun-worship, man-worship, emotion-worship, blood-worship and *fear,* infantile, terrible cryings in the night. And then the Middle. God the spirit and power, woman-worship, reason-worship, control-worship, and no fear but fear of death. And then—*the End!* What will it be? And are we even at the Middle, or very near, still very near, to Stonehenge? Am I at the joining of the Middle and the End? Am I to start the End coming? Or is there no End, and is all I feel, and all I think, an illusion like that monstrous God-Illusion that helped those groaning children to draw those stones along? And this thing that lies in my mind, *in my mind alone*—as yet—this little embryo of a vast change—it lies there like that little lump of life that was Neil once lay in my womb—will it be born, and grow strong and tall like him, and have a will and power like mine, and *do*? Or will it be stillborn, just a sad little carcass, useless? And not *do*, only be thought, by me alone? It might be I was to die tonight. Who would go on with it, if it *is* in me alone? Who will, when I'm dead, if I fail altogether, completely, as I may? And what *will be* the End?"

A thought, an Old Man's thought, came into her mind. The meaning of the thought, but not the shape; the English words were lost, lost in a patch of darkness (blacker than the night-darkness), that lay somewhere, in Time, between her and Stonehenge.

"*Oh, that a man might know the end of this day's business ere it come. But it sufficeth that the end will come, and then the end is known.* O wise Old Man," she thought, "the End will come, in God's time, not mine. And in God's time, not mine, the End of my day's business will be known. But not by me."

A quiet exultation took her, a deep breathing of the spirit, because her conflict, as she sat beside Neil on the veranda, had gone the way it had, and was now done.

"I shall doubt," she thought, "a thousand times more, and be in reasonable agony, because both the beginning and middle and the end of my day's business may be only the coiled serpent of a diseased brain, leading nowhere but back upon itself. I am too female to be a fanatic or a believer, and have steady faith in a rightness I cannot prove to be right. I shall see, a thousand times more, other sources of my life-passion than foreknowledge of what is to come. I shall believe myself mad nine times for the once I shall feel myself the only sane woman there is. But I shall *never turn back.*"

She stood there so straight and sturdy and motionless, and so filled with the psychic power of her finally released will, that a woman who had only just come and had not seen her before thought, "Grania's back. She's bigger than ever. I believe she's bigger than a man, the largest kind. She makes one think of one of the stones of Stonehenge. A weird woman altogether. But one is proud of her, of course."

While his Mother was enjoying this sad and lonely exultation, perhaps rather like the triumph of Satan over Eve, Neil was having a far simpler and more vivid exultation in the midst of the throng. He knew, the moment he left Andreas and hurled himself shouting into the maelstrom of masculinity, that he was happier than he ever had been since he was a youth of nineteen. He was like a penitent absolved from years of sin. His trust in Grania was as absolute as a devout penitent's trust in a priest. She was a woman, he had been always very fond of her, her ordinary female power and wisdom was enhanced for him by her age, her experience and her fame, and there could be no doubt at all that whatever she said must be true, whatever she commanded must be done. She had not promised him happiness, but a thing he prized more highly, something to be done, and with her. She had not scorned him for his glooms and shames, but told him that they were a sign that he was above other men. So, whenever they came upon him again, and he supposed that they must, as she had said he was never to be happy, he would rejoice in them as the signs of his superiority over ordinary manhood. And for the present, they were gone. He felt lighter than the air, lighter than the flames that flowed up like rivers from the bonfires, lighter than the smoke that blew away before the little wind. Of all that noisy, happy crowd no one was happier and no one was noisier than Neil. He organized a large boy-throwing ring, where stalwart men threw the little boys that chased round the bonfires from one to the other over yards of ground, round and round, without any mishaps until the boys were tired of it or sick. When he was tired of that he took off his coat, put it on the ground, and, roaring like a bull, challenged any man in the crowd to pick it up. That meant a friendly wrestling match. A stranger came forward and picked it up. He was strong and agile, but Neil was so full of joy that he had even more than his usual strength. He overcame the stranger easily.

Later, when the bonfires began to die down, people started to jump over them. A dark figure would shout to clear the way, take a long run, a vigorous leap, and disappear into the flame and smoke.

There was no serious risk if the solid part of the fire could be cleared, but to land even on the edge would mean bad burns on the legs. Neil jumped over one or two of the smaller ones easily.

"These are no good!" he cried contemptuously to his companions. "I'm going over the big one!"

"You can't yet," one said. "It's not low enough. A champion jumper couldn't get over it as it is now. There's no sense in jumping deliberately *into* a fire."

"I can get over," Neil boasted, "and if I can't I'll go into it."

But when he walked round the big fire to see how wide and high he would have to jump he was somewhat appalled at his rashness. The flames were nothing, but the solid part of the fire seemed to be about four feet high in the middle and eighteen feet wide. It would have to be a prodigious leap. But now he had said he would jump it he must try or the other men would think he was afraid of burning his legs, and also he would be set down as an idle bragger. So he retired for his run. The men on each side made a lane for him. Neil hesitated. The fire looked enormous. If by any chance he caught his foot in the burning logs at the top he would fall face downwards and be half burned to death before anyone could drag him out. "I *must* do it, I *can't* do it, I *must*," he thought, in a frightful conflict of indecision. "What a *fool* I was." Then suddenly he thought: "I *can* do it. I'll only land in the edge and get a bit scorched. I *will* get over the top. I can."

He ran. Faster and faster till he was at his quickest possible pace; then, beautifully judged, he took off. As he soared into the air, with his eyes closed against the flames and flying sparks, he knew with blissful relief that he had cleared the top of the fire. For an instant the flames were all round him, hot on his face, then he landed with a crash on something wooden that broke beneath him. He stumbled forward and fell on his face, outside the fire, not burnt at all. He picked himself up in the midst of a roar of cheering from the men who had seen his feat of courage and agility, and looked to see what he had come down on. It was something *in* the fire, he was sure. There it was, a half-burnt plank, lying on the top of the deep red embers.

"I don't believe I saw that plank when I walked round," he muttered. "What amazing luck."

"Ah, you're a lucky young fellow, you are," said a well-known cracked old voice in his ear. Neil turned round and saw Andreas, grinning and nodding his head.

"Did you put it there?" Neil asked, putting his arm round the old man's shoulders. Andreas wriggled away from him.

"No, you dolt. It flew there by itself. Well, I just happened to see that bit of wood lying about and I put it on opposite to where you were going to jump from. Of course you might have missed it by yards. But we're just naturally lucky men. Now don't paw me about. Go on now, the men want to give you a drink."

"Come too, then."

They went to the long tables at the side of the field where beer and wine and more solid refreshments were being served out by boys. Andreas soon vanished again, and when Neil had had as much beer as he wanted and looked for the old man to ask him if he were tired and would like to go away, he was nowhere to be seen.

"Where is Andreas?" he asked people. No one knew. One suggested with a chuckle that he was over the other side of the field, where the trees were.

"He's too old," snapped Neil, suddenly angry. "Who'd look at the old goat now? Of course he isn't there."

But his anger and coarse unkind speech hid an uneasiness. Against his will, it seemed, his feet were carrying him past the bonfires and over towards the trees. He had not forgotten his promise to go home with Andreas. He very much wished that Andreas had not disappeared. He would find him. They would go home now. After all he had jumped the biggest bonfire long before anyone else dared to do it. Unless he had a fight now there was not much else to do that wouldn't be an anticlimax and disappointing. A fight, *or Bernadine!* His feet went quicker. He was halfway over the field now. He wanted to see her there, he wanted her, *now*, to look at him in the dimming light of the bonfires as she had looked at him in the morning, over the gate. At the same time he didn't forget that when he had taken that sudden resolution on the way to Salisbury, which Andreas had sneered at, and Grania had warned him against, there had been a reason for it. A reason that really had nothing to do with Andreas. It was to do with his old shame and new pride. If, he had thought, I can *not* see Bernadine tonight, I shall be again more marvelously different from other men, because such a thing would be unheard of, unless a man wasn't attracted. And I *was*. I liked her, only not the way she looked at me. But now desire had grown stronger, and his new pride subtly faded. It didn't seem to matter so much. His old pride, which the jumping of the big bonfire had enhanced, was strong in his head, his heart and his loins. He deserved something for that mighty feat. He deserved Bernadine. It would be the most ridiculous folly, quite wrong in fact, to disappoint her and himself, for—for nothing. But then he remembered crying in the midnight on Old Sarum, and telling Grania of his misery and shame, and all the extraordinary events of this most amazing day. His will went on with the struggle, but his feet kept on walking towards the trees. He was nearly there. He forced himself to stop and think. He tried to understand why it was he could not make up his mind one way or the other. On one side he had his new pride, Andreas' grins and sneers tomorrow morning, and Andreas' loneliness among strangers tonight (a little thing this, hardly worth bothering about, the old man wouldn't really mind); on the other he had Bernadine and the natural wild pleasure of lovemaking, and his old pride in himself as a man of unusual strength and virility and sexual magnetism. It would hurt this pride rather to go away from the Field with Andreas, as if he were old, or a callow youth, or a weakling who found it difficult to get any woman to accept him. "But if I *go* myself," he thought, "then that's different. It's me sending myself away, not them sending me away." He decided, "I do *really*, with the most of me, want now to find Andreas and take him home." And as if this was a signal to his feet they once more began to walk towards the trees. He stopped them again, much bewildered. "Why can't I do what I really want to?" he asked himself, sighing in his distress. "I made myself jump over the bonfire when I was afraid of being badly burned. So why can't I make myself *not* go to find Bernadine, *there,* and go to find Andreas who must be somewhere behind me? Why can't I walk where I want to, when I could make myself run where I didn't want to? That is extraordinary."

The solution came to him at last. He thought: "It's because I've been doing that all my life since I was a boy, making myself fight bigger boys, and never seem afraid of getting hurt. But *this,* I've never done before, because no one ever does. It's wrong to be cowardly, but it's never wrong to make love to any woman who will have you. It would be, most times, just silly not to. Silly and impossible. But this time, *just tonight,* is different for me, and me only. And I shall do a thing no man has ever done before. But if I do but catch one glimpse of Bernadine I *can't* do it. I must go back, and *at once.*"

His feet took two more steps towards the trees. Then with a sort of growling furious noise he turned right round and almost ran back towards the bonfires and the men.

Grania had been watching him. She was too far away, and the light was too uncertain, to see any expression on his face, but his actions told the small heroic tale. She wondered if the woman, Bernadine, Neil had called her, were watching too. But perhaps *she* did not know that that hesitating figure was Neil. It would be hard to recognize anyone at that distance in this light unless one knew him very well indeed. Grania felt rather sorry for Bernadine, who was not at fault in any way, but she was far more glad for Neil. She thought: "If that boy had lived five thousand years ago he'd have been what they called a 'great' man. How has he managed to develop so much character and will? He's marvelous."

Maternal pride made her feel happy and warm. She left the trees and went to the gate Neil would pass through to reach his house. Here she concealed herself in a patch of shadow and waited. Presently Andreas and Neil came through, arguing furiously. Neil sounded sullenly venomous, Andreas was irritable and irrepressible, as usual. Neil was walking very fast and dragging Andreas along by the arm. As she watched them, Andreas suddenly tore himself away and stopped dead.

"I shan't go to your house at all," he said. "Not with you in this foul temper. No. I'd rather get myself to my own house or lie in the Field all night. I wish I'd let you burn your legs now."

Grania moved out of the darkness towards them. Neil looked almost as if he might proceed to violence, and that, she thought, would be a pity. No *man* could make Andreas do what he didn't want to, and he would never forgive a young man for bullying an old one.

"Was that you, then, who jumped over the big bonfire?" Grania asked, taking an arm of each and urging them gently along.

"Yes," said Neil sulkily. He added: "*He* put a plank for me to land on. But I don't care. I'd *rather* have burnt myself than be obliged to him."

"I thought it might be you," said Grania, squeezing his arm. "But couldn't really see. It was fine. Wasn't it, Andreas?"

"That's all very well, Grania. But since then he's gone quite idiotic. Abusing me for leaving him while he was drinking his beer, and saying I must go home now as if I were a little boy and he was my Mother, and dragging me along like that making a show of us both. I wasn't in any particular hurry to go now. It's quite early, and I don't feel tired."

"Perhaps Neil does. It must have been an effort, making up his mind to—jump the fire." Again she squeezed Neil's arm. "I'm *very* proud of him. He's a remarkable man."

"Remarkably ill-tempered," said Andreas, but in his habitual sharp way, not with any real annoyance.

Neil said: "I'm sorry, Andreas. But I really would rather like to go home now."

"Well, we're going, ain't we? I don't *mind* going, since you want to. But I won't be hustled and dragged about and abused."

"He won't," said Grania. "I'm going home, too. Goodnight, my friends." She pulled them gently towards each other and watched them walk away slowly and amicably. She sighed. All this masculine companionship was rather exhausting. She felt a desire to talk to a woman before she went home to the large studio, with small living arrangements attached, that she occupied, by herself, when she was in Salisbury. But she did not want to talk to just any woman. She wondered if Carla, Old Carla, not the young daughter, would still be up. A sister was just the one sort of woman she wanted to talk to. She went to Carla's house, which was not far off, and found her still up, fiddling about with an electric sewing machine. Bits of it were strewn all over the table. Carla was absorbed, frowning and humming.

"Hullo, Grania," she said, when her sister came in, "a woman said to me today, I've seen Grania and she's twice as big and twice as dirty."

"You don't need to pass those sort of rudenesses on. What's all this?"

"Carla's sewing machine. That girl has no mechanical sense

whatever, and that wouldn't matter, only when things go wrong she mucks about with them herself before giving them to me."

Grania looked at her small neat sister, and her delicate but strong hands.

"It would be very boring if all women were electricians like you."

"Of course. I didn't at all want Carla to be mechanically-minded. What I object to is amateur bungling. Supposing some hopeless amateur artist brought you a picture to put right?"

"Oh well, that's different. That machine *can be put* right, even if Carla has tinkered with it. The picture never could. I've been down to the Field."

"To see how English men compare with Russians? I can't be bothered with that May Night nonsense now I'm getting middle-aged. It's all right for young women."

"I went down with Andreas."

"You and Andreas! Well, it's an old scandal everybody's used to."

"And Neil. Does that make it more respectable, or less?"

"Do you mean you met Neil at Andreas' house and walked down with them both?"

"Yes, wasn't it awful?"

"Oh, that. It doesn't matter, seeing it's you. But why wasn't Neil playing about with his pals?"

"He likes Andreas better, perhaps."

"He's a funny boy, Neil is," said Carla, squinting along a tiny piece of metal to see if it had got bent. "A very good boy, but odd in some ways. His affection for Andreas is quite unusual. Almost as if he knew he was his father, and felt about him as, I suppose, men used to when they *did* know."

"However, he has no Old World filial respect or fear of him," said Grania, laughing. "They get furious with each other, and I have to part them. Look, Carla, I've told Neil I'm his Mother and that you're not."

Carla dropped her little bit of metal on the table, stood up-right, and looked at Grania in some astonishment.

"Of course you've a right to do that, seeing he's over twenty-one. But why?"

"He's twenty-four today," said Grania. "He was born on May Day."

"But why have you told him? You're not here very much. And he really couldn't love you any more than he does, and always has. I often think he loves you more than he does me."

"I wanted him to know. But he doesn't *feel* me his Mother, at all. He just knows it, that's all. He'll be just the same with you as he always has been. Only next time he sees you he may be a little shy."

"You're not going to tell me why you wanted him to know."

"No. Deep inexplicable psychological reasons, perhaps."

"Perhaps. Then of course he knows Carla isn't his sister."

"Yes, but that doesn't matter at all. He'll never think of her as anything but his sister."

"I told Carla, when she was old enough to keep things to herself, that you were Neil's Mother. But as you say that doesn't matter. What does matter is that you now can't prevent Neil from guessing that Andreas is his father. Because of their fingers, and your extraordinary intimacy with the old man, which must have *started* with love."

"I knew he would guess, so I told him."

"But that's not good for Neil. And it'll make a *real* scandal if he tells people you told him, Grania."

Carla looked rather worried.

"He won't tell anyone, Carla."

Carla looked at her, then shrugged her shoulders and returned to her bits of machine.

"It's your business, of course. Grania, why do you *like* men so much?"

"Well, I don't know. And after all I only like Andreas and Neil. I've never made friends with any other men. And I do find them a bit wearing after a whole day in their company, so there's grace in me yet. Do you know anything about a woman called Bernadine? I don't know her other name."

"She's a friend of Carla's. She hasn't been here long. She teaches. Transferred from some London school."

"What's she like?"

"Oh, rather attractive to look at, and of course she must have ability or she wouldn't be a teacher. They don't take fools. She's about twenty-eight, I should think. Quite an ordinary sort of person. Why?"

Grania yawned, stretching her arms out.

"I think I'm going home to bed after my exhausting day. I feel better for seeing you, Carla."

"How long are you going to stay in Salisbury?" asked Carla, looking at her in unobtrusive sisterly affection.

"I don't know. Oh, quite a time I shouldn't wonder. Perhaps a year. Perhaps forever. I'm nearly as middle-aged as you."

"*You'll* never stay anywhere forever. Not at the age of ninety."

"Well, I had a foreign father, and you had an English one. The German blood flows restlessly in my veins making whirlpools with the English and it drives me to wandering. But I shall be here for a while. I want to do some studies of Neil. By the way, when you see him, Carla, will you tell him to come to my studio at eleven o'clock next Sunday. He's a beautiful man, my son."

"Have you only just noticed it?"

"Oh, no."

"You've never wanted to do studies of him before."

"Well, Carla, you know what men are like. Modest and shy, and then the really manly ones like Neil always despise men who are willing to take off their clothes and sit as models. I think he won't mind so much now he *knows* I'm his Mother, even though he doesn't feel it.

"It was for that, then?"

"If you like. Carla, would you like to walk up with me to Stonehenge tomorrow?"

"Of course I can't. I've got to work tomorrow. You artists never do any steady work so your time's your own. But you couldn't run power stations on artistic principles."

"Nor mend sewing machines," said Grania, looking at the table full of bits. "Thank God I haven't got a mechanical mind. Goodnight, Carla. Don't forget to tell Neil."

II

GRANIA MIGHT MAKE UP HER MIND to do this or that, and say this, and risk that, but when Neil came to her on Sunday morning she discovered she did not know how to begin to tell him what she wanted him to know. The thing was too big and too difficult; the sheer mental labor of getting it even a quarter understood by an infantile mind like his appalled her, and there was still some resistance in her own mind. It was really resistance to the difficulty of her task. If she could have pressed a button and thereby transferred her knowledge to Neil she could have done it, but to get it into his head, and not only into his head but into his emotions, by word of mouth, seemed now too impossible to attempt.

She made him sit down, and to occupy herself and reassure him, for he was in a mild state of alarm, while she was thinking she did a charcoal sketch, but when she had finished it she thought: "Now I know the outside of his head better. Granite outside and soft as a rotten apple inside. Poor Neil. He is a beautiful fellow." Aloud she said, quite forgetting her real task for a moment: "Take off your coat and shirt, Neil."

Neil colored up, and very slowly began to take off his coat.

"Must I really take off my shirt?" he asked unhappily. "I—I shall be cold."

39

Grania looked at him in silence. Neil, submissive and obedient, and very shy, began to undo his shirt.

"No, no. Leave it on. I'd forgotten you wouldn't like it," Grania said, frowning heavily. "Perhaps some time—I know you have a lovely torso. But never mind that now."

"I believe if I could more think you my Mother I shouldn't mind," said Neil, very anxious to please. "Perhaps I shall after a bit."

"Well, put your coat on for now, anyway. But why *do* men mind uncovering their chests before women? If a woman was doing hot work she wouldn't mind wearing the thinnest possible vest, or no vest at all, even if men were there. So why should men mind?"

"*Some* don't mind," Neil said. "I know there are men models. But they're not very modest or manly people. I mean—I expect the ones you have are quite nice, but—"

"You don't think much of them?"

"Well, I don't think men ought to go stripping off their clothes before women."

Neil grew red again from the embarrassment the subject caused him.

"Shall I tell you the real reason, Neil? I know it, but you won't believe it."

"I shall believe anything you tell me."

"It's because you *really* are, inside you, ashamed of your sex. Ashamed of those portions of you which most markedly differ from women's bodies. You're ashamed that you have a flat chest which is of no biological use, and so you like to keep it out of sight. Women are not ashamed, but proud of their breasts which can feed children."

Neil took this without much apparent astonishment.

"I *did* feel, that morning when I was splitting the logs, that I didn't like myself. I told you. But then that's just *me*. Other men don't feel like that, I'm sure, but none of them would like to be models, none of the fellows I know."

"It's only that you are more conscious. What they feel miles underneath, you are beginning to *know*. And by the way, Neil, have you been seeing Bernadine?"

"Yes," said Neil. "Was it wrong? Would it have been better not to?"

"No. Of course it wasn't wrong. I don't want you to try to be a celibate. It would only upset things in that granite-rotten-apple head of yours."

"What is a celibate?"

"A person who has nothing to do with anyone of the opposite sex."

"There aren't any. Or not any men, certainly."

"No, it's a bit difficult. Women *could* do it, if there were any motive, but they don't. Men *couldn't*, now, but they could have once."

"I—Grania, really I know it's true if you say so, but I don't *believe* it. And what for, anyway?"

"Oh, lots of reasons. But those men had wills. Now you, Neil, have an extraordinary will for a man, but at the same time even with your modesty to help you, you have to take your shirt off if I tell you to. And I'm not your real Mother, only your think-Mother. You could go away, or you could simply stand there and refuse, but you *can't*. In any reasonable order you have to obey any woman, because her will is a giant, and yours is a child."

"Well, it's perfectly natural to obey women," said Neil, greatly bewildered. "What else would we do? I certainly wouldn't obey *men*."

Grania sighed. Her task reared up like a mountain, and even when she had got something into *Neil's* head it was hardly begun. He was, after all, an exceptional man.

"Look here, Neil, if you had two kittens, a tom and a she, and fed them both equally, in the end wouldn't the tom be bigger than the she?"

"Yes."

"But supposing you fed the she well and gave the tom only *just* enough food so that it could *just* live and *just* crawl about, the she would grow the biggest and strongest?"

"Yes. But it wouldn't be a very decent thing to do, to starve the little tom."

"No. Very indecent. But now supposing you fed the tom with everything it could lap, cream and lots of raw meat later on, and starved the little she so that it could *just* live, there'd be a *very big* difference between them, wouldn't there?"

"Yes."

"Well, that *very big* difference is the difference there is now between women's psyches and men's."

"But you said the tom—the he—the *tom* was the fed one. No, I don't understand that at all. And what is a psyche?"

"It's a part of the mind. The soul, if you like. The seat of the will. If you have a very small, weak psyche you have a very small, weak will. It has nothing to sit on, so to speak. If you have a giant overdeveloped psyche you have a giant overdeveloped will. But about the tom and the she, that was only an illustration. The female psyche is the strong tough one *naturally.* The male is the weak soft one. It goes the opposite way to their bodies. Even in animals who are not conscious and have not got psyches like ours this rule holds good. It's for the protection of the young. Nature cannot trust animals to be kind or chivalrous on all occasions, and if the female, who is usually weaker in body, could not develop a tremendous psychic savagery, an inflexible *will*, when her young ones are threatened they would be frequently eaten or injured even by their own fathers. But the fathers, and often other animals too, are afraid to touch young animals when the mother is there. Any of them would rather attack a male of the same species, who is stronger physically, but less cunning and savage in anger, and less utterly determined to prevail. But at one time, Neil, the females of the human species were so starved psychically that their natural psychic power was not there. They could protect neither their children nor themselves, and were as weak and helpless as the little tom kitten would be. They were meant to be psychically very vigorous and healthy, but they *could not grow.* Any more than you can now."

"How was it done?" asked Neil, with much interest, but, as Grania saw, with no real belief that such a thing had ever really happened. She thought: "I might be telling him an Old World fairy story about giants and witches. Nothing will ever make him *understand*. He can't. He's not conditioned to understand anything." But she went on:

"By making the infant psyche ashamed of its sex. Not ashamed of being sexual, though that happened too, but ashamed of the kind of psyche it was. A psyche *cannot* grow unless it's content with its sex. If it's *proud* of it and thinks the other is inferior it will overdevelop, if it's ashamed of it it can't develop at all, if it's content with it it will develop naturally, to the strength it's meant to be. It *must* have this content. It's like milk to the kitten. Its first and most necessary food. Animals are always content with their sex, neither regarding the other as inferior. In leadership, if the qualities wanted are male, physical strength and swiftness, males will lead. If less strength and more cunning is wanted, females will lead. The wisest of all the wild animals, and the most mysterious to us, the elephant, is led by females. In neither case does the nonleading sex feel any shame. But among human beings, who have always *human* nonsexual values, if you make one child think, *believe,* that in human values it is less than a child of the opposite sex it becomes ashamed of its sex, its psyche starves, its brain is dulled, and its will is weakened. Supposing your idea of God is a pantheon of gods and goddesses headed by a Father-God—"

"I don't think you could ever think of that," Neil said, so much interested he had to interrupt, "but I *have* thought that God *is* rather like a Mother, perhaps."

"This is going to be terrible, Neil. Terrible. Well, but listen. Supposing you *did* have a Father-God at the head of this pantheon, the girl-children, when they came to know a bit about religion, couldn't identify themselves with the Father-God, but only with the lesser women-goddesses, so they would begin to feel ashamed of their sex, and their psyches would starve. But supposing there was *only one God,* and this God was purely masculine, and they had *nothing* divine to identify themselves with, then they would starve worse. And supposing this God thought women unfit to serve him, in his ritual, because they were somehow dirty and not so noble as men, then do you see, they would be still more ashamed, and still more starved?"

"Why, I see that they might be. But what is ritual, and why should God be *served?* What does it mean, serving God?"

"It was a Man-God that had to be served and praised," said Grania, first frowning with worry, and then laughing.

"If it was one or the other it ought to have been a Woman-God. Now it would seem just possible to serve and praise a Woman-

God, but who would bother with a Man? Neither the women nor
the men can ever have done that."

"Well, they just did."

"I don't see how."

"Neither do I *see how,* because of course we don't think of God
as needing service or ritual or praising from people any more than
It needs it from animals. But supposing your Mother had told you
when you were a little boy that God was a Divine Mother and
always called this God She, you'd have been quite ready to serve
and praise Her. Because men's minds are infantile, and an-
thropomorphism would present no intellectual difficulties. It
would be Carla who couldn't think of God as a Woman, not you.
But now listen, supposing in addition to this difficulty about God
and religious uncleanness, the infant psyche comes to know that
besides being somehow rather distasteful to God it is debarred by
its sex from knowledge, skill and responsibility, all human joy, in
fact, then it becomes yet more ashamed of its sex, more starved,
more dulled in the brain, and shrinks from even the thought of
those things which as a healthy human being it should be striving
for all its life. If I were to say to you, now Neil come along and I'll
teach you to pilot an airplane, or manage a power station as your
Mother does, or I'll put you up next year as a representative on the
Salisbury Council, you'd think me quite mad. Men couldn't do any
of those, you'd say. It's not *men's work."*

"Well, of course it isn't," Neil said. "We don't *want* to do those
things. We've got our own work."

"Because you're so starved with sex shame and so uneducated
that you can't contemplate doing anything that's more than semi-
skilled, or undertaking anything at all that entails responsibility.
You always have to work under the direction of women."

"None of us would work under the direction of *men.* If Magnus
was my boss—well, it wouldn't *do,"* said Neil firmly. "I don't
believe men could ever have bossed men."

"If you learn as a child to be ashamed of your sex, naturally all
your life you despise the other people who are of your sex, who are
like you. No human being *can* live without some self-esteem, so
you none of you consciously despise yourselves, but you despise

other men. There's as much jealousy, contempt, suspicion and hostility among men now as there was once among women. In fact there's far more, for women always had the bond of motherhood to draw them together, giving them, at times, a feeling of sympathy and solidarity. You have nothing, for your only part in sex must drive you always further apart. You're always quarrelling, and often fighting."

"Well, fighting is fun. We like it."

"So do male animals at certain seasons. You are allowed to concentrate a large part of your attention on your sexual attraction and ability and your feats of male pugnacity, because the more successful as a sexual animal a human being is, with a starved psyche, the less will he or she want to be a *real* human being. That's why you, Neil, are quite remarkable, because you *are* a successful animal, singularly so, and yet you do show signs of wanting to be a human being."

"I shouldn't, if it meant being bossed by men and not by women. But of course that could never be. And, Grania, I don't think men are ashamed of their sex, because if they were they'd be unhappy. But they're not. I am, but only sometimes. It's gone off now completely."

"Was there ever a time when you were a boy that you wished, for a single minute, that you'd been born a girl?"

"I do remember just one time when Carla was teasing me, and I did think for a minute I wished I didn't have to be a boy. But I know it didn't last. You shut Carla up, I remember, and I thought just that I'd been very silly."

"If you'd been more conscious, if all men were getting a little more food for their psyches, all of them would wish, as children, that they'd been born girls. At present they're too depressed even to be consciously envious of the privileged sex."

"They're not depressed," said Neil.

"Neil, do you or don't you think I know what I'm talking about? Am I or am I not wiser than you? How do you think I knew what you were going to do when you told Andreas you were going home with him?"

"Oh, you *do*, you *are*," said Neil humbly. "I know you know all about everything. But it's so *difficult* for me to understand. You've no idea. You tell me men are depressed and ashamed, and I see them hopping round as merrily as rabbits. It was only *me*. They're all right."

"They're better off in one way than you, certainly. And of course you *like* to think you're the only one. But try and understand this. It's what happened to the unconscious part of, say, Magnus. He was born, and from the very first time he could remember his Mother was the only adult that meant anything in his world. She provided his food, his clothes, his play, his pleasure and the love he needed. Later he grew to understand that it was she who worked for him to feed him when he was too young to feed himself. He learned to obey her as absolutely as a young animal obeys his mother, because, if he does not, he will very likely not live to grow up. To Magnus, as to the young animal, his Mother was all-wisdom, all-power, and all-love. Women are reasonable, if they are real women and not starved weaklings, and it is very improbable that Magnus' Mother ever required him to do anything he could not do, or to refrain from anything, such as scuffling with other little boys, that was part of his male-animal nature. So he trusted her implicitly. It was always perfectly natural to him that people like his Mother should rule the world, and not people like his father, whom he has never seen and does not know. He sees men about the streets, but he has nothing to do with them till he is fourteen, and he takes really no personal interest in them until he is beginning to grow up. Then he thinks, I should like to be big, like that one, or a good runner, like this one, or very handsome, like the other. But long before that, when he was quite a small boy, he could see that there was a difference between himself and his Mother and his sister. Between boys who would not be Mothers, only men, and girls who would be Mothers and rule the world. The differences in dress, hair, size, carriage, gestures and movements all arise, he *feels*, he does not think exactly, from the main difference in the structure of the body. So he feels, unconsciously, that what is so different in him is not, as it would be in the reverse case and the reverse starvation, a sign of power, but a *deformity*, a thing it would have been better to be *without*. Mothers are *without*. He is *with*. The lack is far better than the possession. He becomes modest, and is not discouraged, he would not *like* to be dressed as girls are, or to be as careless as girls are as to whether they show their chests or not. Of his chest he is again unconsciously ashamed, but this time of a lack, not of a possession. Mothers have soft breasts, he has none, only two attempts that came to nothing. So he grows up absolutely bound in an unconscious shame that does not make him at all consciously unhappy, because he so loves his Mother, and because he has a happy physical life which suits his male body, and even when he comes to know that his deformity is useful and necessary and the source of great pleasure, and that the race could not do without men, yet still his sex shame holds him. And his Mother-bond. His psyche is starved, his brain is dulled so that he never could learn what girls have to learn, and his will is almost nonexistent, compared with his Mother's and other women's wills. Also, he can really never be an individual. He is an undifferentiated *man*. For the psyche, besides being the seat of the will, is the soul of the *you-ness* of you, the Neil-ness of Neil, and if it is starved you cannot really think or do things because you are Neil, but only those things that other men think and do. At least *you can*, but Magnus could not. He is on the dead flat level of masculinity, undifferentiated except physically, and unindividual. He has no Ego, except that minute portion necessary to his existence as a human being. If he had none at all he would be a complete animal. As it is he is little more than a docile contented hardworking pleasant animal. The average woman on seeing Magnus doesn't think, 'how I despise Magnus,' any more than a cattle-breeder keeps on thinking, 'how I despise my bull.' She thinks: 'That bull's a fine bull,' or 'a not-so-good bull.' If you men got discontented and uppish women would despise you consciously, but *as things are now* you are all so hopeless that they never think of you at all except sexually, and then of course they admire you. Now do you understand *anything?*"

"Not much, I don't think," said Neil despondently. "I told you it would be too difficult for me."

"Shall I get Magnus and try to get *him* to understand? Or Andreas?"

"Oh, no!" said Neil instantly. "Of course they'd be no good. Magnus is a perfect fool, really. I—perhaps I shall sort of grow to understand. But what do you want me to *do?*"

"Be discontented and uppish. I want all men to be, but I start with you."

"But then are you going to change the world so that I have to be ordered about by men, as if I were a boy in boarding school?"

"You seem to think I can change the world very easily, young Neil. It's flattering. No, I can promise you that all *your* life you shall be directed by women. By me."

"I shall like *that*. But now *you said* that at one time the girls were starved and the boys not and that—did you say? That men ruled not only other men, but *women too?*"

A light of horrified excitement came into Neil's eyes. Grania thought: "My exhaustion is not for nothing. Something is *at last* getting through."

"Yes. They were the Lords of Creation," said Grania. "And if they hadn't turned themselves into Lords of Destruction they might have kept their place." This sarcasm was incomprehensible to Neil.

"How long ago was it?" he asked.

"Since their time of absolutely unchallenged supremacy? Roughly, about five thousand years."

The excitement and horror died out of Neil's eyes.

"That's a long time," he murmured. "Too long. Five thousand years. Why, I can't *think* of more than about fifty. The women and the men must be absolutely *different* now. After all that time."

"They are, absolutely different mentally. But it isn't the length of time so much. And, Neil, do think of this. You can change men, or you can change women, almost unrecognizably, by sex shame and starvation of their psyches, but *human needs* are always the same. The human need for the self-esteem necessary to full mental and moral development never changes, any more than the animal need for enough food to develop the physical body as fully as possible. So, you see, while the *need* is there, and it always will be, nothing is permanently irremediable. Women and men can go up and down like children on a seesaw, but *human nature* is like the boy that stands in the middle. Do you see?"

"I might be beginning to. Grania, would you tell me something? Answer a question?"

"Of course I will, if I can."

But Neil couldn't get his question out. He hummed and hawed, rubbed the back of his head, pulled his beard, and got red.

"I don't want you to think I'm prying into women's affairs," he said at last.

"But that's just what you've got to do, however much it alarms you."

"Well, then, is it true that women have a secret language?"

"Quite true," said Grania. Her thick eyebrows lifted in astonishment. "How did any of you find that out? Surely no legend could last among you men for four thousand years."

"It was something a man told Magnus, that he'd heard from someone else, that women could talk among themselves a language that wasn't French or German or Italian or any of the ordinary ones. And that they all knew it, so that whatever country they belonged to they could understand each other. I don't know how he knew. What is the language?"

"It's an old one, older than English or French, called Latin. Italian is derived from it, but no Italian boy could understand it without being taught it. No boy is ever taught it. All girls are. Some of your names are Latin. Magnus is one."

"Does it mean anything?"

"It means 'great,'" said Grania drily.

"He is not as big as I am. You ought to have called me Magnus."

"You weren't very big when we had to start calling you something. Now you'd better go away, Neil, and think about what I've told you, and try to understand it as much as you can, and remember you're quite different from other men and that I have great hopes of you. And Neil," Grania added casually, but with a serious look, "remember too that if you tell any woman *anything,* even the tiniest hint, it'll mean my death. Perhaps yours, too. But certainly mine."

"Death!" whispered Neil, staring at her in horror. "Your *death?* They would—would *kill you?*"

"They wouldn't take my life in an abrupt, violent and barbarous fashion. But I should have to lay it down, like Socrates. This civilization is not run on sentimental lines. And we're a great deal harsher to ourselves than we ever are to you."

"But *death*," repeated Neil, unable to take it in. "Why, people are punished sometimes, but never *killed*."

"More people than you think, Neil. But all female people."

"I shall hardly dare to speak to a woman."

"Nonsense. Speak to them just like you always do. But be careful. You've got wits enough for that."

"Can I speak to Magnus or Andreas?"

"Not yet. And not ever to Andreas. He's too old. I made up my mind he was too old four years ago, and he is now four years older. Andreas must be let alone. And you're not to speak to anyone till I say you can."

Neil pondered.

"Does Mother know, that you're telling me things?"

"No."

"I wish she did."

"So do I. You don't know how much, Neil. But Carla wouldn't help me. And don't think that because she is my sister she'd hesitate to denounce me, because she wouldn't. She'd feel she had to."

"It'll make me very uncomfortable with her, having a fearful secret like this I can't tell her."

"Well, I warned her you would be shy, because I let her know I had told you you were my son. And you needn't think Carla is at all suspicious. She trusts me absolutely not to go beyond a certain point in eccentricity. Absolutely. It's a pity—all that part."

"Are you sad?" asked Neil. His very blue eyes were full of love and anxiety.

"Rather sad. No, not really. Anyway, someone's *got to be*."

"You should go to Old Sarum. It's a nice place for being sad in."

"I went to Stonehenge instead."

"And did you cry? Do women ever cry? I've never seen one, except little girls."

"Most don't. I do sometimes, but I didn't at Stonehenge. I think my affairs have got a bit too serious for weeping. Now go along, Neil, and when I'm ready to teach you some of the past history of the human race, not what *you* learn, which though it goes back a long way is really all the present, I'll let you know. Goodbye, son."

She kissed him and pushed him gently out of the door. She shut it, and stood for a little while in meditation when a loud mew from outside roused her. She opened the door and a young, handsome cat walked in. He purred wholeheartedly and rubbed himself against her legs. It was Grania's cat, which had been living with Carla while his owner was in Russia, but had now returned happily to the studio.

"Well, Pharaoh," said Grania, picking him up. She stroked him absentmindedly with one hand. She sighed with fatigue. "I really would rather try to teach *you* elementary sex psychology. You'd take it in about as well as Neil, I'm sure. But if he can't understand the elements, how can he understand the history?"

Pharaoh purred even louder at the sound of her voice. Grania gave him some milk. She lay down on a flat, hard divan that stood by one wall of the studio and relaxed every muscle and tendon of her body. She banished all thought from her mind. Very soon she was sound asleep, and never noticed when Pharaoh came up beside her and after purring and cuddling for a bit, went to sleep also.

When she woke up, an hour later, she felt much refreshed, but a very familiar feeling of restlessness pervaded her. She prowled up and down the studio for some time, then she changed her clothes, put a few things in a small bag, and taking Pharaoh under one arm she left the studio and locked it. She went to Carla's house, who exclaimed, not at the sight of her sister, but at the cat.

"I thought you meant to stay here for a year or forever," she said.

"I want to go to London for a day or two."

"Why don't you do some work?"

"Oh, I can't."

"What did you do with Neil?"

"I drew a sketch of his head. But I don't know quite what I do mean to do with him yet. Nothing more for a few days."

"Well, as you are here come and have some food. Have you telephoned for your seat in the plane?"

"There won't be many people in it on Sunday. Don't bother,

Carla. Haven't you got rather a crowd here?" asked Grania, as a door opened and the sound of women's voices came through it.

"Only Carla and a few young women."

"I hate young women," said Grania viciously. "I'm beginning to feel about them like Andreas does about young men. I think I'll go away, perhaps."

But Carla took her arm and made her come into the dining room, and sit down and eat. One of the young women was called Bernadine. Grania looked at her with concealed gloom. "If Neil can't hold his tongue," she thought, "and be as discreet as a woman, there's my death sitting opposite me eating an orange. But I can't keep him away from women, so it's no good worrying. She's very attractive."

Grania hardly spoke during the meal, though all the young women were prepared to listen to her with respect. Soon afterwards she went away down to the airport, and after what seemed a very long time of waiting the Eastbound plane came in. After that it did not take long to reach London. She went to the great Central Women's House, where the government of England had its head-quarters. It was a new building, very new. She looked at the decoration of the outside.

"I did that," she thought, feeling for a moment or two quite peaceful. "I shall never do anything big again. But it's quite a nice traitor's memorial. Better than a moldy head on London Bridge. Lasts longer."

She went inside, passing the women at the inner door with a nod. In a very big library she spent what remained of the day, reading.

Later, she went to a certain flat in a big block on the edge of the river. The owner was there, alone, very pleased to see her. It was a German woman, a permanent resident in London representing the German Council.

"I thought you were in Russia, Grania."

"I believe I still am," said Grania moodily. "I know I wish I was. Can you put me up for the night, Elisabet?"

"Certainly. Are you off somewhere else tomorrow?"

"Not out of England. Back to Salisbury I expect."

"What have you come to London for?"

"Oh, to see you. Or hear someone speak German."

"If you want to hear German, why don't you go to Germany?"

"I haven't been there for five years."

"Why not?"

"I don't know. I don't know. Or I can't be bothered to find out."

"You are in a mood, aren't you?"

"Yes."

Grania went to the window and opened it wide. She leaned out. Elisabet came and leaned too. It was dark and cold. Lights shone in the water of the river. London was very quiet.

"Isn't it extraordinary to think of *this place*," said Grania in a low voice as if she might wake somebody, *something*. "How old it is. What a long time people have been living on this ignoble little river. All the cities that have been, bits falling down and bits being built up until it's all in the end a new city and yet never new all at once. Even after the Fire. They might have had a better *piece* of city then, if they'd had any sense. All the cities, foul ones and smoky ones, and clean, and noisy, and quiet, and for it to be London all the time. People being born and dying, and water flowing. Foul water and clean, poor sick savages or sound civilized human beings, but all water and all people. But the water is much the oldest. The people might pass away and the water be left. So it would go on running just the same, without any bridges, any ships, any London."

Grania pulled her head in and stood by the window. A cold draught blew in. She shivered.

"Let's shut it," said Elisabet.

Grania stared down at her, but said nothing. Her eyes looked enormous and dark and quite blind.

"What's the matter?" asked the German, touching her gently on the arm.

"Elisabet, I—I *knew* something, then."

"What, then? Come back to the fire. These damp English May nights are very chilly. There, that's better."

She shut the window.

Grania said: "I knew something that's not happened, so it must be going to. Something to do with a window, and looking out, and its being cold, and someone shivering. *Me?* I don't know. But it's very important, Elisabet."

"You artists are all inclined to be unbalanced and neurotic. Your imaginations are overdeveloped."

"It was knowledge," said Grania. "I know how my *imagination* works. And you German not-artists are like lumps of cold clay."

Elisabet laughed.

"That doesn't come so well from a half-German. Not kind. By the way, I had a letter from Anna K. this morning. Do you want to read it? She asked me if I knew where you were."

"You can tell her I'm in Salisbury," said Grania carelessly. "I am going to be there. I shall settle down now. Yes, my wanderings are quite over, you can tell Anna."

III

On the next Sunday Neil was again summoned to his aunt-Mother's studio. He went in a condition of eagerness, excitement, and some pride, for as he told her as soon as he saw her, he had now asserted his individuality and independence of other men to the extreme extent of refusing to fight when challenged.

"No, Neil!" said Grania, really astonished.

"Yes," said Neil. "I was swaggering, and Magnus and the others got fed up with it, and Magnus smacked my face at a meal. So of course I challenged him, and I said I'd fight two of them together if they liked, because Magnus can't beat me alone, and they wouldn't, and we went outside, and there was a cool wind blowing, and I suddenly decided I wouldn't fight at all, because there was nothing really to fight about, so I told Magnus I was sorry I'd been so aggressive, and he said he didn't care for that, and that I must fight him. But I still said I wouldn't, and that they couldn't make me, so of course Magnus said if I wouldn't fight I must be kicked. So I was. It was awful, Grania. I never have been kicked like a coward before."

"So I suppose you turned round and knocked Magnus down."

"No, I didn't. If I'd done that I wouldn't tell you about it because it wouldn't *mean* anything. I just went away. And next day

Magnus asked me why on earth I'd done such a thing, because of course he knows I'm not afraid of him, and I couldn't tell him because you've told me not to say anything, and he was very much puzzled, but friendly in a way. I think he'd be a good person to start telling. He wasn't so terribly shocked with me as the other men. But of course he's rather a fool."

"Well, I think it was quite amazing of you, Neil, and if you go on the way you've begun, with having even occasional control over your sex desire, and refusing to fight *every* time you're challenged, we'll be able to make a man of you before you die. But you don't know enough yet to tell Magnus anything. Now look at these two pictures."

Grania had two small pictures on separate easels. Even Neil, quite untutored as he was, could see that they could not be by the same hand. The subjects only were alike, a cloudy landscape.

"Which of those two do you like best?" Grania asked him.

Neil thought.

"I don't know. They are very *different*, aren't they? That's one of yours. I saw it last Sunday. I think I like the one that's not yours best. It gives me a funny feeling."

"You have some intuition, Neil. That picture, the one you like, was painted in a different age of humanity altogether. It's a reproduction of a picture painted about five thousand years ago. It was painted by a man."

Neil was astounded.

"Do you mean men were *artists?*" he cried. "They couldn't have been."

"Any human being can be an artist so long as its psyche is sufficiently developed to split into the bisexual psyche necessary to the artist. A very weak, starved psyche cannot be bisexual, can't ever become an artist psyche. So if one sex is completely starved it cannot produce artists. So in the days when that picture was painted, the men were everything, painters, poets, sculptors, musicians, writers, and the women were nothing, just as you are now nothing. But you can see from those two pictures that when women's psyches are so fully developed that they can form their own art, instead of being, as they were at first, completely bound in the tradition of masculine art, their work is quite different. The psyche of any artist is bisexual, but the offspring produced by the two sides of the psyche are always either all male or all female. The base of *our* rhythm and design is the masculine figure, not the feminine. The hard, strong psyche reaches out naturally to the hard, strong form, angular, not rounded. What attracts us sexually is the base of the form of our art. We use the masculine figure in composition, we draw and paint and use for sculpture far more male models than female. With men it was of course the other way. Unless they were inhibited by religious scruples they used the feminine form more than the masculine, and their design was curved. The soft, weak psyche, for even when men's psyches were overdeveloped as far as they possibly could be, they were still soft and weak, reached out to the soft, curved female form. Their art was more flowing, more gracious, and weaker than ours is. No Childhood Age man, unless he were conditioned to like it, could possibly admire my picture more than that one. It would strike him as harsh and graceless. But when women first started to be artists they were absolutely bound in the masculine tradition. They couldn't get away from it to do what they really wanted to. Their psyches were only just beginning to develop properly. So they did bad imitation masculine art. It was no good at all."

Neil listened earnestly, but understood almost nothing of this.

"I don't think I shall ever understand anything about art," he said. "But why did the women in that time so long ago *let* the men rule and be artists and everything? It sounds so frightfully unnatural. The Mothers must have brought the boys up, just as they do now."

"Well, not quite. There were fathers as well. But the Mothers brought the boys up to despise them. That is the central point, the relation between Mother and son. If the Mother brings up the boy to regard her as inferior to himself, men rule. If she brings him up to regard himself as inferior, women rule."

"But I don't see *why* she did make him think she was inferior."

"Because *her* Mother had made her think she was of less importance in the world, of less human value, than her brother or father."

"But how did it *start?* When did it begin? I can see that once it started it would go on by itself. But it must have had a beginning."

"We don't know. It's so long ago that there are no trustworthy records. It seems just possible that at the very beginning of the Childhood Age, when people were so primitive as to be almost animals, there may have been in some tribes a kind of matriarchy. Not like ours, of course. Not nearly so complete, and not founded on reason and knowledge. But we have no real evidence. The thing we *know* about, all we women, is the patriarchy of the Childhood Age, which went on, varying in completeness from time to time, and from place to place, for thousands upon thousands of years."

"It must have been awful," said Neil, trying to think of men being fit to rule; not succeeding.

"It was necessary," said Grania. "Now I'm afraid I may make you blush. But in those days women, who looked more or less like they do now, but who were mentally absolutely different, had no control whatever over their own sexual life. They had to bear as many children as they conceived, and they had to conceive as many as their owners wanted, or at any rate as many as their owners begot. This again was necessary, because an enormous number of the children died in infancy, or before they were old enough to beget or to bear. So the women had no time or strength to do anything but keep the race going. By the time they were past childbearing they were worn out, useless, like an old horse. Childbearing was their job, all through the Childhood Age. And there was more to it than that. Men, whose psyches are of the soft, weak kind *naturally,* could not *do* without somebody to admire them humanly, not only sexually, while they were undergoing the terrific physical and mental toil of subduing the forces of nature to the needs of civilized peoples. Men had to do it, because the women could not do anything but just keep the race alive, and to do it they *had* to be looked up to, almost as gods. You learn as much history as we think you ought to know, and as much truth as we think good for you. You think women civilized the race. They did not. It was done by men, and the price that *had to be* paid was the humiliation of women. Yet, because no individual or group can do a wrong thing (whether it is recognized as wrong or not) without the consequences of wrong ensuing, that necessary humiliation, every tear and drop of blood and sweat and agony, has to be paid for again, by you, by men."

Neil struggled to get his unused brain to work, and after a long frowning silence said: "Then civilization was a wrong thing to try to do."

"We don't look at it that way. We believe that the Will of God is behind everything that ever happens on earth or in the whole universe, and that it is what *we* call a 'good' Will. We don't, of course, believe that *God* thinks in that human way. But we believe that the struggles of the human race are all good. We two, Neil, we two tiny little specks, in a line of hundreds of miles of specks, are good, part of God's Will. I feel it is right to talk to you, and you feel it is right to listen to me. Therefore we are good, even though everyone else, as far as I know, would say we are bad. But if it is God's Will that this cold and reasonable female tyranny is nearing its end, then we two specks shall be able to start something large; and if it is *not*, then we shall end in futility, having done nothing. But whatever happens will be right and good. Just as it is right and good that the women now believe absolutely sincerely that though men were meant to rule in the Childhood Age, women *are meant* to rule in what they believe is the maturity of the race, forever and ever, or rather, for as long as the earth is habitable. They believe, quite as strongly, and far more reasonably than any of those Old Men did in *their* 'natural' right, that it is God's Will women should rule. The Old Men emotionally felt that it was impossible and unnatural that females should rule, but it had never been tried. The women *know* that it is not impossible for men to rule, but they also know that when a certain stage of civilization was reached men's rule meant disaster. Their objection is not emotional, but purely reasonable. And you and I are up against not only that force of reason, but also women's pride. Each sex in power has its own fault. The men's was vanity and arrogance. But the women's is pride. It's the difference in the natural strength of the psyches. Men were inclined to be subconsciously uneasy, not quite sure of themselves. They very often cared what women thought about them, apart from sexual thoughts. But women do not care in the least what men think of them. They care what other women think, that's all."

"It seems quite right to me they should be proud and not care," said Neil. "I shouldn't like *you* to be unproud."

"But you don't like being unproud either."

"No."

"Can't you see how it's my proudness that makes you un-proud?"

"No. You help me to be proud. You tell me things, you trust me, I'm fearfully proud."

"*I* do, but other women don't. There've got to be more me's and you's, don't you see, Neil?"

Neil thought.

"I believe," he said, "that you must have the most pride of all of them, because you don't mind giving me some of it."

"That sounds like sense," said Grania, rather gloomily, "but I know perfectly well that there may be deep, dark, bloody reasons for what I do that aren't half so complimentary to me. But I needn't bother you with them. You couldn't understand me."

"Could I understand why the men's rule ever stopped?"

"It stopped because men's rule, in the end, implied the exter-mination of such large portions of the civilized races that a lapse into barbarism, and a complete loss of all that men with their fearful toil, and women by their constant humiliation, had gained throughout the centuries, was imminent, and not for the first, but for the *second time.* Civilization would have been ruined by the *civilized men themselves.* Do you understand?"

"It seems quite probable," said Neil, out of his ingrained contempt for his own sex.

"Civilizations, before this time I'm speaking of, had often been ruined, but by war from without. By barbaric, that is, more back-ward, peoples sweeping in and overcoming the civilized race by force of arms. But in the time I mean there was no backward nation in the whole world that was strong enough to threaten the huge powerful civilized nations. Civilization was for the first time im-pregnable from without. So, out of that peculiar fundamental male silliness, a kind of ghastly silliness which characterized men's rule from the first to the last, they made two magnificent attempts to destroy it from within. The first nearly succeeded. The second was in the nature of a lost cause. It was after the second that the women finally realized that men were not fit to rule, and never had been. Ruling, as we understand it, was the one thing they never could do. All their government was based on some fundamental silly male idea, such as that God was masculine, or that a king was divine, or that one set of people was inherently more noble than another, or that one nation had a natural right to bully other nations, or that one race was better than another race, or that one kind of male idea about God was much better than another kind. So, even when at times their rule *seemed* reasonable, it never was so, for at any moment the emotion always arising from the fundamental silly idea might completely fog what judgment they had. Men's rule was always emotional and always based on physical force. Women's rule has always been reasonable, and based on psychic power. They rule the world now, as one or two of the exceptional ones used to rule their own households in the Childhood Age, absolutely, but reasonably. But had women, whether exceptional or not, ruled their households then as men were ruling countries, they would have boiled the children for soup because it was too much trouble to go out and buy some bones. But while men were still subduing the powers of nature to their needs their emotional misrule did not threaten the *race*. Wars were fought—"

"What are wars?" Neil asked.

"You know what a fight is?"

"Of course."

"Supposing a group of men should undertake a fight against another group, without any personal quarrel between any man on one side and any man on the other, and all have knives in their hands, that would be a war. A very primitive one."

"But how could you fight a man without any personal quarrel? And they were very cowardly, unmanly men to fight with knives. *We* never fight with knives. I think those men were contemptible."

"They wanted to kill each other, and the women wanted them to kill each other too. But we don't want you to kill each other, so we very early teach you that fighting with weapons or superiority of numbers is cowardly and unmasculine. But I was telling you that these early wars did not really matter to the race. Some men were killed in them, some women and some children were starved in sieges or maltreated and massacred by victorious armies, some towns were destroyed and some countries laid waste. But all on a small scale, owing to difficulties of transport and the comparative inadequacy of their weapons. Each man in a day's fighting could only kill the number of men his physical strength sufficed for. Later on, one man, by no means particularly strong, could easily kill, or cause to die, a hundred men in a minute. The deadliness of the weapons came with the final subduing of the powers of nature to the needs of civilized men. Men, with the aid of machines, could produce, easily, all the food and necessaries required by the sum of the people on the planet at any given time. It is true that at first they could not *distribute* the food. They found it far easier to distribute the death from their weapons of destruction than the life from their engines of production. And because they found it difficult to distribute the life, their fundamental emotionalism became a death-hysteria, which was a serious threat to civilization. But long before this death-hysteria became acute there had been a gradual rise on the part of European women, a slight increase in self-esteem, caused, we suppose, by the Christian religion becoming formal, and losing its vital power. It lost its vital power owing to scientific discoveries which made men, but not women at first, distrust its dogma. When the religion was formal, though women were still unclean (that is, less acceptable to God than were men, not allowed to approach God except through a priest who must be male) they *felt* their uncleanness less, because it was a formal and not a vital uncleanness. They became less deeply and unconsciously ashamed of their sex. They began to wonder if they were not, after all, human beings with certain human necessities and human rights. They still thought men must always rule, and they still felt themselves inferior, but they set up a demand for education and political power.

"This women's movement caused a reaction in the men of the nature of which they were not themselves aware, for they knew at the time very little of the working of their own minds. But it made their emotional misrule still more emotional and still less reasonable, and the end of the first women's movement came in a vast war during which death was distributed to ten million men, and the necessities of life withheld from millions of men, women and children. It was quite the most efficient distribution of death that had yet been seen. There was no reason at all for this war except the hysteria of the male rulers. Nothing was settled by it which could not have been settled by reasonable people without having a war at all, and the peace which followed this highly emotional war seems to have been the most emotional and least reasonable peace that was ever made. But the women of Europe, who were naturally all brought up to be male in their ideas, could not help a great accession of inferiority-feeling owing to their physical bodies being better fitted to produce life than to distribute death, so they all threw up their own struggle and entered into the men's. They had no solidarity with the women of other countries; they accepted the male death-hysteria, made it their own, and behaved in a completely male way from the beginning of the war to the end.

"But in this war, which owing to improved transport was conducted with very huge armies, so that enormous numbers of men were engaged on purely destructive work, it was discovered that women must help with the productive work in the countries or the war could not go on. It was also discovered that women could do anything within their physical strength so long as they were taught. So they did endless things of which they had been believed to be naturally and forever incapable, and while the men were relieved at the time, even pleased, after the war they became very nervous. The prop of religion had been knocked away from their superiority, and now the supposed mental incapacity of women to do and learn certain things was seen to be a fiction. And though the women had behaved in a most exemplary male way during the war, and had been quite as hysterical as the men, there was no certainty that they would go on being male forever, *if there were no more wars*.

"A new and very extraordinary issue for humanity began to emerge, too horrible to look at. It had to be veiled in fogs of sentiment and emotionalism, confused by a vital but, as it turned out, less important economic issue, and yet in all the fog and mist and the unwillingness of both women and men to face it, it was there, after what we call the Big War, to distinguish it from the Last War. The issue, now that men had conquered nature, was, should men go on ruling by emotion, based on physical force; or should women rule by reason, based on the superior power of their psyches? And was the world to be a pleasant place for men, or was it to be a safe place for children to grow up in? The fundamental object of all purely female governance is to protect the young; but the fundamental object of all purely male rule is to protect male power.

"So, though this issue was not recognized consciously by anyone, because no one dared to look it in its hideous face, as soon as the nations had a little recovered from their devastating war, the men started a deliberate cult of violence, emotionalism and unreasonableness, and now openly admitted, what men had never admitted before, that not only did they rule the world by emotion, but that it was right to do so, and that any even seeming reasonableness must be eliminated as soon as possible. Rule must be as instinctive, as emotional and as violent as possible, and the noblest violence, which was war, must be worshipped. This doctrine naturally included the complete resubmission of women, and the loss of the partial independence they had gained as a result of their efforts in the war. A new generation of women had grown up whose psyches had been badly starved in their war-childhood when, for more than four years, man-worship had been inevitable. Women could not be soldiers, and whatever useful work they did counted for very little against the risks and agonies and glories of the soldiers. So the girls of the war-period despised themselves more than the former generation, and there was a cleavage between the older women who wanted to keep the independence they had, and those younger ones who threw it cheerfully on the altar of fascism. Also the young women hoped that their submission would relieve the growing tension they had felt in the years after the war between themselves and the men, and make the young men more willing to marry and support them.

"This doctrine of the rightness of emotion and the evil of reason, the goodness of blood and the badness of brains, the innocence of male will-to-power and the devilishness of female will-to-power, was first stated in this country by a man who had every incentive to hate the big war, and who objected in his own person to physical violence. His work is so male and so fundamentally silly that it is very difficult for a woman to read, especially as I'm sure it doesn't translate well, but we do read it because Lawrence, this English novelist and poet, is historically important. He was the English prophet of the cult of emotion and blood and instinct which later on, after he was dead, swept over most of the European nations like a disease."

"What's that?"

"Illness."

"Illness doesn't sweep about," Neil objected.

"It doesn't now, but it did then. They had rows of catching illnesses which people could pass from one to another. And they caught their mental diseases, patriotism and fascism and death-hysteria, in just the same way."

"And did they die of them?"

"Ten million men died of patriotism between 1914 and 1918."

"But what *is* it?"

"It was a morbid growth on the natural love a woman has for the language, climate, and kind of country in which she passed her childhood. One country is home, the permanent dwelling-place; other countries are foreign, delightful perhaps, but not so lovable as one's own. We all have that sort of love, and various national characteristics which mean ourselves to ourselves. An English-woman doesn't speak the same language as an Italian, she doesn't speak *like* the Italian, either. She gesticulates less, and speaks more slowly and monotonously. I could tell whether a woman was an Italian, a German or a Russian if I saw her eating a meal with a companion through a glass window. After more than four thou-sand years of peace and far more mixing up than there ever was in the old days there are still marked national differences in ways of thought and speech and habits and manners. But we *like* the differences. They make the world an interesting and exciting place to move about in. But what the Old Men meant by patriotism was a feeling that the *people* of their own country were *better* than the people of others, and that therefore the others were contemptible and hateful, and it was not wrong to kill them. So once they became really irritated with the people of another country the natural differences, which we like, became an aggravation of pa-triotism and hatred and contempt. Also patriotism implies fear, and the greater the patriotism the greater the panic, so that in those days when a country really had the disease badly the people would believe, think, say and do the most senseless and amazing things.

"The Fascist cult of instinct and violence was patriotic, and the country where it flowered the most gloriously, which was my well-beloved Germany, was so stricken with patriotism that she committed a spiritual suicide and destroyed herself from within. Germans are queer people. Whatever they are doing they do with all their might, they never can think of two things at once, they must be thorough. It isn't just an accident that the Supreme Council of Europe always sits in Munich, nor that the General Secretary for Europe has been for a very long time always a German woman. They're as superior in female reasonableness, and female psychic force, as they used to be in male emotionalism and silliness and male violence. The most vigorous opposition to your freedom is certain to come from Germany, because now the whole nation is reasonable through its women none of them will be able to grasp that there may be something to be said against pure reasonableness; just as in the old days when the whole nation was male and emotional none of them could ever see anything but evil in reason and nonviolence. A slightly non-German German might see something that wasn't quite in the direct line of vision, but your true German, never. There'll be trouble in that quarter."

Grania was silent. Neil watched her. He had understood very little of the foregoing, and had almost stopped listening. But he was not at all bored. He liked watching the shades of expression pass over Grania's face. Her face was so familiar to him; he had known every contour of it since childhood; yet now, when she had broken for him her feminine reserve, he found that her face was changed, that he must learn it over again. As he learned it he loved her more. He almost worshipped her, and yet he was not at all afraid. Now, as she thought of the "trouble in that quarter," she was frowning a little, and the corners of her wide sensitive mouth were drawn down. Neil thought: "It can't be a happy thing to know so much and think so much. I shouldn't have liked to be a woman when it means all this thinking and knowing. I'm better as I am even if I did get miserable fits."

Grania went on: "I suppose, Neil, that the thirty years between 1914 and 1944 of the Christian Era were the worst, mentally, that the race has ever had to go through. Or at any rate, the worst in Europe apart from Russia, in America, and in China, and in Japan.

They were like people who had with terrific toil got themselves up a precipice to a flat place where they could rest and take their breath, but they *couldn't* rest because what was on the top of the precipice simply scared them to death. They had, with the invention of mechanical power, put themselves beyond danger of famine and attack from barbarians; and with the advance of science they had a far better control over disease; they could make sure that more of their children grew up, and that people should have longer, healthier and materially happier lives. But *because* they had conquered nature and now had or could have complete control over their environment, their old way of life, the life they had lived struggling up the precipice, was now no longer possible. They were *on* the flat place, and every single thing, economics, morals, education, the whole of their social science, had to be changed. The old system simply would not do for the country and climate that was at the top of the precipice. But the mere idea of this huge change appalled them.

"To go on with the metaphor, there was a horrible dark wood at the top of the cliff, where they would not have to climb with terrible labor, but where, they felt, they must be lost. Lost. That's what they were. Lost for thirty years. It's a very little time in history, just a flash, but imagine what it must have been like for the people *in* the wood. Is there any wonder that hordes of them tried to go back down the precipice, screaming: 'Anything, *anything* is better than this awful dark wood that's looming in front of us. How do we know whether there's anything good on the other side of it? How do we know we shall ever get through it? Back, back, back! Back to barbarism, back to our terrific toil of hill-climbing, back to animals, but *back!*' So away they go to the edge and try to get down again. But now they find that the ropes which served them so nobly to help them *up* the cliff are rotten, not trustworthy, they look sound but they are rotten inside. Their religion, the unquestioned dominance of men over women, and one class over another class, all the ropes have been rotted inside, and they can't get back down the cliff. And the more rotten the ropes get the more the frantic, panic-stricken people yell out that they're sound really and that in just a minute or two they *are* going down the cliff again, but the wood comes nearer all the time and swallows them up. So then they plunge about in the wood trying to find even the edge of the cliff, with the rotten ropes hanging on it, because even the sight of the cliff would be comforting, but the wood *is* the Great Change they dreaded so desperately. They are in it. They can't get out."

"Oh," said Neil, round-eyed. "*That* wasn't very nice. I'm glad I wasn't alive then."

"But then, Neil, there were a few people who walked straight on boldly into the wood and left the panic-stricken ones screaming behind. Because they knew there was some good country beyond. They stumbled about, and bashed their heads, and suffered terrible things, but they were not *afraid*. They hadn't the least desire to get back down the cliff again, so though they had endless physical misery to put up with they were mentally far happier than the cowards. These were the Communists, the Fascists' deadly enemies. No really great change, however inevitable, can come about in human society without there being a terrible enmity between the people who accept it and the people who are afraid of it and oppose it. There was a hostility between these two groups which was quite as fierce and cruel as any religious or national enmity, and actually in the end it brought down nationalism and patriotism in ruins. For as the struggle between the two ideas became more and more passionate every person in every country had to choose between the two, and be either a Fascist or a Communist, for no weaker party could live, and there was more sympathy between Fascists or Communists of all the countries than between people of the same blood and language but opposed in political ideas. The Communists admitted this internationalism, but the Fascists were far too emotional and unreasonable to see that Fascism in itself contained the seeds of internationalism. All Fascists persecuted Communists, and all Fascists who had many Jews in their countries persecuted Jews. This gave them an international fellow-feeling for other foreign Fascist persecution."

"What were Jews?" Neil asked. "Just an odd kind of Communist?"

"They were an odd kind of race with a tremendous spiritual power which seemed to come from their long established monotheism."

"What's that?"

"Believing God to be one and indivisible. The Jews' God was masculine, personal and with human qualities, but the fact of this God being One, instead of Three, like the Christians', seems to be the source of the Jews' power. It was a power that nothing ever broke except in the end their loss of faith in this masculine personal One God. While they had him, they could do without a country, without the respect of other peoples, without land, without safety, without happiness, without health, without freedom, and almost without food. They produced a long line of great men, one of whom was part of the Christians' Three God."

"What? How could a man be, even if it was a Three God?"

"It was quite easy, because their God was a man anyway. When they said 'God,' they didn't mean what you or I would mean. You must understand that."

"Well I don't. But anyway, why did the Fascists persecute Jews?"

"Oh, Christians always did, off and on. And the Fascists were Christians in name, though they didn't preserve any of the spirit of the religion at all. But they were just Christian enough to persecute Jews."

"But I thought you said part of their Three God *was* a Jew."

"He was, though the Germans afterwards said he was German. But you see, whether he was a German or a Jew, the Jews killed Jesus, or rather were responsible for his death. So the Christians always had that excuse. It's rather interesting about Christians and Jews because it shows the sort of way the male rulers used to reason. These Jews were dispersed from their country for turbulence, and it was seized by other races, so that for many hundreds of years they could never go back. They had to live about in other peoples' countries, and were often not allowed to own land or practice crafts. So they had to trade in money, and developed a peculiar kind of money-character, whereupon all the Christians united to abuse them for the character they themselves had thrust upon the Jews. Also, under persecution and imprisonment in foul ghettoes and other cruelties, they developed the mentality and manners natural to people who live in constant physical fear, and the Christians blamed them for that too. Of course the real trouble with the Christians from first to last was jealousy, because they could not break the Jews' spiritual power, nor could they prevent them from becoming rich, nor could they stop them from producing great men. Jesus was the greatest, but he was not the first, nor was he by any means the last."

"And didn't they produce any great women?"

"Oh, no. A Jewish woman was more deeply and unconsciously convinced of her inferiority even than a Christian woman. She was nothing but a cow who might one day bear a Messiah. The Jewish boys' psyches all profited very much by the complete starvation of their sisters'. But for all that, the Jewish women were not unhappy while they were still good Jews. They were not conscious of humiliation unless they failed to have sons. And any son *might* be the Messiah, though of course the chances were against it."

"What is a Messiah?"

"It was a man who was to lead them forth out of all their bonds and make them a great nation. They did not realize that they were always a great nation, the greatest nation, in fact, and that when their bonds were finally struck from them they would cease to be Jews, or a nation at all. There are no Jews now. There are some people in Palestine who are descended from Jews who went there during the last persecution, but they're all mixed up with Arabs, and they're all called Arabians. The Jews that stayed behind in Europe just became Germans or English or French."

"Then they never did get their Messiah?"

"They got three, but they had the same difficulty in recognizing their Messiahs as they had in recognizing their own greatness. The mass of the people rejected all three Messiahs, who each in his turn wished to strike off some of their bonds. Jesus wanted to deliver them from the oppressiveness and harshness of their own Law. Karl Marx wanted to deliver them from the tyranny of money and their usurious habits. Sigmund Freud wanted to deliver them from ignorance and superstition and incomprehensible guilt. All these three great Jews were rejected by the really religious Jews and had to do their necessary work for the world through the Christians. It was largely the ex-Christian Marxists, or Communists, who finally delivered the Jews, for good and all, from Christian persecution, from the oppressiveness of their Law, from their usurious habits, and from incomprehensible guilt. Then of course, without their fetters to hold them together, they lost their faith in their personal masculine God, and their spiritual power, and their racial feeling, and their power to produce great men, and were absorbed completely into the life and blood of other nations. It's a very strange history, the Jews'.

"But I was telling you really about the Communists, the people who accepted the Great Change made necessary by human mastery over natural environment. Russia, which as you know is a very enormous country, leaped straight into the far edge of the wood, as it were, from below the top of the cliff. Russia was always doing things like that. Staying behind the rest of Europe in a bog of backwardness, and then doing a terrific grasshopper leap to catch up, having missed all the intervening stages, and arriving in utter confusion standing on her head. So instead of having the Big War; a period of pseudo-pacifism, pseudo-socialism and pseudo-feminism; a period of Fascism; and then Communism, she jumped straight out of the middle of the war into Communism, passing in this leap all the other nations by many years, and after the most desperate civil war and cruelties and starvation and agonies she got up on her feet an established Communist country, ready to modify Communism and make it more humane and reasonable before the other nations had even got as far as the fanatical male-emotional Communism that replaced Fascism. So, when all the nations of Europe were Fascist, there was this one very large country to give moral support to the harassed Communists in the rest of the world. Of physical support Russia could give none. She had Fascist or capitalist enemies on every side and had therefore to keep Communism going in a Fascist world and also support a huge army, so she could do nothing to help anyone else. The Fascists seemed to have it all their own way.

"The old economic system was breaking down, because it was not suitable to a planet which had now plenty of people and plenty of goods. The worse it worked the more miserable the working class in every country became, and then there was a natural tendency on the part of some of the workers to put in a government that would, or might, look after them. When that happened, or before it happened in some countries, the prominent no-men, that is, the people who wouldn't accept any real change whatever in economics, or morals, or ethics, rallied all the other no-men and no-women to their sides, and seized the power, sometimes emotionally, sometimes by force. Moral cowardice is always popular and in every country there were more no-men and no-women than people who wanted a real sex-equality, a real class-equality, and a real race-equality. So one country after another went Fascist, and in an orgy of male-emotion robbed women of their very partial independence, suppressed workers' organizations, encouraged patriotism, patriarchy, militarism, blood, instinct, violence, and the form of the Christian religion. But most of their ideas were like knives to the poor old economic system, which was dying for internationalism, a common standard of living, and the freest of free trade, so it got worse and worse, and at last a lot of people had nothing really to live on except patriotism, pure womanhood, virile manhood, drums, flags, speeches, battleships, machineguns, airplanes, gas-bombs, tanks, uniforms, Armistice Days, and the form of the Christian religion. They became more and more miserable, even the soldiers, who were the best fed, but still they were panic-stricken at the thought of any Great Change.

"And yet, with all this endless parade of militarism, soldier-worship, and complete degradation of that very wise and gentle Jew, Jesus, no Fascist government wanted a war. Because they, all of them, were afraid *of being beaten*. If any Fascist country lost a war it would immediately become Communist, because the Communists, though always killed or imprisoned if found, were growing always more and more numerous. Yet if the leaders, who were worshipped as gods, could not improve the economic situation, their people must have a war. Death-hysteria, born as usual from a fear of life's difficulties, was rampant among all males from eighteen to forty-eight. This death-hysteria, which is a natural disease among moral cowards, but can be cured, had been deliberately encouraged by the Fascist rulers, and now it became evident to the rulers of Germany and Italy, where the hysteria had been culti-vated the longest, that they *must* have a war. Otherwise many of the men, and perhaps even some women, would kill themselves if they could not die for their country. They would not kill their rulers, because they were still absolutely appalled at the idea of any change in social balances, but they would undoubtedly kill themselves. Indeed, they were already killing themselves, particularly in Germany. Besides this very high and alarming suicide rate it was becoming evident that children born of women who were not only undernourished, but also in a constant state of oscillation between death-hysteria and despair, were inclined to be mentally below the average if not imbecile. The Fascist rulers had encouraged the women to have as many children as they could possibly bear, and though many of the children died in infancy yet enough under-brained children were growing up to alarm the rulers for the futures of their countries.

"The gloom that overcast the Fascist countries at this time, just before the Last War, seems to have been worse than anything Europe had had to endure since in the year 1000 of the Christian Era many people had been convinced the world was to come to an end. The only people who remained comparatively happy in each country were the Communists, for though they were in constant peril, they were not afflicted with the death-hysteria, and their children, though born of undernourished mothers, were not im-beciles. They were spiritually strong, as the persecuted Jews were, and after their years of dogged, rather hopeless hanging on a great flame of hope began to pass from one to another. They knew that Fascism had come to the end of its blind alley, and that every Fascist knew, though no Fascist would admit it, that the Great Change *must* come.

"So, like desperate rats Germany and Italy turned upon one another. The alleged cause of war was an incident on the German frontier of what we now call Old Austria, which is now a part of Germany, but was then a so-called independent state under the influence of Italy. Both Germany and Italy had allies, but while these allies were still making up their minds whether they would or would not honor their agreements, for they thought there was no particular hurry to decide, the war was over. On the first day, when war was declared, every Fascist in both countries went raving mad with delight. The cure for all their evils, war, blood, glory, and death, was at last, after these maddening years of waiting and preparation, to be given them. All their doubt and inner gloom burst out in the form of the most insane ravings of mingled joy in the war and hatred of the enemy. Ambassadors were killed before

they could get away, and German and Italian citizens who happened to be in the enemy country at the outbreak of this terribly
sudden war were killed or terribly maltreated by the lunatic mobs.
Austria, which was of course a German-speaking country, had a
violent blood-revival, pitched Italian influence and all her promises
to Italy to the winds, and let the German troops through so that
they could attack Italy on her own frontier. Naturally all this had
been planned by certain of the Austrian Fascists, and immediately
after the frontier incident, which was in the nature of a stage-affair,
these Germany-favoring Fascists seized the government and declared war on Italy.

"On the third day of the war some German airplanes, trying to
bomb an important railway station behind the Italian lines, made a
mistake, or did not make a mistake, for no one ever knew really,
but they wiped out a small unfortified town, massacring most of
the inhabitants. That started the war in the air, for though no one
but the airmen wanted the war to be in the air, and though it was
essential that the German, Austrian and Italian ground armies
should have a war on the ground, and a long enough war to slake
the nations' longing for blood and death, it was found impossible to
keep the air fleets out of it. The Italian nation cried for revenge for
their murdered civilians, so a general bombing of towns began.
Large fleets of bombing planes, accompanied by quick fighting
planes to beat off any defense, passed and repassed across the
frontiers like swarms of bees. The capitals and big industrial cities
were defended, but defense was found inadequate; they were set
on fire, or blown to pieces, or filled with noxious gas. The Fascist
women could not stand it. The idea of war had filled them with a
frenzy of delight; that men should kill each other and die was part,
and the holiest part, of the Fascist creed, which they had accepted
as a religion. But when they saw their small children being killed,
and day after day the streets littered with dead, this male religion
completely failed them. They went mad and could not be disci-
plined. They walked out of the towns and stormed the trains. The
civilian men caught their panic and there was a stampede away
from the towns which, even in Italy which was less highly indus-
trialized than Germany, completely disorganized the munition
business, the transport, and the whole life of the country. Plenty of

civilians and women were shot to restore discipline and make them go back to the towns, or the ruins of the towns, but they had lived on hysteria and emotion for years and they had learned their lesson well.

"Only the Communists, and the soldiers who were preparing to enjoy a long war at the frontier, and the airmen who were bombing the towns, could keep their heads. The German soldiers were not told what was happening behind them, for fear they might become depressed, but in a fortnight, before they had even reduced by artillery fire the underground defenses along the frontier, no more food came to them. No more food, either, came to the Italian soldiers, or the Austrian soldiers. The countries behind them were ruined. They were ordered to go to their homes. Furious at the lack of food, glory, death and the bloodshed for which they had been waiting so many years, they went back into their countries and killed all the Jews they could find. For, they said, it was the Jews' fault that the war had only lasted a fortnight. But killing the Jews could not bring back stability to the women, or life to those who had been killed, or organization to the country. The Communists were the only people in the country who knew what they wanted, and in face of the general destruction, disillusion and despair a man who knew what he wanted and how he meant to set about getting it was worth a thousand. Many even of the Fascist soldiers now saw that war was, under modern conditions, impossible, and giving up the idea of war meant knocking the heart out of Fascism. They joined the Communists, shot down the armed bands of looters who were roving over the country, and worked heroically to get the wheels of the country turning again. The Fascist leaders were shot or committed suicide.

"There is a very interesting book written by a German of this period. He fought as a very young man in the last year of the Big War. Then he worried through the time of pseudo-pacificism, socialism and feminism in Germany as a civilian. He was not ready for any real change; he was one of those who wanted to go back down the precipice. He became a Fascist—Nazis, the German Fascists called themselves—and accepted to the full the blood-instinct-violence creed. He waited for the blessed sacramental war which should pass all German soldiers, whether they lived or died, into a kind of Valhalla of perfect joy. He went to the front, but was only in reserve. When no more food came and he was told with the others to find his own way back, he nearly killed himself. Very many of the soldiers did. But some remnant of reason and courage remained in him, and he went through ruined Austria in a dull but feverish nightmare. The sufferings of the Austrians did not break his dream. But when he came at last after many adventures to his own home town and saw it half-ruined, with dead bodies still unburied, like a battlefield, and crazy women wandering everywhere, he had a tremendous spiritual experience. His dream, the dream he had lived in for over forty years, broke and vanished. He saw that every single thing he had been taught as a boy of the ruling class, retaught in the Big War, retaught again more madly by the Nazis, was false. He had to take his prides off him one by one, until he was quite naked. His pride as a Nazi, his pride as a soldier, his pride as a man, his pride as a German. He knew now they were false, dirty, like foul clothes. But when they were laid away, and he was stripped quite clean and naked, unarmed, empty-handed, *then* he was proud. 'There is still something there,' he thought. 'Me, a human being. He was always there. Sane, not delirious. Clean, not covered with dirty clothes.'

"He felt no bitterness against the Italians. He knew very well that in Italy there were towns like this, and women wandering about like these, and unburied bodies of children. He felt no bitterness against his father and mother, nor his schoolmasters, nor his superiors in the Big War, nor the Nazi leaders, all of whom had told him lies. 'They told us lies,' he thinks, 'but if we had not been cowards we should not have believed them. We believed lies because we were afraid of the truth, as boys and as men. We were afraid of change. We worshipped death and blood and sacrifice because we were afraid of life. We persecuted Jews because we were afraid of Jews. We put the women back in the kitchen because we were afraid of women. We went about in packs because we were afraid of ourselves. We said Germany was the greatest, holiest, nation because we were afraid of the whole non-German world. And now our fear has its ending, in this ruined German town. Our cowardice has killed the children, and made the women mad, and we, the great brave Nazis, who had four hundred killed in the revolution out of about two million, we the Nazi soldiers, come back from our great war without having fired a shot or risked a fingernail. To meet our cowardice. The strong man armed. But the strong man ought not to be armed. That is another cowardice, for a strong man to be armed. Let the women be armed, or the boys and girls, but surely not the strong men. And anyway, there are no wild beasts in Germany.'

"So he throws his rifle away, but then gets it again, because he doesn't want to die now he's found that he is a sane human being, and the country isn't altogether safe. He goes on into the town and speaks to women sometimes, but most of them don't answer. They're looking for something in the broken houses. He takes no notice of any of the men. Then he meets a woman he knows quite well, and she seems less shaken than some of the others. He asks her how she does, and she stares and then falls into a kind of frenzy.

" 'Heil Hitler, Conrad! Welcome home, soldier!'

" 'Hush, Lisa, hush! See the flag up there.'

"For he has seen, flying from the town hall, a red flag with a hammer and sickle on it. It was the Communist emblem, which had meant death to the wearer anywhere outside Russia.

" 'That!' says Lisa. 'Who cares, now? Just listen, Conrad. In 1932 I had a job and was getting on pretty well. In 1933 I was turned out of it. In 1934 I married because I had to do that or starve, and it's right for women to marry anyway, isn't it? And we were all told that if we were married, and were submissive and quiet and good, and had plenty of children, we should be happy, and the men would be happy, and the children, and Germany. And we did it, didn't we, Conrad? Weren't we good? Didn't we do what we were told?'

" 'Yes, yes, Lisa.'

" 'Well, I had five children, though we never really had enough food for ourselves and two children, and the second and the fourth were born stupid and even the first wasn't very strong, and two died because really we didn't have enough to eat and if they got at all ill they never could stand it.'

" 'I know, Lisa. I know it's been hard times.'

" 'Yes, and why, soldier? Well, then you see we had this war we've all been waiting for, to wipe out the humiliation of 1918, and what do you think? I went into the country one day to see if I could buy some potatoes cheap, and when I came back the three children were in ribbons. The stupid one, little Ernst, and the two sound ones. All just in ribbons on what was left of the floor where I'd left them playing.'

" 'It's terrible, Lisa.'

" 'Yes, soldier. Why did you tell us we must have children if they were only to make red ribbons of? Germany is happy now, and can make red flags out of the dead children. What do you think women are made of? *You men!* It's your fault. Men, men. Soldiers, Nazis, men. You lied, and lied, and lied to us. Everything you told us was lies, and now our children are dead.'

" 'We did lie to you, Lisa. It was no good at all having a lot of children. None of it was any good.'

" 'And you're not even scratched, soldier. We didn't throw flowers at you when you went away in order that you might have them to smell on your little holiday at the Austrian frontier. We thought you were our protectors and our children's protectors.'

" 'We would have been if we could.'

" 'No, you wouldn't. It was *men* came over in the airplanes. Italian men, who cares? You hate us, you've always hated us. You take our jobs away and tell us to have children, and then kill all the children. You're monsters.'

"So she comes up to him to scratch him or strangle him, hoping perhaps that he'll get angry and kill her, but he puts her away from him very gently.

" 'We're cowards, Lisa, that's all. We made you be cowards too. Lisa, is my wife alive?'

"At that she cries and clings to his arm.

" 'Forgive me, Conrad. I—we haven't been ourselves. No, Conrad. Your wife was killed in the first raid.'

" 'And my little girl?'

" 'They couldn't find her, but they think she was in the house. It's all ruins. Conrad, they had some bomb things that dropped and burst, but then things came out and burst too so that you never knew when it would stop. And there was a gas raid after that. They must have had a great many planes.'

" 'So did we. Italy is the same as this. And Austria. All ruined. So my wife is dead?'

" 'Yes, Conrad. And your little girl almost certainly.'

" 'I knew it, when I saw the town. I must go now.'

"So he goes along, very sad, but still a sane human being, passing a good many mad ones on the way, till he comes to the Town Hall. And there he finds some men and some women, haggard and hungry and very anxious, but quite sane. He says he wants to help and hands over his rifle to show he means no harm to them.

" 'Spit on that flag, then,' says a Communist, for he knows that if Conrad has any feeling left for Hitler and the Nazis he'll hesitate. He sees at his feet, all muddy and trampled, the German flag with the swastika in the middle.

" 'It's nothing to me,' he says. 'All we Nazis are cowards.'

"But still spitting at things doesn't seem human or dignified, so he wets his finger at his mouth and touches the swastika.

" 'You might be kissing it, like that,' says the Communist suspiciously. 'Come now, spit like a bloody capitalist soldier.'

" 'He needn't, Karl,' says a woman who has just come out of the building. 'He's all right. Come in here, Conrad.'

"Then he sees it's a woman he knows, but he never knew she was a Communist. He tells her so, when they're alone in a little office room.

" 'It hasn't been safe or sensible to *say* you're a Communist for twelve years,' she says. 'But there are more of us than you think. But not enough, Conrad. Things are in a terrible mess. We simply don't know whether we'll be able to save civilization or not. It depends largely on you soldiers.'

" 'I'll do what I can,' he says. 'I see now that you were the brave people.'

" 'Oh, *that*,' she says, 'you make too much of courage. *Courage* won't save Germany or the world from complete wreck.'

" 'We made too much of it because we never had it,' he says. 'But what shall I do?'

" 'You can go out with our men and bury the dead. It's not good for the town to have so many stinking corpses in it.'

"Well, you see, Neil, that with Germany, Italy and Austria in this disorganized and ruined condition the economic situation of the rest of the world got a bit worse, and between that and the moral despair of the Fascists in every country the World Revolution came at last, twenty-seven years after the Russian Revolution. Russia was by now standing on her feet and not on her head, and though when the war in Europe came the Japanese were on the point of making their long-threatened attack on the Soviet Union, the Japanese Revolution got in first. The Japanese, though very warlike and Fascist in spirit, had really dreaded war just as much as any other Fascist country, and for the same reason, because they could not afford to be defeated. So, as Russia was large and had a very big army and an enormous number of airplanes, the Japanese leaders had put off their attack just too long. And in Japan and all the civilized countries the Fascist government, which had seemed as strong as steel towers, fell down like rotten old sheds. The failure of the war, the failure of war itself, took the heart out of them. Their keystone was the nobility and inevitability and ever-lastingness of war, and now war was finally proved, not to be costly or wasteful or wicked, for that would not have worried them, but just impossible. Indeed, war that killed ten civilians for every soldier, and was over before a sixth of the armies had time to get anywhere near the enemy, was not war at all. There was not even any glory for the airmen, for far too few of them had been killed. Butchery without danger was not distasteful personally to a few of the Fascists, but the mass of them could not stand it. So they came out of their patriotic blood-and-violence dream in every country and either joined the Communists or killed themselves in despair.

"The people now at last accepted the Great Change, and the awful bogy of Bolshevism (that's the Russian name) which had made them sweat with terror for twenty-seven years was now seen from its other side, not as a frightful thing that was being forced upon them by superlatively wicked people, but as their only hope. Some kind of government and way of life must be found in this new warless world; Fascism had failed completely, and the older moderate capitalist parties had all disappeared in the years of Fascist rule. They were dead beyond resurrection. Also the people found that universal Communism was a very different thing from the Communism of one country, maintaining itself with difficulty in face of a completely hostile world. It was different too from the

Communism of a persecuted minority. Still, there was in every country a period of violence and fanaticism, with a certain amount of private vengeance for wrongs committed by the Fascists. This period was naturally longer and more cruel in those countries where Fascism had been very oppressive, or of very long standing. The Communists were most embittered in Spain, Germany, Italy, Japan and the United States, and most ready to make peace in England and the dominions of England, and in the Scandinavian countries, where the Fascist governments had been comparatively mild. In these countries even some of the Fascist leaders were allowed to live, so long as they made complete submission. In the others they were shot, or shot themselves. The time of militant Communism was short because there was nothing to put in its place. The governments did not live in continual dread of counter-revolution as the Russian government had for many many years. It took them a little while to realize that Fascism had collapsed *from inside,* and that the Last War, unlike the Big War, had brought about a real general change of heart, but when they did with joy understand this they saw that their only enemies were the minority of rich people who had been able to live in comfort while the workers were underpaid. And even these were not all enemies, for the condition of Germany, Italy and Austria shocked even some armament manufacturers. Or so it is said, though it doesn't seem altogether likely.

"In some countries, notably Spain and Austria, priests were persecuted for a little while, but not for more than a few months. In England there was no harassing of priests at all. The Fascists had really destroyed Christianity, and even the Catholic church had very little life left in it. The churches everywhere were disestablished, that is to say they were not allowed to own any property, but religion, either the Jewish or the Christian, was not forbidden. If people liked to keep and pay for a priest they could. He might conduct services, but was not allowed to educate children. The poverty the Christian churches now fell into appears to have been the intention of the early Christians, and the enormous wealth at one time owned by the Catholic church seems not to have been part of Jesus' idea at all. So the Communists really did it a service by purifying both the priests and the worshippers, but even that could not make Christianity last beyond the turn of the century. But when Communism was universally established and therefore more sure of itself and more reasonable, there was none of that vilification of Jesus himself, apart from his so-called followers throughout the two thousand years of his deification, which had been so rife in Russia after her private revolution. The world Communists thought of him *as* a Communist, born a great deal too soon, and into an impossible world for Communism, but none the less to be revered. They recognized that it was his followers, the Christians, who had by their greed and blood-thirst and tyranny brought the name of Christ into disrepute. About God they were indifferent. There was no long bitter anti-God campaign, as there had been in Russia. People could believe what they liked so long as they didn't teach other people that God favored patriotism, or private ownership of property, or Women in the Home. For they knew that it was essential for the New World that women should be once more, and properly this time, brought out of the Home.

"The Fascists had taught women that politics was a purely male business, and though the German women, the Italians and the Austrians now knew that the results of purely male politics were disastrous to women and children, they did not yet realize that the state of Germany, Italy and Austria was their fault as much as the men's. An unnaturally submissive woman makes an unnaturally aggressive man, and the submission is as faulty as the aggression. But the Communists, both the women and the men, knew very well that a nonpolitical, economically dependent, will-less woman is the greatest drag on progress there can be, for she will always incline to timidity and conservatism, and by her sexual power can influence her husband and her sons. So the Fascist women had to be brought out of the Home would they or would they not, and reconciled to the new regime with what seemed to them extraordinary privileges and large doses of sex-flattery. That generation of women who had eagerly embraced Fascism developed no powers, and could not be anything but rather frightened and apologetic to the end of their lives. Their psyches had been too starved in their childhood in the Big War. But the next lot, those who had been born either in the Big War or soon afterwards, and had passed their childhood in the period of pseudo-feminism, threw off their Fascist bonds easily enough, and became as Communist and free and happy as those older Communist women who had rejected Fascism from its start. The Communist psychologists foresaw another generation of under-powered women, those who had passed their early childhood under Fascist rule, but they hoped, by education, and putting them to work at trades like men as soon as they were old enough, to redeem these girls to some extent. They also foresaw yet one more generation of young men who would incline to sadism, brutality and extreme moral cowardice, as had the generation which had been very young boys in the man-worship of the Big War, and had later formed the backbone of Fascism. The boys who had passed their childhood in the Fascist youth organizations, and had had the blood-and-violence religion impressed upon them at a very tender age, might cause some trouble later on.

"But at first the Communists had very little time to worry about what later generations would do. They had before them the huge task of re-creating the economic machine, so that the abundance of goods that could now be produced by machine power in all parts of the world should reach the underfed populations in all parts of the world. Under the old system quantities of things that people were almost literally dying for had been destroyed in order to keep up the price of what was sold. Each country, through fear of war, tried to live on what it could produce itself, and a country that had plenty of surplus of one or two kinds of goods, could not sell them, and therefore could not afford to buy what it had a lack of. The Communists had to organize a system of long credit and free trade, based on a common standard of living throughout the industrial countries. The East, for instance, had largely lived, or sometimes starved, on rice, not because they liked living on rice or wouldn't have eaten other foods if they could have got them, but because they *could* live on rice if they got enough. A European man can't live on rice, or cannot work on it. So the standard of living in Japan and China had to be raised well above the subsistence level, in order that, under free trade, the living of the Europeans might not be too low. Under the Fascist governments this would have been impossible, but the Japanese Communists did not mind their workers having, for them, a very high standard. They no longer wanted, for the sake of profits, to undersell the European countries. Part of China had been Communist, without anyone taking much notice of it, for many years, and it formed a useful nucleus from which the Communization of the rest of China could take place. Both in China and India the difficulties were largely religious. The Chinese had a religion which kept the women in slavery and ensured that there should always be more children than the family, or the nation, could support. In India there were many religions, most of which had the same effect. The greatest opposition came from the priests, and the Communists' most valuable support came from the women who had abandoned their religions.

"But with all the difficulties of the first ten years after the World Revolution, the backwardness and slowness of the East, except Japan, and the shortages, and the curious jerky working of the new economic machine (which did most unexpected things at first), people were a great deal happier than they had been for the thirty years before the Revolution. They had hope. Not a hysterical death-hope, but a flaming reasonable hope of better life. They had lost fear. They no longer lived in fear of war, in fear of idleness, in fear of the complete ruin of civilization, in fear of each other, or in fear of Communism. Communism was there, and people had not become bloodthirsty fiends, or sexual maniacs, or cold inhuman machines. They were poor and materially uncomfortable for the first few years, but they *liked each other.* If one met another she or he did not feel immediately hostile and suspicious. She didn't think: 'It's a man, or a Jew, or a German, or a Negro, or a Fascist.' She'd think: 'It's a human being, my comrade, my friend.' And that was the main thing. *After that,* people were men or women, or Jews or Germans. This extraordinary happiness and fearlessness, this great outbreak of all the suppressed *love* of the world, is reflected in the literature and art and music of the first hundred years after the Revolution. There was not for long any bitterness or hatred of the ex-enemy, such as there had been in the Russian revolution literature, when she was with difficulty maintaining Communism alone. There were too few ex-enemies to bother about. And people were too happy. Their release from fear and the dull fever of the blood-and-violence dream made their spirits soar, not hysterically, but naturally, like birds singing in the spring.

"People had been constantly preaching in the past that love was no powerful motive, like hatred, that universal love was a coward's dream, and that nothing creative could ever come of it. But, in fact, it was love that reorganized the world and made workable the new economic machine, love that toiled and sweated and went in rags that presently all might be clothed, and love that was at the bottom of the tremendous renaissance of art. Women and men *had* to pour themselves out, to relieve themselves of their excess happiness and faith and valor. There's no greater contrast, I think, in the history of European literature, than that between the literature of the thirty years of dark panic and hatred, and the literature of the early Communist period. The first falls into two kinds, sadistic and cynical. The sadistic literature was dark, cruel, bloody and miserable. Both kinds were sex-antagonistic, whether the book was by a man or a woman. Indeed practically all of the women writers of the pre-Communist thirty years just imitated men, even to their sexual sadism, which of course was false for them. The men were sadistic because they were afraid of women; the women were not, of course, afraid of themselves, but they were panic-stricken at the fear and dislike the men felt, and in an unconscious attempt to placate them, joined in the violent anti-feminism of the young men. As this literature was based on fear and efforts at retrogression it was not really creative at all. Hardly any of it was worth keeping for itself; only some was kept for historical interest.

"But the next literature, the very first in the whole history of the world to be based on world-courage, and world-love—that was wonderful. It was like—well, we can only guess what it was like, unfortunately. It must have been like a huge roaring golden fire, a fire that never died down for a hundred, well, more than that, a hundred and fifty years. It was the happiest time, Neil. The bravest time. Those women and those men, the Communists, were the most favored of all our race.

"And now I can't tell you any more today. The tale goes into darkness again, and I'd rather leave it in the light."

IV

"WELL, NOW, NEIL, WE LEFT THOSE COMMUNISTS still being happy in a society which was materially comfortable, where the just balance had been found between too much hand-labor (which gives people plenty of work and not enough to eat) and too much machine-labor (which can give them a luxurious standard of living but no occupation for half of them). And a society too where there was no class-distinction, and no sex privilege, and where every person was first a human being and a friend, and then of a certain sex, nation or race. But they couldn't stay happy, and sometimes when I'm miserable I think, well, human beings never *can,* and sometimes when I'm hopeful I know they can get back, or rather get forward, to another good place, like, and yet not like, that Communist period, but a *good* place, from whence they will never drive themselves out. After all, what's four thousand years in the history of the whole race? Just nothing. A little breathing-space.

"When the Communist governments had been ruling for about a hundred and twenty years the old sex issue, which appeared to have been completely settled by the collapse of Fascism and patriotism, and by the love and friendship and fearlessness that had arisen between women and men after the Revolution— that old hideous monster now rose up again, and was at last seen in

86

its true form. *Were men or women to rule?* The Communist idea had been that when women were fit for it both sexes should rule in cooperation. (In the Communist parties, when they had been outlawed and persecuted, there had been perfectly friendly relations and comradeship between the women and the men. A person was either a Communist or not. There was no special woman's branch of Communism, subordinate and inferior, as there had been in Fascism.) But now, with four generations of women having grown up completely free from sex-shame, and regarded by their mothers as every bit as valuable human material as the boys, the sex balance had completely changed. Women's naturally strong psyches had developed as far as they could, while the boys', without the overdevelopment caused by their Mothers' feeling of inferiority, had very much weakened. Women's brains, no longer hopelessly dulled by sex-shame and psyche starvation, were proved to be stronger and better on the average than men's, and their wills and moral power were far tougher. By sheer ability women rose in the structure of the Communist societies until three-quarters of the people in high places, both in the governments and the skilled trades, were women.

"Now had the men let things be all might have been well. The women were so happy in their new self-respect, and in the marvelous flowering of their powers, that they were not in the least inclined to bully or force men with their superior wills to take the old place of women. They could do very well without keeping men in an artificial subjection. The women said, let the best human beings rule. If you're the best, you shall. If we're the best, we will. That's fair, and according to Communist principles. But the men, though Communist, *could not forget.* They could not, quite, let the Old World go. They could not forget, with their emotions, making it but a reasonable remembrance, the glorious history of their sex, how they had tamed nature and civilized themselves, and ruled the world as unquestioned Lords of Creation, for thousands upon thousands of years. They knew now, for sexual psychology (the science founded by the third great Jew, Sigmund Freud), had made great strides, that men could not have done what they had without the extra strength gained from women's admiration and acceptance of their own humiliation; they knew now that the idea of women's *natural* inferiority had been false from the beginning; they knew now that there was no *reason*, human or divine, why women should not rule, and rule justly and humanely. But they *could not* reason about it. Male emotionalism was still there, even after more than a hundred years of Communism, which is a reasonable way of life. They just *felt* that they couldn't bear their time of glory to pass away. So the second Fascist reaction started. The old ideas of patriotism and militarism were revived. No one knew by personal experience what war was like, but many of the men banded together to drag it out of its dishonorable grave and crown it once more with glory, and make it generally revered.

"But it could not be done. The food of militarism, what it must have to exist at all, is the admiration of women. The women, however, would not admire the new Fascists. They admired themselves now. And besides this feeling of superiority they could no longer have any respect for a heroism that implied destruction of human life. They could not think in a male way, because they were now wholly female. What they admired was heroism that either saved life or produced more life, so this attempt at reviving the old death-hysteria revolted them. They boycotted the militarists and the New Patriots, who could march and sing and make speeches as much as they liked, but had to lead celibate lives. They suffered very badly. The women suffered too, but the mass of them held on until the new militarism had died a natural death and the men had capitulated. But the happiness and fearlessness of the world had been broken, and nothing could restore it. The women were afraid. They were horrified to find that men did still in a way despise them, that they still were not willing the best human being should rule, if it were a woman. The reaction had failed, but it had made them suffer. There might be others. They might, through some contingency no one could foresee, be forced back by the superior physical strength of men into complete subjection. They might again suffer all the miseries and humiliations of women's lives before the Communist era. The control they now had over their sexual lives might be taken from them, the control they had over their young children; prostitution might return, economic helplessness, forced monogamy, legitimacy, male religions, psyche starvation, unnatural stupidity and debility—all the old horrors might come back upon them. And if these old horrors came back while they still had machine power there was nothing to stop the men making a general Last and First War, and precipitating the whole race back to barbarism, to start the whole round over again. And besides this very appalling danger, there had been, during the few years when the men were trying to revive patriotism and militarism, a good many ugly incidents of violence. Women and girls were frequently caught by the militarists and maltreated, and though this naturally did the militarist cause no good it made the women very angry. A woman in a healthy state of psychic development is proud; she is not frigid, nor in the least masochistic. She does not tolerate violence from men as the old type of woman did. The sadism of the militarists produced no masochism in the women, but it did produce among practically all women, whether they had been themselves ill-treated or not, an enormous blackly bitter resentment.

"It is possible that there is a race-memory in human beings, and that it may have been the accumulated resentment of centuries. There may have been in it the pain of little Chinese girls whose feet were deliberately deformed, or that of small Indian girls forcibly married before they were mature, or that of women whose girl-children had been murdered, or that of all the countless hordes of women who suffered personally at the hands of masters or husbands or slave-owners, or that of all those unproud unfortunates who had to trade themselves sexually to live or keep their bastards, or that of all the women who saw their young children massacred by soldiers in war, or that of little girls who felt themselves a useless burden to their mothers.

"But if it were so, this resentment was dormant in the years of pure Communism, and there seems no reason, had it not been for the emotional jealousy of the men, why it should not have slept and slept, until it slept itself away. But the women who had watched the second Fascist reaction, in the mighty power of their resentment and their dread that their long slavery might somehow begin again, were determined to make themselves and all future generations of women safe. And that could only be done by making the men so weak psychically that they could never use their physical strength against a woman, and would, besides, accept women without resentment or jealousy as their natural rulers. The women now knew, what they had never known in their long period of subjection, that *any* human being can be kept in moral slavery by early inculcation of sex-shame. The work started by Freud had been continued, largely by women, since the Revolution. They had been, perhaps naturally, more interested in it than men, and had been able to give a correct account of normal feminine psychology. For of course Freud and all his disciples had been studying the psyches of starved women, and their conclusions were no more correct for psychically healthy women entirely free from either conscious or subconscious sex-shame than would be the conclusions of an anthropologist who went to study the physique of a certain race and concentrated his attention entirely on undernourished hunchbacks. Masculine psychology had also modified somewhat, seeing the male psyche was no longer over-developing itself at the expense of the female, but in spite of the enormous change in the character and ability of women, and the lesser change in the character and ability of men, Freud's main theory still held, that the relationship between the Mother, the son and the father will determine the life and character of the son.

"From this trinity the Communist women eliminated the father. A father is not necessary in a family unless he's needed for its protection, or is responsible for its support, or has some religious significance. The Communist women had no need of him for support, because they could now easily earn enough themselves to keep the small families they had. He was not needed for protection, as conditions were civilized. Neither had he any religious significance. Communists had never recognized any difference between children born within or outside marriage, and a few women had, through all the Communist period, preferred to live by themselves and be entirely responsible for their children. Now, in their very deep resentment and fear, they all began to do the same thing. The children had fathers, of course, but they were not told who these were. The fathers themselves were naturally not certain, for the women were free and able to do what they liked, and go with whom they liked. Now the boy in the Christian or any Old World family, who had a father, reacted to his Mother-bond in one way, but the boy in the very late Communist period, after the second Fascist reaction, who had none, and whose friends and companions had none either, reacted quite differently. There was no conflict and struggle, no jealousy or envy or admiration of the father, because he didn't exist. The son could *accept* his Mother-bond, and no longer had to fight against her power to become an independent masculine motherless adult like his father, nor had he to love his Mother feverishly and pathologically because he was so jealous of the father. As a child he accepted his Mother as the *sole* provider of love and of the things he must have in order to live, and learned to regard his own sex, the sex that could never be Mothers, as of less importance. So he must come to despise himself, because he could never be a Mother.

"After this elimination of fathers, the women did nothing more for about forty years. For you must understand that the subjection of men by women was not an accidental and not-understood thing, like the subjection of women through religious uncleanness, nor was it an emotional and sudden thing like the resubjection of women carried out by the Fascists; it was a cold, logical and slow process, passed from Mother to daughter, and spreading over some two hundred and fifty years. It started in the Secret Society of Women which had been formed during the second militarist reaction, and it ended in the form of rule we have today. This secret society was first made by the German women, but it rapidly spread all over the civilized Communist world. Any woman over the age of seventeen could belong to it, but no man whatever, even if he detested the militarists. In their horror and resentment the women could not trust any man not to be a militarist at heart. The women took an oath on joining the society not to reveal any of the discussion that went on. The organization was the same as the Communist; the villages sent a member to the county town society, and the county town to London, and the head London groups to Germany, where the European center was, and so on all over the world. At first it had no buildings and no press; its proceedings were informal and verbal, rather like the Fascist and patriotic murder-societies before the Revolution. But, unlike in the murder-societies, there was no compulsion. It was suggested that certain things might be done, but no woman need do them unless she wished. Nor, at first, did they do or suggest anything essentially uncom-

munistic. Resistance to militarism was part of Communism, and
the elimination of the father from the family was not against it.
Communism always had been more concerned with protection of
children than protection of fathers. The only other things women
did in the first forty years after the militarist reaction was gradually
to withdraw themselves from all the men's sports and games. This
again, though uncommunist in spirit, was not a breaking of any
law. Women need not play games with men unless they liked to,
but in the early Communist period, when women and men loved
each other, they had enjoyed it. But they gave that up, as they gave
up much else, in their dark brooding powerful resentment and
fear. They gave up love itself. It had been said of Christian women
that they considered the world well lost for love, and that love was
their whole existence, meaning of course love for some particular
man. The Communist women had not thought of love in that way,
for there were so many other things to do, so much friendship and
liking and happiness and work and achievement, that love was no
more a woman's business than a man's. And perhaps because it
was then equal in importance to both sexes, and free, not bound by
religion or women's economic helplessness or any theory of legitimacy, there had been much faithful, deep and happy love, an
inspiration and joy to both partners in it. But the women gave this
up, because their trust in men was shattered, and whether they will
ever regain that kind of spiritual sex-love, God only knows. But it is
not possible, as men knew in the days of women's greatest inferiority, to love a person who is mentally and morally vastly below
yourself, except in a physical way, as a Mother, or just a temporary
mate. Besides that, it is not possible to love a person really if you do
not live with them for at any rate part of the time, and the women
would no longer live with the men, or share their social lives. So
they gave up love to make their new, safe world.

"When some of the boys who had been brought up without
fathers were nearly middle-aged the women made their first attack
on Communism. The women printers everywhere refused to take
any more boy-apprentices, or to work with men who did. This was
absolutely against the Communist principle of equality of opportunity for both sexes, but the men had no remedy. Women were in a
majority in both the trade and the governments. The men could

not make the women teach boys, nor could they stop them teaching girls. Besides, though the older men were resentful, the younger men and the boys accepted what their Mothers told them without questioning it. If women said that printing was not fit work for men, then it was not. It was, after all, rather finicky work, and a man's muscles might be put to better uses. For the women in those forty years had been impressing on the boys a sense of pride in their *physical* strength, and encouraging them to develop it to its utmost by sport and games, though such masculine pursuits were beneath the serious attention of girls. So the older men, who knew that physical strength is only an animal quality and not to be compared in human values with mental and moral power, were helpless in face of the moral inertia of the men brought up without fathers, and had to submit. They were in the same position as the older women in the Fascist period who saw all that they had gained lost by the inertia of the younger women who in their war-childhood had worshipped their fathers almost as gods.

"So after a time, when the older men in the printing trade had died or retired from work, the entire trade was in the hands of women. They could print what they liked, and refuse to print what they did not like. They gradually did the same thing in all the skilled trades, pushing men out of responsibility into unskilled or semiskilled work. The boys thought it quite natural that they should be put to heavy dull laborious work which exercised their fine muscles, and put no strain on their dulled minds. They thought it quite natural that they should be allowed to clean airplanes, but neither pilot nor design them, that they should be allowed to work on ships, but not navigate them, that they should be allowed to mind machines, but never understand them. And though their pay was almost always less than women earned at their work, the men had no children to support, and had ample enough for their own needs. The men, at this time, still knew that formerly they had done all the skilled work, and had all the responsible positions both in trade and government, but their fall from power now seemed a natural historical process. As, indeed, I suppose it was. But it seemed natural that men should have ruled in the Childhood Age (as the women now began to call it, rather than the Capitalist Age), because women had to have so many children that they had no leisure; that there should have been a period when women were getting ready to rule; and that then women, their Mothers, should rule. But the women would not leave it like that. They had decided in their cold, slow, logical way that they could never be really safe until the men could no longer *remember* the great male civilizations of the past. So they changed the old education laws, and taught the boys and girls differently. There were certain things boys were not allowed to learn. Latin was forbidden to them. The women wanted a secret language.

"So, when men were reduced by the strength of their accepted Mother-bond, and by lack of skill, and by their too great emphasis on the value of physical strength, and by contempt of their own not-Mother sex, to a state of extreme psychic enfeeblement, the women set about in a reasonable thorough and female way the destruction of all memory of male civilization in the minds of men. They translated some of the old books into Latin, and gradually collected and destroyed all the originals. The statues, monuments, pictures and music they left alone. No boy could know, unless he was told, whether a woman or a man had painted a certain picture or designed a certain monument or composed a certain piece of music. It was true that women's art and music and sculpture, which had developed naturally along its own lines once women's psyches were strong and healthy, was quite different from the men's, but the men and boys were by now too stupid and depressed in spirit to take any notice of the difference in rhythm between the old male art and the new female. They had ceased to be artists themselves, as their psyches could now never develop far enough to become bisexual.

"This destruction of masculine literature, the fruit of men's minds, was perhaps the terrible vengeance taken by the female life-loving spirit for the endless destruction of sons, the fruit of women's bodies, by war. But the women who did it did not think like that. That's a male-emotional way of thinking, and comes from my split personality as an artist. The women did it for a reason, so that no man ever, even if he had the temerity to go into the sacred-against-him Women's Houses where these Latin books were kept, should be able to find out anything about the old civilizations in any language he could understand. One literature was left standing amid the ruin of the others. If I were to teach you Latin you could read all the old Roman poets and prose writers in the original. But our own poets, the English poets, you would have to read in Latin, good translations, well done by most scholarly women, for only the very best Latinists were entrusted with the work—but still, translations, and into a most unsuitable language. Once when I was a young woman I got a friend of mine who was a very good Latinist to translate an English poem, a lovely poem that was written about five hundred years ago. The English poem lost itself. It was not the same, a mere shadow of its former self. The Italian and French literature perhaps lost less, the German more even than the English, and the Eastern literatures in Latin perhaps lose most of all. We have the *meaning* of the old books, but not the spirit. If we retranslate them, as I have done with some of the German poems, a thing which is strictly forbidden by the way, we cannot be at all sure of getting them right. The man's mind, the over-developed male psyche with its split personality of the artist, is lost to us. It was a terrible destruction, but there is no evidence that the women engaged in it, even the women who so very carefully, almost lovingly, translated the best, or what they considered the best, books, felt any remorse or misgiving. They were being reasonable, and were no more remorseful for their female reasonableness than the Old Men were for their male emotionalism, or its results.

"The women kept also, in the headquarters of their secret society all over the world, the collections of war-pictures which had been made by the very early Communists. These had been, after the Revolution, shown to both girls and boys, to drive into their young minds the evils of capitalism and patriotism and consequent wars, and during the second Fascist reaction a good many of the war museums had been destroyed by riotous mobs of militarists. But there were plenty of pictures left after that died down. The old negatives had been reproduced on steel plates, and these from time to time are replaced by new plates, so that I shall be able to show you some exact representations of deeds done a good deal more than four thousand years ago. But men and boys have not been allowed to see them for a very very long time. They most of them contain evidence of male power. The girls have always been shown these war-pictures to harden their hearts, stiffen their pride and make them absolutely resolved to keep men down and themselves up. They also read sworn statements by women as to what happened in the second Fascist reaction.

"The women were lucky in one way. They had a knowledge of psychology, and they could profit by the mistakes men had made in their dealings with the sex they were always trying to keep in subjection. And you men are lucky in another way, because matriarchs are physically much fonder of their sons than patriarchs were of their daughters. You have far healthier, happier lives than women ever had in times of complete subjection. You are not drowned at birth, though we do not really want as many of you as there are. Your physical development is never interfered with, you are never shut up in houses without proper air and exercise, you are never either overworked or not allowed to work at all, you are not either encouraged to be sexually precocious or kept completely without sexual experience for the whole of your lives, which was what happened to very many thousands of women when men were still trying to combine monogamous marriage with war and large-scale male emigration. You are not kept economically helpless; your money's your own, and you can all of you earn enough to keep yourselves in comfort. You are all free to go where you like if you choose to save enough money to buy a ticket on the air or ship lines. Your natural male combative instinct is controlled, but not repressed. When women first began to rule men, they knew and had known for a long time that the combative instinct in men is part of the sex instinct and cannot be separated from it. It is indeed the root cause of male emotionalism. The male part of sex is an emotional display of beauty, a violent and emotional conflict with any other male that may be interfering with the courtship, and then a highly emotional act of loving. The female part of sex is a long, cold, slow, logical process which requires no emotion at all to bring it to a successful conclusion. And if boys are brought up to abhor *all* violence, and at the same time cannot sublimate the destructive instinct by religious fervor, or art, or skill, transforming it into a creative purpose, the result will be a neurosis of some kind. Impotence or sadism. The women would not let the boys have any skill, for it brings a sense of power and feeds the psyche, so they allowed them to fight each other as much as they liked, to play the most violent and dangerous games, to wrestle and run, to box with the naked hands or with gloves on, and to fight with sticks under certain rules. The girls and women had withdrawn from all violent sports, so that the boys and men never got any sense of power over women by their fighting and playing games, only over each other. They knew that the women despised roughness and violence as masculine, but at the same time sexually admired a man with a fine, strong body. The women did, as they do now, keep healthy by walking and swimming and certain exercises, but they are not nearly as muscular now as they were in the Communist period. Only some seem to be *born* muscular, like me, and then it's a disaster.

"Then again, you are far luckier than the women were because your natural sex instinct is never interfered with, or made to seem wrong to you. You are ashamed, unconsciously, of your sex, of being male, but you are not ashamed of being sexual. Women were terribly burdened by men's emotional admiration of virginity, which is a purely negative condition, natural to the immature, but growing increasingly unnatural as years pass by, and chastity, which really meant a frigid and perverse condition of not enjoying lovemaking at all. So that women were not only ashamed of their sex, but also ashamed of being sexual, and yet had to conceive and bear any number of children. Women, of course, are perfectly reasonable about sex; seeing they have far the largest part in it they always would have been, if not infected with male ideas, and they know that if you are not to be allowed to be human beings, you must at least be allowed to be happy and free animals. You are all of you allowed to make love to any mature woman you can get to favor you. No one expects you to be faithful. The women never bother you with jealousy. You are not expected to live with one woman or any women, you are left absolutely free to do as you like. Your sexual life would seem ideal to some of the Old Men who were most irked by the Christian ideas about sex. Yet they would be wrong to envy you. Because now you have no more real control over your sexual lives than women used to have over theirs; you must go where the wind blows you, and bow down when it blows too hard. You are never allowed to develop will enough to have control over your sexual desires, and yet if a person *cannot* say 'I will,' or 'I will not,' to them, he is not a human being. There's no woman probably in the world who can't say 'I will' or 'I will not,' and there's no man who can, except you, Neil. So you must be a genius.

"The world under women has been well ruled. Naturally there have been no wars, and populations have been kept stationary, with the economic machine that a stationary population demands. Hugely expanding populations must lead in the end to land difficulties and disputes, while rapidly declining populations set up practical difficulties and also create a feeling of pessimism, as if nothing were worthwhile. In the period of Communism the balance was found between too much machine-labor and idleness, and too much hand-labor and poverty, so the women kept it so. There is no luxurious living, but no idleness either. But naturally, to keep that balance, inventiveness has been checked, as there is little incentive to invention if you know that it cannot be used without condemning some people to live without any occupation, and therefore will not be used. Pure science interests comparatively few women. They like to *make* things; they do not care particularly just to know things if nothing can be made out of the knowledge. They are not nearly so interested as men were in the nature of the universe outside our planet, so pure science, mathematics and physics have been really stagnant all these centuries. On the other hand, they have been intensely interested in biology and anatomy and all the sciences that have to do with the life that exists on this planet, for out of them something can be made of value to human beings, which is health. They never have wanted, naturally, to make human life in any way but by ordinary animal procreation, because it would undermine their own power, but they have cultivated all sorts of other life artificially, outside the womb, to study fetal growth. In the same way, though it would be possible to predetermine the sex of children they will not do it; it needs the cooperation of men, and women will not cooperate with men in any way except one. So we still go on having girls or boys, hit or miss, and I don't think anyone often minds very much. Then they have been passionately interested in the study of the mind, and the science of sexual psychology started by the old Jew. This, the fact that women know how their own minds work, and how yours work, but that you know nothing about any of it, is one of the chief sources of their power over you. They are in a far higher state of consciousness. A girl of sixteen is a great deal more conscious than a man of sixty. Then they were always interested in medicine, preventive and curative, and by good hygiene, sex-freedom, and their knowledge of psychology they have made a race which is at any rate physically healthy.

"There probably never was at any time a race of such constitutionally sound and well-developed men as you, and while the women do deliberately keep themselves unmuscular in order to be as different from you as possible, they are constitutionally of an iron robustness. The mass of ailments peculiar to women in subjection, which were caused by unhealthy lives, wrong clothing, sex-repression, and either unwilling childbearing or no childbearing at all, are now unknown. We do not have many children, because our children live, but we could easily have a dozen each and suffer no inconvenience. The human attitude towards having children has completed the change which was begun in the Communist period. In the pre-Communist era, when women were ashamed of their sex, pregnancy was always concealed as long as possible, and treated as something rather immodest and disgusting, even though women were always being told that it was their only important function in human society. But when women rule pregnancy is regarded as highly honorable, the proof that you are a real woman, and not a barren creature rather like a man. Women advertise it by wearing a special dress long before they need to for convenience or grace, and when any of you men see a woman wearing one of those long cloaks you fall into a sort of superstitious terror. Your Mother-bond rises to your throats and almost chokes you. It is the sign, the symbol, of her power over you, and women's power over men. None of you would dare to speak to a pregnant woman unless she spoke to you first.

"But for you to understand the height and depth of women's power I must tell you something of the upbringing of girls, which of course is a sealed book to you. You boys are not allowed to leave your Mothers except to play in Nurseries and do a few simple lessons in day-schools until you are fourteen. Then you do go to live with other boys in a boarding school, where you learn a few more things. But your poor brains are so like putty that it takes you from eight to sixteen to learn to read, write, and do simple arithmetic, and a little geography, hygiene and elementary physiology; and to learn to cook and keep your houses clean and your clothes clean and mended, and really you spend quite half your school days scuffling with each other and playing games.

"But a girl's education is absolutely different. She goes to a boarding school at eight, for women do not want to keep girls in the Mother-bond. The bond between Mothers and daughters is not so strong as that between Mothers and sons, because of the sameness of sex, but it is there, and has to be broken if the girls are to develop as fully as they may. Women do not mind the girls leaving them so early, because though a woman may be disappointed if a son is born, unless she has some daughters, she usually feels more tender towards him than to a daughter. Women are proud of their girl-children, but they love their boys more. This, being admired more, but loved less, sets up a kind of hardy independence in the girl-child, and she usually goes to school quite willingly, not knowing, poor baby, in the least what she is in for. The girls work very hard, and as their brains are as good as they can be, not dulled by any shame of sex, but sharpened by pride of sex, they learn more in one year than you could in three. They learn Latin as a matter of course, but not from the old Roman books. They learn from translations. They usually learn one or two other languages, and geography and mathematics and anatomy and hygiene and a few other routine things. They are taught about the literature and art and music of their own age, that is the last four thousand years, but no history, not while they're still at school. They develop special aptitudes usually at about thirteen, and learn the elements of whatever it is, engineering or art or biology, they want to work at when they're grown up. The education, apart from book-learning, is all directed to one purpose, strengthening the will. They come to school with naturally strong wills, because they have hard, tough female psyches, and these wills are developed by every device known to humanity. They have to gain a control over their emotions which is absolutely rigid. They have to get complete control over their own bodies. This science, for it is exact, has been enormously developed by women. Men knew about it. Certain Easterns in the old days could control their bodies to a very large extent. But *all* women can. For instance, the weakest-willed woman in the world can by will power expel a fetus from her womb. In ancient days women had to resort to the most comic expedients to prevent conception. They had not really any control over their own bodies. It was all artificial. Now it is real.

"Besides this very stiff training in control, which is very often both mentally and physically painful and fatiguing, the girls are made to understand certain things. They come to school thinking boys are rather inferior, because their Mothers are women, and this sense of female superiority is increased in every possible way. They get a rigid idea of the honor of women. The honor of women in the Christian era was concerned entirely with sexual behavior, and the self-control of women was limited to one thing, control of the sexual impulse. Otherwise they had no honor, and were taught no control, and so came to be regarded as naturally uncontrolled, weak, impulsive, unreasonable and lacking in scruple. But our girls are only taught that they must control the sexual impulse till they are women, and *be able* to control it at any time after that if circumstances make it wise that they should, and their honor is not concerned with that at all. It is, however, dishonorable for a woman to show any emotion, except sex-love or motherly love, before a man or boy; to lie to other women; to intrigue against other women; and to display sex jealousy before men. This last is the most important. Sex jealousy is a most disruptive influence; if women were allowed to be possessive with men and openly hostile to their rivals the women's solidarity would be shaken, and the men would get a feeling of power. A woman can display sex jealousy to another woman privately, though it is considered rather undignified, but never must let any man know she is jealous. If a man is tired of her and wants another woman she must let him go without a sign of distress. Men in all their days of power never could control their sex jealousy, because they might have had other men's children foisted on them as theirs. Women have not this difficulty. So, though women are very jealous sometimes over a peculiarly attractive man, they can, and do, control and conceal it.

"The end of this education is, that women have a will so strong, compared with men's, that there is no possibility of conflict between them. If a woman tells you to go, you must go. Or to come, you must come. Or to do this, or to do that, you must do it. But it is considered extremely dishonorable to use this power capriciously, to tease men or boys, to mock them, or to be anything but kind and, within the limits of the form of society, just. For instance, it is not only dishonorable, but a capital crime, that is, a crime punishable by death, for a woman to break a promise to a man. One of our lines of power over you, and one of the things that keeps you contented and happy, is your trust in us. You all know from boyhood up that if *any* woman promises to do a certain thing that thing will be done unless circumstances make it physically impossible. This trust is not allowed to be tampered with. Women, in the old days, might be able to trust certain individual men, but they never could have any confidence whatever in men in general because it was rarely considered particularly dishonorable among men to break promises given to women. There again, we have been able to profit by their mistakes.

"Well, then, Neil, at the end of this very hard training the girls go to their Initiation in the Women's House and become women. First of all they promise not to reveal, to any girl, man, or boy, what they shall see and hear. There's nothing very formal about the taking of this oath. They just stand up and say it, one by one. There are no amusing ceremonies; they don't ask God to help them keep it, because they know God doesn't care for humans in a personal enough way to help them either to keep or to break an oath. Sometimes one seems to need a lot more help to break one.

"But without any ceremonies, or invoking God, or praying the devil to catch their souls, the whole thing is fairly grim. The knowledge that all women all over the world take the oath makes it ponderous. When all the oaths have been taken by that particular batch of girls, someone, usually the Secretary of the Council for the town or city where the Women's House is, casually announces that the penalty for breaking the oath, besides complete moral degradation, is death. Of course no one shows any emotion at this idea, but the affair gets several shades grimmer. Then they tell the girls about the Childhood Age and the Rule of Men, not all at once, of course, but day by day for about a month, and they look at all sorts of pictures, faithful representations of those far-back, filthy deeds, and then they know where they are, where they *were*; where men are, and where *they* were. It's a shocking thing. One doesn't show it, but the shock is there, for every girl. You see, they are so proud. It's terribly humiliating to them to know that once women were treated by men like slaves or animals or children or dolls. They don't think of those Old Women as the *same* as themselves, because *they* know that they wouldn't live under such treatment. But it hurts them very badly to think that anything in human female form could ever have been so low. Then apart from the blow to their pride the pictures are very shocking. Women now consciously detest wanton destruction, physical cruelty, and unnecessary ug-liness. The sheer, foul ugliness of some of the war-pictures is astounding. Well, they see all these things, and they are told what I have told you, and they get, on the heels of the shock, an abso-lutely iron-hard determination to keep the world as it is, with the life-bearing and undestructive sex in complete power.

"Then after this month's startling revelations they are given their circlets. The practical use of it is that you men can see at a glance whether a very young woman is really a woman, or a girl who's forbidden to you. The other use, the inward spiritual value, is that it is a symbol. It's like a girdle of purity, of mental integrity, to prevent, by its acquired moral power, any weakness on the part of the oath-takers. Not that much weakness is there. But it is, anyway, a symbol of women's honor. If—*when*—anyone finds out that I have broken my oath, my circlet will be taken from me, and my hair fall all about my face. It will be very shameful. I was trying to find out what it *would* feel like that day on Andreas' veranda. But it doesn't matter.

"Well, then, these women, for they are women now, have the freedom of all the Libraries in the Women's Houses and they can read the Latin translations of the old books and explore the real history of the human race. Lots of them don't bother with it. Engineers and navigators and such rather whistle it down the wind. They say, 'Well it doesn't matter much what *they* did, so long as we go on doing as we are.' They get the shock and the deter-mination, but it goes down underneath. But some women, mostly girls who want to be writers and professional psychologists, do get down to history and read a lot. The psychologists get a perfectly impersonal thrill when they get back as far as Freud. They laugh at his psychology of women but they admire him all the same. They get more thrills when they read about Jesus and Plato and Gautama Buddha. And I, though I was not going to be a writer, but an artist, and though male art is not so interesting to me as female, I read and read. From when I was seventeen till now I've spent a great deal of my spare time in Women's Libraries reading the Latin books. And I got a feeling, even at first, and it grew, of intense admiration for those Old Men. Not only for the exceptional ones, but for the whole toiling mass. Naturally I don't underrate the price women paid for the men's *ability* to toil so nobly. I often think that the price women paid that the race might be civilized was too heavy. That *no* civilization was ever worth it, and that we had better have remained animals. But it was not God's will. But with all that, I began to admire the Old Men and still admired them, even when I had a pretty fair understanding of their ghastly male silliness. So I began to think—when? Well, Neil, I sometime began to think, and now I finish to think, that women's retaliation, women's perfectly reasonable and logical enslavement of men, lest they rise up in all their old panoply of ghastly male silliness and destroy the whole lot of us, root and branch, as they *once tried to do*, has gone far enough. So, you see, I broke my oath. I see that it is the safest thing for the whole race that women should rule forever, and yet I have broken my oath. And while I believe it was right that women *should* rule these last four thousand years, while I believe that their en-slavement of men was no more *wrong* than men's enslavement of women, but necessary and inevitable, and therefore according to God's will, yet I believe that when women begin to think it wrong, and a condition to be changed, then it does *become* wrong, and the change itself is started.

"I have a strong belief, Neil, which is not shared by, as far as I know, any other women, nor even wholly by you, that women and men are not as happy as they might be. They may be happier now than they were in the Childhood Age, when a great deal of the best and most moving literature was tragic, and death was constantly being extravagantly praised. I think they are. But there is that glimpse of a real happiness in the Communist times, though even it *cannot* have been a complete happiness, or the men would not have felt the smallest temptation to destroy it. This female world, I think, is not *right*. It is safe, reasonable, uncruel, loveless and *dull*. The men's world was not right either. It was absurd and too unsafe, cruel and stupid, and at certain times as entirely without spiritual sex-love as ours is. I think it was not often dull, because where male silliness is paramount there never can be any longstanding monotony. There was always fear of either God or hell or Inquisitions or other peoples' soldiers or starvation to keep life brisk and entertaining. But then, you see, we do really die of boredom. There's nothing to kill us, neither violence nor disease, and yet we don't live much longer than they did. We die because our old age is unhappy, and our old age is unhappy because our world is *too* reasonable and *too* unemotional. In a right life, no one would hate old age, and no one, though this sounds ridiculous, would dread death, except physically, when it was actually upon them. So there never has been any right life yet for human beings, because they have always, in all ages, hated old age, and have always dreaded death spiritually and in the abstract, unless they were under the influence of death-hysteria. But though there never has yet been any right life for human beings that does not necessarily mean that there never will be.

"Karl Marx's theory of history was, very briefly, that there was a constant push up of power through the strata of society. I know you can't understand that very well, because our society has no artificial strata at all, and is simply divided into a ruling sex and a ruled sex. But in former times there were several layers in society, sometimes rigidly divided, so that people could not pass from one to another; sometimes fluid and intermixing. In English history the earliest form is a König who is chosen from among the most powerful and able men, and the people he rules over. Then comes the King by birth, the chief men by birth, and the people. That's a rigid form. If a man were not born King, or born into the chief men's group, he could not gain power or land legally, only by violence and usurpation. The next form is the Crown, the Barons, merchants, and serfs. The Barons were always trying to do down the Crown, but in the end the Barons were dispossessed as a ruling class, and the form became the Crown, the gentlemen, and the people. The gentlemen broke the power of the Crown and dissipated its holy mystery, and then the gentlemen ruled. But meanwhile a new class was arising among the people, which when it had consolidated itself was neither gentlemen nor people, but with bits of both in it, and that new class was called the bourgeoisie. It dispossessed the gentlemen, by land taxes and political changes, so now the form was the bourgeoisie and the people; for the King, the Barons, and the gentlemen had no longer any special power. They had all had their day. So there was only one class left that had had no day, and that was the people, those who lived on a wage and worked with their hands. Karl Marx said this class *must*, by the historical law, come to power, dispossessing the bourgeoisie, and that then after a period of rule by the people in their own interests the bourgeoisie would either be dead or have become part of the people themselves, and society would be classless. All that came to pass; the Fascist reaction of the bourgeoisie failed after the Last War, the lowest class did rise to power, did rule, and society became classless. There, this historical process was supposed to stop, being finished. But it was not, because there was one more class of people who had never had any power, never ruled in their own interests, and had been so very poor and downtrodden that they had sometimes even been denied the possession of immortal souls.

"These were, of course, the women, and unfortunately the Marxian process went on as inexorably as an avalanche; this last class rose till it became threatening, there was a reaction against its growing power, a war (none the less bitter because it was largely a spiritual war) and a revolution (none the less complete because it took so long). So now there should have been not only a classless, but also a sexless society, for all classes had had their day, and both sexes. But of course a sexless society is physically impossible. I believe, though, that it is not morally impossible. I believe that after this extremely long Dictatorship of the Women there might be a society in which there was no sex-antagonism. For it was the *antagonism* between classes that made the low one rise and the high one fall, and the fact that the ruling class will *always* rule in its own interests, leaving the non-ruling class to pick up the scraps. Then again Karl Marx said that no ruling class ever abdicates, that is, gives up its power voluntarily, and he was right; but a ruling *sex* can do it. Men abdicated in Communism, though afterwards they wished they had not, and what men have done, women can do. Men voluntarily stifled their tremendously powerful emotional feeling that they ought to rule; so women can stifle their tremendous reasonable certainty that women ought to rule. Then there would be at last the classless society without sex-antagonism, and we don't know at all what it will be like. Only right, somehow. Not emotional and cruel. Not reasonable and dull. Happy, we suppose, and nearer to the full feeling of God.

"Now I'll tell you more about the secret country where you never can come, without me to guide you, where women live. Just as a Mother treats her daughter with far more severity than she does her son, expecting a great deal more of her and consequently punishing her more harshly if she fails in what is expected of girls than she does her son for any little fault of immodesty or unmanliness, so society treats women severely, and men indulgently.

"There is no crime you are able to commit that is punishable by death, except Treason against the World Order. And you cannot commit that unless you are helped by a woman, because you have neither the knowledge nor the will even to *wish* to change the World Order by yourselves. I am committing treason, and you may be by merely listening to me, probably you are. I'm very sorry and it seems a shame, I'm a very unnatural Mother.

"Apart from this treason, which you *can't* commit unless dragged into it, you're safe. Even if you run amok, as very occasionally one of you does, under the influence of wine or strong beer and some unsuspected inferiority feeling, and you kill a man, or even a woman or a child, with a knife or some other edged tool, you are not executed. You are arrested by other men at the order of whatever woman is in charge of the district, and taken to a place of detention to be psychologically treated. The position of women as a whole is no more shaken by these incidents, even if a woman is the victim, than the position of humanity as the supreme power on the planet is shaken because people are occasionally gored to death by irritated bulls. The only reason why we put dangerous bulls to death is because no one has yet succeeded in psychoanalyzing a bull. But you, I mean this accidental murderer, is not considered to have been in his right mind, and by finding out *why* he fell out of his right mind under the influence of alcohol, his right mind is restored to him, it is suggested to him by a professional psychologist that he should not again get so very drunk that he wouldn't know what he was doing, and after a while he is released, chastened, and determined to behave in a manly way for the rest of his life. The same with your lesser crimes—stealing things belonging to other men, or destroying their personal belongings, hindering them in their work, bullying boys and the like—these petty misdemeanants are all treated in detention houses by professional psychologists. And it may interest you to know that no one is allowed to undertake the psychological cure of a man unless she has had a son. Because maternal tenderness, a physical but unsexual love for the male, is essential if the woman is to make a good job of it. But for you, the mere thought of having to spend some hours every day in an unsexual and mental contact with a woman who is not your Mother or your sister frightens you so much that the mere thought of psychological treatment is a good deterrent. And should a man, through injury to his head or other cause, go completely and permanently out of his right mind, and become for ever inaccessible and intractable, he is not killed, though his life is but little use to him. He is kept away from other people and guarded as gently as possible by other men under the direction of women. Men are only killed at their own request, if they are very old, painfully and hopelessly ill as the result of some accident, or completely crippled and done for as men.

"But among women there are a number of crimes which are punished by public loss of honor, and death. Breaking a promise to a man, I told you of. Another is political intrigue. This is necessary, because if we allowed any careerism and personal grabbing for power among women there might always arise some very selfish and unscrupulous woman, who to gain her own ends might train and even arm a group of men, and get her will by force. So in our governments, from the village councils to the Supreme Council of Europe, the women who wish to represent their village or town or city or country are allowed to do nothing more than send in their names. They may not canvass, publicly or privately, or write pamphlets, or make any speeches anywhere. All that is political intrigue. It is also political intrigue to say publicly, or publish, any adverse criticism of members of councils during their term of office. If they're slack or annoying or stupid the remedy is to wait and not choose them again, but their authority must not be undermined while they are still in office. The system works quite well. The villages and small towns know who are the women most fitted to govern, and a woman who is not fitted to govern, but who merely would like to govern, does not get elected. The towns choose one of their number to represent them at their city, the city chooses two or three for London, and London chooses two to represent England at the Supreme Council of Europe, which sits at Munich. But political intrigue might upset the whole thing, and you might in the end get a woman sitting in Anna Karenstochter's place in Munich who was not the ablest woman in Europe, as Anna is, but that one who had the most passionate desire to sit in the highest place. But women are not often seized with a passion to dominate large masses of other people; that sort of ambition was more characteristic of the softer emotional male psyche in a state of overdevelopment. It is an offshoot of vanity, not of pride. Most women want to do what they're fitted for, and I don't suppose many of them have been executed for political intrigue.

"Then, should a woman kill another woman, as they occasionally do, usually from an outburst of some fearfully vivid sex jealousy which has had to be suppressed before the man, the murderess is not treated psychologically. If her crime is proved she is condemned to death at once. Killing men or children is unknown. I remember a woman killing another woman when I was in Germany long, long ago when I was twenty. They went out skiing together and only one came back. There were enquiries, and at last she confessed that she'd shoved the other over a precipice. So she was degraded from her estate of womanhood and left alone with the poison which no woman, even when dishonored, has ever refused to drink. It would be thought the extreme of spiritual cowardice, and so however undignified and dishonorable are our crimes, our executions are always decent, womanly and civilized.

"Now, Neil, you have heard, though I know you cannot understand, the worst we do to you. Now I'll show you something that may make you grasp a fraction of what men did to themselves, and to women and to children."

She went to a chest of drawers that stood in a corner of the studio, unlocked one of the drawers and brought back five pictures.

"I am not supposed to take these outside the Women's House," she said. "I had to steal them very cautiously, and I can't get many at a time. Fortunately they're used to me going in and out carrying a sketching satchel. And fortunately, too, I'm such a great woman in Salisbury that no one likes to pry into my affairs. Now look at this first one."

The picture was of a large building with the roof fallen in and the sides somewhat knocked about. Neil looked at it with interest, but no alarm.

"That must be after an earthquake, like they have in other parts of the world," he said. "I don't see what that's got to do with it."

"It wasn't an earthquake. That building was made like that with shellfire. It was a deliberate man-caused destruction. It's the old Cloth Hall at Ypres, and that is a picture from the Big War. Houses, farms, trees, villages, towns, were all made like that, or worse, over a very large area of France, and a piece of Belgium and in central Europe. The people who lived in the houses had to go, the animals had to go, the whole place was devastated, good fields and careful drainage all ruined; the country was made a sticky, slimy desert where nothing could live but rats and soldiers. Now look at this one."

Neil looked and cried out, and put his hands over his face. It was a picture of the head of a man, a live man, but so appallingly mutilated that his face was more terrifying than the most obscene imagination.

"What *is it*?" asked Neil, trembling, his face averted.

"It's a man whose face had been hurt by shellfire or a bomb. That's another picture from the Big War. Thousands of men were left like that, so that no woman or man or child could bear to look on them. They had to be shut up, or wear a mask. Some were left without arms and legs, or blind, or castrated, but the fate of those who had become a horror to their fellows was the worst of all."

"Don't show me any more!" Neil cried. "Please, Grania!"

"No, you must look at them, Neil. You must realize, as far as you can, what we're doing, and what the risk is, not to ourselves, but to humanity."

The next was a picture of a woman, wounded and bleeding, with a dead child in her arms. She was looking at the camera, staring blindly out of a mask of fear and pain and grief.

"That's from the Last War, after an ordinary bombing raid, not a gas-bombing raid, over a city in Germany. The Communists took a lot of photographs in the Last War. They wanted records, for they knew what was coming *after* the war. They took fearful risks to get these pictures and preserve them. Thousands must have been lost, but some got through. And Neil, plenty of women in all the wars of the world were made to look like that. Millions of women, and children dead. Not because of wild beasts or earthquakes, but because of men. Now see this one."

Neil looked, shuddering, but tried to control himself.

"Grania," he said, "*those aren't human!* They're—they're *things!*"

It was a picture of a soldier in a gas mask bayonetting a civilian, also in a gas mask, who was lying on the ground. There was a ghastly impersonal cruelty and horror about the figures, as if a fiend were killing a fiend, without normal male fury or blood-lust, but from the depths of some cold pure malignity unknown to human life.

"They are *men*," said Grania. "Men, in shape like you. They're wearing gas masks. That's to keep away from their lungs the deadly gas that has been released from airplanes over the city. The original photograph was taken on the eighth day of the Last War, when there was an abortive Communist rising in a part of Berlin. The soldiers who were still in Berlin massacred the Communists, but in the middle of the massacre there was an air raid, so the soldiers and Communists both put on their gas masks. One thinks now, looking at that picture, that men might have known from its hideousness that war had lost all human justification. Nothing, one thinks now, could ever justify a human being running about in a public place looking like that. Even without a bayonet to poke into people. Now see this last."

The picture she now showed him was not ghastly. It was just a flat piece of land with orderly rows of little pale crosses, as far as the eye could reach.

"What are they?" Neil asked.

"Graves."

"But what is a grave?"

"We burn our dead, the people and the animals, because we think it healthier. But they buried theirs under the ground. That is a fraction of the great graveyards in France and Flanders where some of the millions of men who were killed in the Big War were buried under the ground. The graves have those little crosses on them because they believed that the wise and gentle Jew, Jesus of Nazareth, was divine, part of their Three God. They believed also that Jesus had told people, *everyone*, to love their enemies, and that peacemakers were blessed, so after the war, in memory of Jesus, whose enemies nailed him to a cross, they decorated their graves so. It was the least they could do, you see."

"I don't understand," said Neil, still looking at the flat peaceful monotony of the graveyards.

"I don't wonder, my poor boy. You're hardly male enough in spirit even to be silly."

"And is there really a dead man under each of those little pale crosses?"

"A dead man, or most of a dead man. But numbers were so blown to bits they couldn't be identified or buried at all."

"It makes me feel very queer," said Neil. "But it's not frightening like some of the others."

"Dead men are beyond fear and cruelty. They can neither give it nor receive it. But now do you understand that it was this thing, war, that made houses and buildings like this, and men's faces and limbs like this, and women and children like this, and city scenes like this, and made large tracts of land a burying ground like this? And do you understand that for many years this destruction was glorified as the highest and best possible human activity, that peacemakers in every country were persecuted with the utmost vindictiveness, and that armed men were the aristocracy, the ruling class of Europe?"

"But what if we do—whatever it is you want us to do—tell men and boys about all this, *must that come back? That?*" repeated Neil, touching the pictures with the extreme tip of his big, blunt-ended forefinger.

"I believe not. But no one could say that it was quite impossible, and women say, reasonably, that the risk mustn't be taken. And there is another thing. There is no reason, apart from the human reason of wanting all human beings to grow as far as they can, physically and spiritually, why this civilization ever should be overset. Men, the Old Men, had an idea that if a civilization did not keep on changing, it must degenerate. From *their* knowledge, the facts *they* had to argue from, they were right. Male civilizations must change all the time or they become degenerate. But they knew nothing about a female civilization that includes the whole world. This civilization is not degenerate. It is as sound, morally, mentally and physically, as it was three thousand years ago. That may be owing to the greater vitality and stability of women. It is no more degenerate, no more likely to weaken and decay and split up from within, than the earth, which brings forth different things every year, which are always the same things. Generations upon generations of women have been born, lived and died, but their civilization remains as stable and healthy as the earth itself. So to move it or change it is not like moving a mountain on the earth, no, not merely that, but moving the earth. And it is no good waiting, hoping something will *happen* to change it, for nothing can happen. In the past five years, since I made up my mind at last that whatever the risk men *ought* to be made free, I've talked to all sorts of women, guardedly, about the status of men, and have always come up very soon against a blank wall. And nothing can happen against the women's will. I can break my oath and talk to you, and you can collect a few other men whom you think trustworthy, and I'll talk to them, and we can make a little nucleus of conspirators, but I don't see that it is going to be much good, really. It's the *boys* we ought to talk to, but we can't, because they'd straightaway tell their Mothers. And Neil, I want you to tell any other man that you let into this, that the time he's *most* likely to give us away is when he's been making love. When the woman, after being for a little while his equal, is soaring off again into her remoteness and superiority. Boasting might happen then, you see. But I don't for a moment expect the conspirators to be celibate."

"You never warned me like that," said Neil.

"It's different for you. I trust you absolutely because you love *me*. Whether I'm only your aunt or your think-Mother, you love me and always have, and would think of me even if you did feel like boasting. But you see, Neil, how it all seems so hopeless. And yet, in another way, it isn't, for the very fact that I feel as I do *does* show that the women's civilization *is* beginning to break up from within, because I am a woman, though rather a peculiar one. And if it's beginning to break, it'll go on. There'll be more me's as time goes on, and under God's will things will be changed. On the other hand," she said gloomily, "it may not be God's will that things should ever be changed, only that I'm a mad woman and doomed to attempt the impossible. As to that, I shall probably never know."

"I'm quite *sure*," said Neil very seriously, "that you can't be mad, Grania. You must be the sane one, and the others must be mad."

"Thank you, my son. Without irony, your belief in me is a great help."

V

BUT EVEN WITH NEIL'S BELIEF IN HER, and the growing *human* love she felt for him which made her certain that wherever she wandered in the future, however far, Neil must come too, the next few weeks were extraordinarily miserable. She was oppressed by a sense of utter futility and impotence, and saw with ghastly clear flashes of vision that she had broken her oath and put not only her own life but also Neil's in danger for nothing at all. She was like a person after a fit of hysteria, who wonders how he *can* have been so terribly silly. But with all her misery she went on with it, concealing her misgivings from Neil and the minute band of conspirators he had collected. There was Magnus, the man he had refused to fight, and three other men, Harold, Joseph and Rolf. With the exception of Neil, who did grow most amazingly in dignity and humanity, so that every day he seemed to gain in spiritual stature, none of them, Grania felt, were any good at all. They were hopelessly thickheaded and infantile. They sat at her feet metaphorically, and of course believed all the things she told them, and found it all very odd and curious, and sometimes horrible and alarming, but never did they *understand* anything at all. They said, as Neil had at first, that it was all a very long time ago. Grania knew they felt no kinship whatever with the Old Men who had civilized the race, neither with their good nor with their evil deeds. She might have been telling them about either animals or angels. Magnus, she thought, might understand something in time. Harold, Joseph and Rolf seemed hopeless.

The excuse she gave to Carla and other people for having these constant male meetings in her studio was that she was doing a large picture with a group of masculine figures in it. She had drawn Neil's head so many times she knew every smallest detail of it. Now she sketched the others, and one day, being fired by the extraordinary grace of the young man Rolf, she persuaded all of them to take most of their clothes off and pose for her. Their beauty, the loveliness of their male bodies, and her awareness of the pathetic helplessness of their starved male minds, almost brought her down to tears. This emotionalism surprised her, but it went on into a wild passion of feeling during which she made a great harsh, savage sketch of them on a huge piece of paper she had pinned on the wall. She had no mercy on them; made them go on posing in boredom and physical strain till they were quite worn out. She wouldn't speak to them, either, except to tell them to stand or sit still. She went on drawing, white-faced and sweating, until it began to get dark. Then she stopped suddenly, wiped her face with a dirty rag in mistake for her handkerchief, and came back to the self they knew, controlled, and always gentle. She apologized to them and sent them away, even Neil, though she gave him a very loving hug and kiss.

She turned on the light to see her sketch.

"That's rather good," she thought. "If it were to be the last thing I ever did, I shouldn't mind. Poor men. Poor me. Poor world without love."

But she slept very well, and next morning, as all the men were at work and there was nothing to do about either the picture or the state of the world, she went for a walk up the bank of the Avon.

It was a perfect midsummer day. She remembered, when she had left Salisbury behind and was alone with the river and the hills, that it was June 23rd, Midsummer Eve. She wondered if she would walk all the way up to Amesbury and from there to Stonehenge, and stay there by the stones for the night and see the sun rise on them in the morning. She had done it often before. But today she felt a little not at all unpleasantly tired. She thought she would not walk so far, but just idle up the Avon until she felt tired of moving and then sit down and eat the food she had brought with her, and go to sleep under a tree in the hot afternoon when the chalky hills threw out too much heat and glare, and idle back to Salisbury in the evening.

As she moved along, very slowly, often stopping to look at a flower or at young sheep or up at the lines of the downs, she began to know she was released, a prisoner set free. The invisible dark bonds which bound her to the wrongness of the human world were relaxed, not perhaps broken, she did not know, but loosed. Nothing had significance except the thoughts called up by patterns of line and shapes of mass and light. Her eyes saw by themselves; they were swift and keen as eagles in flight. Her ears heard by themselves, her body moved, her feet gripped the earth cunningly, so that no matter how fast she ran or over whatever stony ground, she could not fall. Released from the dark bonds, her spirit breathed. She thought, "This is the feel of God. This is how all of us might live. *You fools!"*

Even that thought brought no pain, not even a mild regret. She was alone and holy. Nothing could spoil or break this hallowed wandering by the river.

Presently, feeling the sun hotter and hotter, she took off her clothes and walked into the water. She swam and lay languidly, being carried down the stream, looking up through the sparkling drops on her eyelashes at the blue deep sky. The drops made fiery colors shine. Cooled, she came out again, wrung out her long hair and dried herself. The water was holy, and so was the earth where she now lay, and the tree, an oak tree, which arched above her, and the food she ate.

"We are better than we know," she thought, "and when we know, we shall be better still."

She went to sleep.

When she woke, her time of release was over, the dark, invisible bonds bound her again to human sins, she was once more concerned with the world. But she had attained somehow to a robust placidity, and no fear or misgiving seemed likely to make an entrance through this strong guard she felt round her faith and purpose. She felt passionate with life and strength. Fit to walk to Stonehenge to see the sun rise on Midsummer Day. But when she rose from the earth she turned her face to the south, and went back to Salisbury.

It was four o'clock when she got home. She had left the studio unlocked, and when she went in she saw two women standing there, looking at her sketch of the five men, and instantly knew that the little futile conspiracy had been discovered. Her heart gave a great bursting leap, then settled down again to a steady beat. She wondered if these two women, both of whom were members of the Salisbury Council, had broken open her chest of drawers. There were some pictures there she had not been able to return to the Women's House. The chest looked all right.

"None of us," she thought, "has the faintest idea how to conduct a conspiracy with proper ingenuity. In a world where there are none, except one huge one, no one can take the necessary steps to learn."

One of the women said: "Hullo, Grania. We've been waiting for you. You're wanted at a special meeting of the Council."

"What for?" asked Grania, again glancing at the chest of drawers.

The woman shrugged her shoulders and made no reply.

"Can I change?" Grania asked. "These are my painting clothes, and I've been rolling on the earth in them, too."

"Well, yes, I should think so," was the answer, given after a moment's hesitation. "That's a fine sketch," she added, with a casual glance at the artist.

"My last?" said Grania.

Both of them nodded. Nothing more was said, and one with an apologetic smile went with Grania into her bedroom to watch her while she changed her clothes. She dressed herself in her nicest things, brushed out her long dark hair carefully and then with a stiff stare at her jailer put her circlet on again and twisted the hair in and out.

"Now then," she said, "I'm nearly ready. Can I get a handkerchief out of the chest of drawers in the studio?"

"You could if you kept them there, but you don't. I saw them in this chest of drawers. But don't fuss, we've got what was in the studio chest."

"Oh, well, I'll have one of these, then."

Grania took a handkerchief. Nothing more was said until the party got to the Women's House, and into the Council Room. Grania knew now that she was not to be confronted with any of her fellow conspirators. If any of the men had been there this extraordinary sitting would have been held in that part of the House where men were allowed to go, to get books or travel tickets or to make complaints about anything that worried them.

All the Council was there, with its Secretary, a woman called Vivien, whom Grania liked. Also there was another woman, not on the Council, whom Grania had known for a number of years and had never liked at all. Her name was Pipistrel. Grania was still in her state of robust placidity; indeed, things looked so bad that no female worthy of the name *could* have felt anything but placid about them, but she felt a shoot of anger rise like a little flame.

"And must this loathly Pipistrel," she thought, "trip me up at every turn of my life? Which of my lovely pathetic young men has she been with? If it's Neil I won't ever forgive him. But it can't be Neil, anyway."

Vivien said: "You'd better sit down, Grania."

Grania sat down and looked at Pipistrel, who looked back at her. Both glances were equally contemptuous and haughty. Then Grania looked at Vivien, and her hard heart softened. The Secretary was not showing any emotion, but she did seem to find it difficult to begin.

"Get on with it, Vivien," Grania said encouragingly. "What do you want to say to me? And why have people been barging about in my studio in my absence?"

"Well, the fact is that a man called Magnus Eveson told Pipistrel that you've been telling him and four other men all sorts of things they aren't supposed to know, and showing them war-pictures."

"*That* isn't what Magnus told Pipistrel," said Grania coldly. "That's what she wormed out of him afterwards, in quite as unfair and loathsome a way as the old way Fascists had to extort confessions from Communists, or Christians had to get money from Jews."

"This isn't an anthropological discussion," Vivien reminded her.

"I'm going to say what I like to Pipistrel, as there aren't any men here," Grania said pleasantly. "What Magnus, the poor fool, *told* her was that men once ruled the world. Isn't that so, Pipistrel?"

"Yes, but after all he must have got the idea from somewhere, mustn't he?"

"Quite so. But you got him to implicate other people by a sort of psychic scourging. Naturally Magnus couldn't stand up to you if you were determined to make him say things."

"Grania, this is all unnecessary and rather undignified," said Vivien. "Of course we've got to know how far this has gone."

"People like Pipistrel are dirty," said Grania, now including even Vivien in her glare of wrath. "Dirty people, dirty methods. Cowards and bullies, just like the worst kind of Old Men."

"I think you're mad," said Vivien, "though that won't help you, of course. Your sort of madness is too dangerous. But do you admit that you have talked to these five men, Magnus, Rolf, Joseph, Harold, and your own nephew, Neil Carlason?"

"Her own son," Pipistrel put in.

"Is he your son? I thought he was Carla's son," said Vivien, rather surprised.

"You haven't been in Salisbury as long as that loathly Pipistrel," said Grania, now quite reckless about proper manners. "She's been poisoning the place for twenty-five years and more; which is one reason why I'm always abroad, and you'd think she was too old for a baby boy like Magnus, wouldn't you?"

"This is impossible," said Vivien. "Is Neil your son or not?"

"Certainly he is. He knows it too, but that wasn't illegal, for he is long over twenty-one. And I shall go on being impossible, Vivien, so long as you keep Pipistrel here. You can put her out of this Council meeting. She's said her piece, she's not on the Council, and she must go."

"It's for me to say whether she is to go or not."

"Do as you like, but I shan't say any more while she's there."

"You'd better go," said Vivien, after a long pause.

Grania took no notice when the door opened and closed again behind the back of her enemy. She seemed to be thinking deeply of something else.

"Well, Grania, you admit before this Council that you've broken your oath, and told these five men things you were sworn not to reveal, and taken war-pictures out of the Salisbury's Women's House, and shown them to these five men. Do you admit it?"

"It's no good not admitting it. You found some pictures in my chest, and you know from that sketch on the wall that those five men have been in my studio. It's a clear case, and we're very bad conspirators. By the way, Vivien, will you see that Carla gets my pictures? That last one is good."

"Yes, I'll see to it. What have you been doing all this for, Grania? Of course you needn't answer if you don't want to."

Grania looked at them, one by one. Their faces were controlled and cold.

"It's no good me telling *you* why I've been doing anything. But I believe things have got to be changed. That's all. It was just the stupidest, most futile way to try to change them, but I didn't know what else to do. I never could get anywhere with women."

"Of course not. When did you start this?"

"About May Day. Oh, and look here, Vivien, don't go bothering Andreas, because he isn't in it. He's as innocent as the unborn, the poor old man."

"I'll take your word for Andreas, though there's no reason why I should take your word for anything. Are there any other men in it besides those five?"

"No. What will happen to them?"

"I don't know. But I should think nothing will happen to the four that are not related to you, except perhaps a short detention."

"During which they'll be made to believe I'm a mad woman with hallucinations?"

"It would be suggested to them perhaps that nothing you said mattered very much."

"The authorities needn't worry. They really understood nothing at all, and are prepared to do nothing at all. They'll just forget about it, and it'll be to them like a tale you tell children if they can't get to sleep. But what will happen to Neil?"

"He's your son, and they may doubt that you brought him up properly."

"Carla brought him up. I was only his aunt until just the other day."

"Still, you were there very often when he was a child. But it's no good asking me, Grania. It isn't in my hands. I shall have to get into communication with the London people."

"What would you do, if it *were* in your hands, about Neil, I mean?"

But Vivien wouldn't answer. She just shook her head. She got up and said: "Well, that's the end of this meeting. Grania, will you go and wait in the room at the back of the men's library? You can give me your word not to walk out, and then you can be by yourself."

"Well, that's very good of you, taking my word for so many things. But can't I go into our Library?"

"I'm really very sorry," said Vivien impassively, "but it's reserved for women."

"Oh, well," said Grania. She sighed, then made a small movement, a tiny shrug of the shoulders, and went out of the room.

In about three hours Vivien came in, alone.

"I've done all that," she said. "It was really very quick."

"I suppose I've got to go to London. Or did they give me leave to be poisoned in my own home town?"

"Well, neither. They want you to go to Munich."

Grania stared. She could not speak for a little while.

"*Vivien!* Oh, no, I can't do that. Bring me my swill and I'll be no trouble to you whatever. But I can't be sent over there to Anna K."

"Didn't you ever think you might be?"

"Of course not. I did think I'd be sent to London, of course. But Munich! Why should I ever think of such a thing? Can't we manage our own affairs in England and kill our own women? These Germans are too damned interfering for anything."

"It is an unusual case, you know," Vivien said, almost apologetically. "You aren't an obscurity. We—as a matter of fact, we've always been rather proud of you, I think. I think we'd just as soon you did go to Munich."

"Poor Viv. You're a nice, gentle creature, for a woman. Not like that godless Pipistrel. Tell me, will you connive at my escape, not from justice, but from going to Germany? Will you get the dog's-wash or whatever it is we drink, and bring it here to me? Will you do that, Vivien?"

"No. You know I can't do that. But why do you mind so much?"

Grania sighed, and said nothing for a little while. Then she said: "I shan't know what to say to Anna. I shan't like her to look at me, unless I can make her understand I'm right and all of you are wrong. I shan't like any of it. I can't think of any greater calamity in the last few days of my life, than that I should be sent to Munich. And you say there's no remedy?"

"None. Because she, Anna K., seems most anxious that you *should* see her. It's her personal order that you are to go, and she spoke on the telephone herself."

Grania got up and paced distractedly up and down the room.

"Who would have thought of such a thing? Blast all Germans, all Germans, beginning with my father. What a country, what a nation, what a—oh, well, excuse me, Viv, I'm upset."

"I suppose," said Vivien, feeling rather sorry for Grania, treason and all, "that you know Anna K. quite well?"

"Too well for this sort of thing. It's sheer indecency her dragging me to Munich when my own countrywomen can perfectly well put me to death at home. I feel all English and annoyed, Vivien. Look here, do be English too and get me out of this."

"I can't. I'd like to, but it wouldn't be right. Perhaps when you get to Germany you'll feel less English, as you are half German."

"I don't *want* to be German again," said Grania, in distress that was all the deeper because she didn't like to show it much, even before Vivien. "I haven't been to Germany or seen Anna for more than five years. Of course I understand all that now. I saw Elisabet in London and she said, why didn't I go to Germany. Well, now I am going, and I assure you, Vivien, that I'd rather be going to the Old Men's fiery hell. I assure you, Vivien, that if I hadn't met God on the bank of Avon this morning I should jump out of the plane."

"It's a shame to kill anyone as mad as you are," said Vivien thoughtfully. "Quite a shame. But will you give me your word not to leap out of the plane? Otherwise I shall have to make all sorts of ludicrous arrangements."

"Yes, I will. But why do you go on taking the word of the dishonored?"

"Oh, I don't know. Well, we shall be starting quite soon, so you'd better let me send for your coat and a bag."

"What do you mean? Shan't we be going up to London on the night plane, and on in the liner?"

"You're to go in a special private plane from here, and it'll be ready for us in half an hour."

"How important I am. And what about Neil?"

"He's not going with us."

"Is he being taken to Munich too?"

"Anna K. seems rather interested in the family."

"So he is?"

"Yes, but he's going the ordinary way."

"Can I see him before I go?"

"No."

Grania meditated. She did not want to stress Neil's independence of spirit, as it might make things worse for him, but if he was taken to Munich in the ordinary way used with erring or lunatic males, under a guard of men directed by a woman, there was no certainty that he would not commit some quite useless violence.

"Can *you* see Neil? Is he arrested?"

"Yes. I should have time to go and see him, I think. What do you want him told?"

"Tell him, I'll see him at Munich."

"I will tell him, but it seems rather a shame because you may not be allowed to."

"Oh, yes," said Grania absently, "Anna will do that for me. So tell him he must get safely to Munich to see his Mother. And just send someone for my warm coat and a bag, because it may be cold in the plane, though it'll be fairly hot in Munich, I expect. It's my birthday tomorrow, Midsummer Day."

"What about Carla?" Vivien asked, hesitating at the door.

"No," said Grania, shaking her head. "I'd rather say goodbye to Pipistrel than Carla."

"What's the matter with Pipistrel?"

"My dear Viv, in the short time you and I have left to talk in this world, I couldn't begin to tell you why I hate Pipistrel. Besides, it's a very humiliating story."

"I do wish it had been someone else."

"Oh, I don't mind that any longer now. This is merely a day of calamity mixed with Paradise. A very queer day altogether. Go on now, Viv, or we shall keep our special private plane waiting."

It was a good flying night, the little swift plane was in perfect order, the seats were comfortable and only by a soft humming was one made aware of travel. Vivien soon went to sleep, as Grania seemed disinclined for conversation, though had her prisoner wished to talk she would cheerfully have sacrificed her own comfort and talked all night. She could not understand herself. Grania was not only disgraced, an oath-breaker, but also had been doing a terrible and dangerous thing. She was an enemy of society, unashamed. And yet Vivien felt sorry for her and worried for her, particularly about this going to Germany, and could not make herself feel with any passion of reprobation that Grania had been doing anything *wrong* at all. "It must be," she thought, just before she went to sleep, "because she really *is* mad, and naturally one never can feel contemptuous of or angry with mad people. But no one ever was so mad and seemed so sane."

Grania had forgotten Vivien, Carla, Andreas, the whole question of men. She had even forgotten Neil. Now the little airplane was flying so fast and so softly and so inexorably to the southeast, now there was no escape and she must be in Munich in the morning, tides of what she called to herself "German-feeling" began to flow. The past five years dropped out of her mind. She went back to her childhood, when for no discoverable reason she had felt as much will to learn German as she had to learn drawing. She remembered telling her Mother about the extraordinary liking she had for the language, and her Mother, who was reserved even for a woman, just nodded, saying nothing at all. But later, when Grania had done her school time and her initiation and could go where she liked, and said she meant to go to the Munich Art School, Carla, Oldest Carla, now dead, did speak. She told Grania that if she met a man, a very tall, blonde man about forty now, called Hans Margaretesohn, she must not have anything to do with him, because he was her father. The young Grania was quite indecently interested in this German father, and wanted to know all sorts of things, but her Mother had retreated into her reserve.

"Well then, just tell me where you were," Grania remembered asking.

"In Munich."

So there it was. The long routes of her life began and ended in the same place. In Munich she had been conceived, and there, unless this little airplane impossibly fell to the earth or into the narrow sea, in Munich she would die. And then five and a half years ago being with Anna on the veranda of her little country cottage up on the Ammer Lake and telling her that she knew that she, Grania, had to do something very weird and extraordinary before she died. Anna saying it was just a big picture or something. But no, no, Grania knew it was more extraordinary than that, but not knowing what. It was the discontent, divine or merely lunatic, she could never know for certain, of her whole life since she had grown up, rising at last in spite of ponderous down-pressings near to the top of her mind. She left Germany soon after that, and as if it had been a haunted country, laying a spell on her, when she got away from it and away from Anna, she knew what was wrong. So, she thought, that was why I never went back. I was afraid of that terrific German thoroughness, and their conscientiousness in whatever they do, and their spiritual strength, and Anna's abominably strong character, and the power she had over me. For this new business *can't* start in Germany, and I must have known that, even before I knew what *it* was. If they're being reasonable they'll go on being it till the equator freezes, or till something cracks them over the head. But then, I don't know, I had power over Anna, too. My mysterious, frivolous, islandishness part has power over her. Not the German part. That's where we meet. But the other part, that's where we *might fight*. She doesn't understand it. It's unknown and queer and attractive and has a power. But what of that, when, for the good of the whole world, Anna will put me to death?

She began to wonder what death would be like, and slept at last, and had a very strange, long dream.

It started in a dark cave, which yet was lit in some way, because she could see, though not very clearly. She saw an enormous and horrible-looking creature, rather like an octopus, flabby, fleshy and obscene, which vomited forth at terrific speed through its great hole of a mouth, a stream of the most various life. It had eyes, but they could not see, perhaps, Grania thought, because the cave is really always quite dark, but it's just lighted up for me, so that I can see what it is doing. The life landed on the floor of the cave without injury, and ran or flew or crawled away all in the same direction. Grania watched this process for some time. She was not at all afraid of the octopus-thing because she realized that though it was extremely unaesthetic to look at it was not malevolent, and could never be, in itself, dangerous. It just did its job, which was to spew life, and would go on doing it until, in its stomach, or womb, or head, or wherever the life came from, there was no more life left to be vomited forth. Grania even felt a certain kinship with the octopus-thing, because she knew, though its method was unconventional, it was certainly a female giving birth.

A woman appeared at her side and said, "I think we'd better be going." Grania looked away from the octopus and at the person who had addressed her. It was a very small woman, naked, hairy and much deformed. The octopus-thing and the cave both vanished, and they were outside somewhere, battling up a terrifically steep, rocky hill in the teeth of a gale.

"Is it always like this?" Grania asked, thinking she *must* soon turn round and go down the hill and with the wind.

"For my part, yes," said the naked, deformed woman.

"What do you mean, your part?"

But that woman was gone by the time Grania spoke, for she could not get enough breath for some minutes, or perhaps years or centuries, and another woman, quite different, with clothes on, answered.

"She meant, for our part, yes. Always like this."

Grania went on walking up the hill against the wind. It was terrible, an agony of labor, but she had to do it.

"The wind can't go on blowing from this direction forever. Nor can any hill be without a top."

"Perhaps not," said her third companion on this frightfully unpleasant walk. "But for our part it can go on always blowing, and being hill."

"Then I shall never get to the top."

"For your part," replied a fourth woman, "you can if you wish to. This is unreal, for your part."

But it seemed very real, the terrific seemingly malignant wind, and the steepness of the way, the ache in her feet and legs and head and heart and lungs.

"It is impossible," she thought. "I *must* stop." But she went on and on. The hill went on and on. And the wind blew.

Then later, a long long time later, the dream did alter. The rocky steepness became a grass steepness, and it grew steeper and steeper. Grania thought uncomfortably, "I know this bit. The hill will now fall right over back on top of me, and I shall wake up."

The fifth, or perhaps the five thousandth, woman who had accompanied her on her extraordinary and laborious travel said: "It won't do that this time. Now you see."

"Are we near the top?"

"For my part, I believe so."

But now it was as steep as a wall and they were hanging on to bits of grass in really desperate danger of falling. Grania clutched at the top of the hill, gripped it and pulled herself up. She was there. Flat on her face, gasping for breath. The wind had completely dropped. The stars were shining in a clear lovely night.

"That was dreadful," she said.

Another woman, not she who had been with her on the last bit of her climb, answered, "The next is worse."

"On, no, it can't be."

"For my part, it can be. I don't think that hill is anything. The wood comes now."

Grania, still getting her breath, looked at this woman. "Don't vanish for a minute, will you?"

"Naturally not, while you sit here. This *is* my part."

She was, Grania thought, the most extraordinary woman of all, but then, with the exception of the first, the little naked, hairy deformity, she had not been able to look at them attentively. She had been too busy fighting the wind and the force of gravity.

This one was small and meager, and though not deformed she was very badly shaped. Though quite young she had few teeth, and what she had were decayed. Her skin was yellowish-white. Her expression was mean, cringing, sharp and terribly anxious. Her clothes were hideous and dirty, her shoes not only hideous but also quite worn out. Her hair was thin, dirty and dishevelled.

"Well, you are a one," said Grania, but she was no more afraid of or disgusted with this very queer-looking woman than she had been with the octopus-thing.

"Ah, for my part, I am, as you say, a one. But there are lots like me in the wood."

"What is the wood?"

"Where we get lost. I think we'd better be going."

Grania felt afraid of the wood now. It had come a good deal closer while they were talking, and now there was little room between it and the hill.

"Let's go down the hill again," she said.

"Look down the hill."

Grania looked, and was not comforted. It was now a sheer precipice with no bottom.

"You know you can't go back down that hill. You told Neil so."

"Did I? I can't remember that."

"In the wood," said the woman, "everyone forgets things that should be remembered, and remembers things that were—best—forgotten."

The words came softly like a sigh, from far away. For they were in the wood. And as everyone in it was lost, Grania was lost and the woman was lost. For the first time she had no companion, and no path to follow.

"This *is* worse than the hill," thought Grania. "She was right. Where are my women?"

She called. No one answered. And yet, in the half-darkness of the wood, for now it had become daytime outside it, there were plenty of people. But as they were all lost they could not help each other very much. The wood smelled rather unpleasantly; the ground underfoot felt soft and sometimes alive, as if, Grania thought, she were walking over half-dead bodies. But when she looked at it it seemed to be a black, spongy sort of moss. "It is not a good wood to be lost in," she thought. "All these people are frightened. I should be frightened myself if this were my part."

But then, for a few seconds, or years, she *was* frightened, as terrified as all the other people who were lost. "It's become a nightmare at last," she said. "Now I'm bound to wake up."

She tried to wake up, but could not. The horror grew and grew. The fear of all the people who were lost in the wood rushed upon her, forcing a way into her through her ears and eyes and settling like a disease in her womb and heart and blood. She charged a tree with her head down, like a bull, to bang herself awake. The tree splintered and fell, and she fell through the trunk into light, outside the wood. The sun shone, the wind blew soft and mildly; the fear and the wood both were behind her.

"That must have been the very last tree I hit."

"Lots of people do what you did," said a woman. "Butt the trees with their heads instead of going on trying to find a way out. It's a great temptation in there."

Grania looked up. To her intense astonishment it was the same woman, she of the bad teeth and hideous clothes. Her hair was white, and her expression more mean, more cringing and more anxious, but it was undoubtedly the same.

"Are *you* still here?"

"Easily," said she. "That is a very small wood really. It only seems big because it is so bad and frightening."

"I like this part," said Grania.

They were walking over a broad open heath on a summer day. The wind was behind them, the going was easy, there was no difficulty and no fear.

"Yes," said a woman, not she of the mean anxious face, but another, handsome, healthy, upright, and dignified. "But see how the poison of the wood hangs over it."

Grania looked back and saw how the clouds of poisonous vapor from the wood did indeed travel slowly over the heath even to where they stood.

"It's getting thicker!" Grania cried. "It's darkening the sun! Oh, why couldn't they *forget* the wood?"

"They were too frightened *in* it," said another woman, a sad-eyed, grave-looking person. "For my part, there is no reasonable forgetting. Now we must go through it."

They plunged into the rolling dark clouds of acrid vapor. It stung Grania's eyes and nose and throat; it was suffocating and horrible, but she felt no fear, only misery and discomfort.

She was through it. Standing outside an iron gate, leading to some formal, well-kept gardens.

"I'm glad *that's* done," she said, wiping her streaming eyes. "Through here?"

"Yes," said another woman. She unlocked the gate; they passed through and with a somber heavy sound the gate clanged to behind them.

"That's the only gate we've passed," said Grania uneasily. She had not liked the sound of it, and now she was in the gardens she was not sure that she liked them, either.

"It doesn't matter," said her temporary companion. "You can't go back on this journey, anyway. Remember the precipice. But that certainly is a strong gate, attached to a strong ring fence. It's to keep out the wild beasts."

Grania said: "I thought these gardens would be nice after that awful smoke, and the wood, and that terrible walk up the hill. But they are very dull."

She went on walking through the formal gardens. The day was always gray and overcast. There was no disabling wind, but there was no sun either. The gardens were most beautifully kept; everything was tidy and clean and well cared for and protected; flowers grew in profusion; trees were pruned where they needed it, leaves swept up. There was no fear, no appalling labor in travel, no suffocating smoke.

The gardens went on and on; different companions came to her and left her, the sky was always gray, and the gardens always neat, safe and monotonous. The women, she noticed now, were the sort of women she was accustomed to. Not deformed or hairy, or cringing and anxious, or even at all like those she had been with on the pleasant heath that was spoiled by the vapor from the wood.

And at last, after a long long time of walking in these depressing never-ending gardens, she looked round at a new companion and saw that it was herself.

"Oh, Grania, I am glad to see you!" she cried. "I'm absolutely dying of boredom. Do these gardens go on forever and ever?"

"I believe not," said herself. "But then, you know, that hill and the wind, and the wood, and the jolly but poisoned heath, and the last cloud of smoke—*they* weren't too nice, either."

"That's so," said Grania. "The only *absolutely right* thing I've seen yet was the old octopus-thing at the beginning. *She* was right. Nothing else has been. Shall we get back to her cave at the end?"

"For our part, I don't think we *can* go quite as far as that. But there must be something better than the hill or the wood or the vapor, or these damned dull, gray gardens."

"Do you really think so?" Grania asked Grania.

"I'm sure so. Pretty soon, now."

Then herself left her, and she got a slight shock, because now she knew she was dead. And being-dead seemed a bit more shocking somehow than not-having-yet-been-born. But at last she saw that the garden was getting untidy and wild. It got wilder and wilder. It was opening out into real country. And now, curiously, Anna was beside her, holding her hand.

"You lived longer than me, Anna," said Grania, feeling now very happy indeed.

"Oh, a great deal longer. I had to kill you, you know, because you didn't like the gardens."

"Does it matter?"

"Not at all," said Anna. "You've been walking a long time. A very long time. Let's sit down on this stone."

They sat down on a gray boulder in the middle of a moor. But it didn't stay so. Sometimes it seemed to Grania that they were on a Russian plain in the spring, when the flowers came out. And sometimes in a little valley in the Bavarian Alps. And once on a beach she knew with very white sand and a green sea and palm trees and brown-skinned girls and boys. And once on the bank of Avon in Wiltshire between the water and the down. And sometimes it was sunny, and sometimes a wind with rain behind it, or a cold wind with great dark yellow-gray snow clouds, or the snow itself falling, white on the ground, dark against the sky. Wherever it was, and whatever the weather, things were *right*, like the old octopus-thing; there was the feel of God. She was completely happy, at ease, and free.

"Anna, I've never been happier than now. Never, never, *never*, not even when I was a child and had not come to the dark invisible bonds. This is the right place. Better, far, than all those other things, but worth going through them to get to. Shall we go right on and find the dear old octopus-thing at the other end?"

"We can't do that," said Anna. "Well, *you* can. There she is."

Grania looked down. She saw a little grave, dug in soft earth. A little shallow grave. The earth looked comfortable, and she felt rather tired, even with happiness.

"That's a little Old Grave," she said. "But one can't die twice. I *am* dead."

"Well, but," said Anna, very reasonably, "if you die twice you're *quite certain* you are dead."

"That is so," Grania agreed. So she lay down in the comfortable little grave, and died, and woke.

And now the little fast plane was flying through daylight, and over Germany. Grania's dream dropped down through her mind slowly, like a piece of slate wavering downwards through well-water. It might return to her later, she knew, but for the present it was vanishing. She felt quiet and rested in mind, though her body was stiff. She was no longer distressed at having been brought to Germany. She watched the country flowing away beneath her, and the tides of "German-feeling" rose. So that when at last they landed at the Munich airport, and her feet touched the ground, ridiculous and unwomanly tears came into her eyes. She felt light-headed, emotional, all over the place and slightly giddy.

"Vivien, give me your arm," she whispered, not wanting to disgrace her controlled sex in front of the airport laborers and cleaners.

"Some people feel sick, not in the air, but on coming down again," said Vivien, holding her arm firmly.

"That must be it," Grania agreed. She soon felt quite well, and they went forward on the last stage of their journey, to the huge Women's House which dominated the town. Grania thought: "I suppose when I get inside that place the next time I come out it'll be feet first through a back door." But she didn't seem to care at all. She was entranced, listening to the German voices. It was not like a homecoming, it was at once sharper and less deep than that. It was like meeting someone she loved. She felt a strange aching sensation in her breastbone, her cheeks flushed and her eyes looked bright. Vivien, looking up at her, suddenly thought, "Why, she is rather a beautiful creature, really, for all she is so big and coarse. She looks perfectly happy. She is mad, and all this is wrong."

She said aloud: "Do you mind now so much, having had to come here?"

"No," said Grania dreamily. "It's all right, of course. I might have known it would be. This is mein Vaters Land. It cannot hurt me, or do me lasting injury. Only a sharp necessary pain, like having one's first man."

"That sounds rather incestuous," said Vivien, with deliberate lightness.

"I expect incest is a very old thing," said Grania. "Like being born, or dying. Now here we are. And we walk up these steps, and study these exceedingly German decorations, which aren't a patch on mine in London, and we go in, Viv, and then you must go home."

"Grania, I should like to say—" Vivien began.

"What?"

They were standing on the flat space outside the huge open doors.

"Well, that I think you're just mad."

"Don't worry. Even if my madness affects you now, so that you think I'm really an injured party, one of those too, too tedious bloody old martyrs, you won't feel like that when you get back to England. But I should appreciate it if you'll tell Carla you think I'm just mad, not wicked. It's hard on her, and she's very fond of Neil, too, and she brought him up for me. And oh, Viv, if you do ever get the chance of doing anything mildly nasty to Pipistrel, justly, of course, do it in my memory, will you?"

"You don't even hate Pipistrel now," said Vivien, sadly. "You're just making that up."

"Oh, well, perhaps I am. But supposing Anna said to me, 'All right, you're as free as the air,' *then* I should hate Pipistrel again. So I do really. She's a horrid little person, I give you my word."

They stated their names, but not their business, at the enquiry office in the huge central hall, and after a little time of waiting a very young person, only just a woman, and exceedingly pretty, came dancing rather than walking up to their comfortable chairs. Grania stared at her.

"You're very like Anna," she said in German.

"Ich bin Elsa," the little creature half sang. "Elsa Annastochter."

"Do you remember me?"

"Natürlich. I came home from school one week and saw you, the great Grania—ach, like that!" She sketched a giantess in the air to show how very large Grania had seemed, both physically and spiritually, all those years ago.

"You can't have been more than about thirteen. I don't think you were so like Anna then. Well, what are you doing now?"

"I'm about Mother's thirty-second under personal secretary. Oh, I don't know what I am. I just gallop round. She told me to look out for you. But we're being rather rude, nicht wahr? We should speak English with your friend."

"Can you?"

"Be-au-tifully," drawled Elsa. "Look, what will you do, Vivien? Have breakfast with Grania in her rooms? Or do you like to look over this offal great place and see how things work? Or to go out into München?"

Vivien looked at her watch and got up.

"I think I should go back to the airport. I must get back today."

Elsa raised her eyebrows comically.

"But what so friendly a friend as to come all the way to München with, just to sit in an airplane with."

Grania laughed, and took Vivien's hand.

"Your English isn't so terribly good, Elsa. I think my German's a lot better."

"Ach, Mother says you are more German sometimes than she. If I were so English I could speak it better."

"And so goodbye, Viv," Grania said. "Love to Carla. Thank you for coming."

"Goodbye," said Vivien, and with a smile she went.

"What came she for?" Elsa asked. "And go on speaking in English. It's good for me."

"Then you must say, why did she come, or what did she come for, and I answer, because I am not well, quite nearly dead in fact, and must have someone with me on the journey."

"Ach, I am sorry!" Elsa cried. "That is owful!"

"*Awful*, not 'owful' nor 'offal.' Schrecklich. So it is."

"Mother never told me you were ill."

"What *did* she tell you, young Elsa?"

"She say you are coming to see her, and not to go to the cottage on Ammer, because of course we cannot go till Saturday, and that you are to stay in München, she tell me what rooms you are to have, and I am to see you have all you want. Breakfasts and baths and books."

They were shooting up in a lift. It stopped at the fifth floor, and Elsa took Grania to a little suite with bedroom, bathroom, and sitting room. The sitting room had a huge wide window fully open and Grania went to it, and looked out over Munich at the mountains.

"I shall see about the breakfast," Elsa said.

Grania started slightly and turned round. Her face looked a little strained.

"Elsa, when do you think your Mother will see me?"

"Oh, an hour or two or three."

"Where?"

"Here. So it is better we don't go anywhere else, because she might come very soon when you've had your bath and breakfast."

"Then I think you'd better go back to your galloping round. I mustn't keep you from your work."

"My work is to look after you. But then if you are ill, you must be tired, and best be alone. Then should I get some doctor to come? We have very good, the best doctors in München."

"I'm past doctors," said Grania gloomily.

Else looked at her and laughed.

"It's all a—a tease!" she said. "You are not ill at all. No one could be so ill and look like you do. It was for some other reason she, Vivien, came."

"It's a mental disease that makes me throw myself out of airplanes."

"Then you'll throw yourself down there," said Elsa, waving her hand at the window. "That would kill you."

"It certainly would. But windows haven't the same attraction as airplanes. You can safely leave me, Elsa."

"I will," Elsa said, nodding to a hint of authority in Grania's last words. "Your breakfast will come. And I shall see you again?"

"You must ask your Mother, child," Grania said. "But perhaps. Auf wiedersehen, anyway."

"Auf wiedersehen."

Grania had her bath and her breakfast, and Anna did not come. She tried to read, but could not concentrate. She walked up and down. She sat on the couch by the big window looking out at the mountains. Two hours passed.

"Can she really not come?" Grania wondered, "or is she doing it to torment me? Now I wish I hadn't sent the child away."

She tried to bring back the condition of robust placidity; she tried to remember her dream. But all thought and feeling was swallowed up at nascence in one thought, of Anna. At last, feeling ashamed of her uncontrol and nervousness, she lay down on her back on the couch, and deliberately relaxing her body she managed, though not without great effort, to bring her will and thoughts under her command. Peace came, and she shut her eyes.

When she opened them Anna was there, looking down at her. Either she had come in very softly or Grania had been asleep.

"Grüss Gott, Anna," Grania said, smiling as placidly and delightedly as a small child.

"Grüss Gott," said Anna.

Grania swung her legs off the couch. Anna sat down in a chair. They looked at each other gravely, without speaking. Anna was fairly tall, taller than the little Elsa, but not nearly so tall as Grania. She was slim and delicately made both in feature and limb. Her skin was smooth and hardly lined at all, pale, but very faintly flushed over the cheekbones. Her hair was thick, dark and straight. Her very determined mouth was wide and red-lipped.

"Anna, you look marvelously young after five years," said Grania. "Do you know I am forty-eight today?"

"I wish you—well, I am forty-three."

"You look about thirty, I think. You know, I think Elsa is very pretty, but she is not so beautiful as you."

"I have a little boy now," Anna said. "Besides the three girls."

"What did you call him?"

"Heinrich."

"Oh, what a stupid German name."

"He's a stupid German boy."

"You like him though?"

"Very much."

"Better than the girls when they were babies?"

"I think most women love the boys more."

"I wasn't asking about most women."

"Well, I think I do love Heinrich more than the others. Grania, why have you not come to see me all these five years? Why haven't you been in Germany?"

"I don't think I *could* come to Germany and not go to München."

"Why have you never written to me?"

"I gave Elisabet a message for you, when last I saw her in London."

"To say you were settled in Salisbury for the rest of your life."

"I was right."

"Not quite. Well, but why haven't you been to see me?"

"How long have you been General Secretary for Europe?"

"Seven years," said Anna, looking faintly surprised at the question. "But you couldn't have minded that."

"I can't be bothered to tell people of such brainpower and ability what they know already."

"How was I to know what you were up to? I knew there was something, of course."

"I told you on the veranda of the cottage that night, Anna, do you remember that night? I told you then."

"I remember. I didn't think it would be—be this," said Anna, looking at her small dainty feet.

"I warned you it would be something extraordinary."

"It seems to be unique," said Anna. "I spent some of last night looking up criminal records. In the last thousand years only one hundred and seven women have been executed for breaking their oaths, and they all did it because they wanted their lovers to have more spirit. They did it for particular men."

"Then see how much better I am than they; I want all men to have more spirit."

"However, it won't make any difference what you did it for."

"But it does to you?"

"Yes."

"Anna, you are going to have me executed?"

"Yes."

"How dared you bring me out here to you?"

"It's my business to find out *why* such things happen. Particularly with a woman like you, a woman who, *apparently*, has everything our world has to give."

"Yes, but how dared you, all the same?"

Anna looked at her steadily.

"It isn't me that's the coward, Grania. You've been afraid to come to me all these years, afraid to come to Germany. Because you knew you couldn't go on thinking, even *thinking* this way, if I was there. I may be the only woman in Europe who can, who could, control your will, but there *was one*, and so you were afraid."

"Yes, I was afraid of you, Anna. But not now, and your control is broken. You'd better have left me to those English women."

"Did you like the idea of coming here?"

"It seemed quite terrible."

"Because you knew you couldn't keep up your fantasy with me, and you knew you'd be ashamed."

"Anna, if you dare suggest I'm ashamed of anything at all, except being so stupid and futile, I shall throw you out of that window."

"Coarseness and violence always increase with age," Anna remarked. "Sit down. It's too hot for even thinking about throwing people through windows, or any other action at all. All right, you aren't ashamed. But you were."

"I was very silly. The fantasy was in thinking I couldn't see you safely. Now I've missed you awfully all these years and—well, how long have we got?"

"Do you mind being judged by the German Supreme Council?"

"I shall be honored. I am sure it is a fearfully august body without the smallest sense of levity."

"If it had one, it wouldn't have much opportunity to display it to you. Well, that'll be on Thursday morning."

"It's Tuesday, isn't it? Why, it was only on Sunday, though it seems months ago, that I did that marvelous sketch."

"What of?"

"My five poor men. Such lovely creatures, Anna. There was one called Rolf who was perfectly beautiful. I made them sit for hours and they got so bored and fearfully stiff."

"Your son Neil will be stiffer soon," Anna said deliberately.

"My dear, I know, I know. You don't need to put things before me as if I didn't care. I know you can't let Neil live, even without me, and it's better so. He couldn't be happy—now."

"Perhaps he could *have* been, if you'd let him alone."

"No. He *wasn't* being happy. That's why I started with him."

"You've got no sense at all, Grania. Nothing like that could ever be *started* among the men. It would have to start with the young women. You ought to have corrupted women, not men."

"Well, I did try, but I never could get anywhere with them."

"That shows how useless and wrong it is."

"It doesn't. It shows I was trying with the wrong sort of woman. Now I shall try with the right sort."

"Grania! Are you thinking—surely you're *not* thinking that because I love you, I shall—*shall let you go?*"

"There is another window-worthy insult. If you were that sort of weak creature why should I ever have bothered with you at all? Ach, you think German, *German*, how stupid you are with all your brains!"

"German yourself," said Anna, recovering her poise. "Well, I'm sorry. But how do you think you can corrupt any women before you meet the Council on Thursday?"

"I don't know how it is, Anna," Grania said seriously, "but wherever I go corruptible women spring up round me like daisies in the grass. And of course they will spring just the same if I *don't* go, because it is a natural law."

"You do talk terrible nonsense," said Anna, laughing, but wiping her eyes. "You make me cry, with your silliness, and being just the same."

"But where is your womanly control, my dear?"

"I doubt if it was designed to meet situations like this. Now look here. If you sign this paper, I can make the Council business very formal and short. I shall ask you whether you object to the Council or to me, and you'll say no, you don't, and then it'll be all over."

"Supposing I said I did object to you, what would happen?"

"I don't know," said Anna. "No one ever has."

"You ought to be prepared for all contingencies. Are you going to be the judge?"

"I have to be, if it is the German Council."

"All right. I won't behave badly. What do you want me to sign?"

"Your confession." Anna took a piece of paper out of her pocket and handed it to Grania. On it was written:

"I, Grania Carlasdaughter, an artist, of Salisbury, Wiltshire, England, admit that I have broken the oath I swore to keep as a woman, and have entered into a conspiracy against the World Order with my son Neil, usually known as Neil Carlason, and four other men."

Grania read this through and said, "The other men aren't going to be named, then?"

"No. Neither named nor executed. Just detained a little while, I expect. But mind, Grania, you could have been responsible for the deaths of all the five, for they are all conspirators, just by listening to you."

"That's an unjust law, Anna."

"It is unjust. And that's why it's hardly ever enforced. But it will be, with Neil. It's unjust, but sometimes necessary. Now just write at the bottom, 'I agree that this statement is correctly written down,' and sign it."

"And supposing I don't, Gen. Sec.?"

"We shall have to get the Salisbury women over here who heard you confess."

"Oh, poor things. No, I wouldn't like that."

Grania took the paper to a little writing table, wrote what was required below what Anna had written, and signed it with a sprawling, rather fantastic "Grania C."

"There," she said, showing Anna the paper, and pointing to

the different writings with the end of her pen, "That's you, and that's me. You are very upright, honorable, and intelligent, while I am stupid and visionary and fantastic. Yet in the end, *that one* will beat *that one*, Anna K."

Anna put it in her pocket and only said, "It's an interesting document. Some people would give me a bit of money for it, the signature, I mean."

"Only very silly people," said Grania absently. "Anna, why should I be tried at all? I don't think it is going to be very nice."

"You should have thought of that before," said Anna with annoying obviousness.

"You could have left me in England," said Grania heatedly.

"I couldn't. A real conspiracy *has* to come to me. Murders and other crimes, yes, but not conspiracy. And besides, I wanted to see you."

"And now, and now, Anna, are you glad you've brought me here?"

Anna hesitated, then said "Yes."

Grania was silent a little while, then went on in a troubled way. "Anna, why should I be *tried?* Can't I not be? I've confessed."

"No. I can't just quietly murder you without any formality. No one can do that. It's as quick as it can be, but form there must be."

"Röhm wasn't tried," Grania said. One of her sudden changes of mood made her face look quite different.

"Röhm, who was she?"

"He was a man who annoyed Hitler, and he was just left in a little cell with a revolver, one of those things that went off bang and made such nasty untidy bloody male messes of people."

"Hitler! You know, Grania, the root of your fantasy is that all your life, long before you got to this dangerous conscious stage, you *would* live in the far past. All those Old Men, good and bad, Hitler and Jesus and Socrates, are more real to you than living people."

"No, no. Not more *real* to me. Not more real than you or Neil or Andreas. But important."

"Well, what happened about Röhm?"

"Oh," said Grania absently, "he just sat there with this ridiculous revolver-thing, but he didn't use it, and just sat there, perhaps thinking that Hitler, who had been his friend, was a tiresome obstinate beast, or perhaps not thinking at all, or perhaps thinking of the future of Germany. And then he was taken out and messed up with one of those long shooting things, rifles, that women still have to use in parts of the world where there are dangerous wild beasts."

"I don't suppose for a moment that I know as much German history as you do, and I can't remember anything about a Nazi called Röhm. But I do remember about Frederick, about Fichte, about Bismarck, Nietzsche, Hindenburg and Hitler. And you want that sort of sequence to start again, and men to be like them. You want Germany, and the world, to go back to *that*."

"I don't. The world *can't* go back. If you hardly knew any history at all, Anna, your reason must tell you that it never goes *back*. Civilizations have been overrun by barbarians, but a whole civilized world *cannot* return on its tracks. Well, the Fascists found that out, didn't they? The world, now, has got to go forward to something *better*."

"Then you don't admit the smallest risk of a return to male violence and unreasonableness?"

"I admit a risk. I don't know what it's a risk of, exactly, but I admit that there is one. But, Anna, it's *got to be taken*. This is a safe world, nothing can happen against our will, and we're safe undestructive people. But it's a *coward's world*. Why, it was right for the women to be resentful and afraid after the second Fascist reaction; they'd had such a little time of peace and freedom and dignity, and their unreckonable ages of humiliation and misery were such a little way, such a very little way, behind them. But it's not right *now*, Anna. It's not right to hold a grudge for four thousand years, and from that grudge and that cowardice to deprive half the human race of its human right to grow. We call ourselves mature, and we say that in the race's maturity women must rule. But no race can ever be mature while one sex is infantile. This is not a mature, or a free, or a happy humanity; God is not with it as God might be."

"You mean that you are not happy, and you say that your son Neil isn't, and so for the sake of two individuals you want to change the whole world."

"I should change it so that there might be more than two individuals in it," Grania flashed back at her. "But I mean, Anna, that *you* are not happy. You send Elsa to me so that I can see how happy she is. Well, she is. But in any time of the world people of eighteen were happy if they had enough to eat, something to do, and were allowed to make love. But you're older, you've had all the things Elsa looks forward to so much, lovers and children and work and fame and admiration, and you daren't say to me, *to me*, that you're happy, because I shall know you're telling me a lie."

"Naturally," said Anna steadily, "I am not happy now."

"No, and what will you do when I'm dead? Not just away, not just avoiding you, but dead and out of the world?"

"Grania, is this your new human fairness and justice?"

"It's my new human way of breaking people to bits. I shall break you to pieces, Anna, and leave you in pieces, and you'll put yourself together differently, when I am gone. Why do you love me so much?"

"I don't know. It is a pity, isn't it?"

"It is, and it isn't. It makes my death certain, but it also makes your *life* certain. But now I'll tell you why you love me, because you *can't love anybody else*. You, people like you, arranged this world where there can't be any but physical love between women and men. And you live in it, but you can't be happy in it. You haven't had my difficulties, Anna. You're beautiful and attractive and men draw towards you like iron to a magnet, but you've never been able to love any of them, not even as much as I love my old Andreas. You have as much natural force to love as anyone that's ever been in the world, to love as hard, and love as long, and you've had to give it all to me for lack of a better receiver."

"I don't regret it," said Anna.

"But I don't accept it," said Grania sternly. "I throw it away, like that. It's no use to me, except for the furtherance of my purpose and my desire."

"That's something to know," Anna murmured. "Well, shall I go, then? I've got things I can do, you know."

"Go! My God, no. I haven't started yet. I'll tell you something that's more interesting than any of the things you can go away and do. When you came into this room, when you saw me you *knew*, not only that I *thought* I was right, but that I *am* right, and that you and all the rest of you are wrong."

"Grania. I can't let you go on talking like this. I really can't. If I thought you were right I should not only let you go, but I should go with you. Of course I don't believe it's wrong to break an oath if the oath is binding you to a course of action you *know* to be wrong. That would be as stupid and as masculine as Herod taking off the head of John the Baptist. If I *knew* you were right, as you say I do, I should break my own oath like you have, and help you in a new and more sensible conspiracy. Which would be far better managed, by the way. And *you know* that I'd far *rather* chuck all this, and break my oath, and be dishonored and anything, than—than send you to your death. And be in a world that hasn't got you somewhere in it. You throw my love for you back at me, but it's there just the same. You can't destroy it. I would do anything in the world, but wrong, to save you."

"You've got a terribly strong defense in your uprightness and sense of duty. I'm not thinking I can break *that* down. I don't have to. Because by Thursday night it will be gone."

"You're a sadist," said Anna. "I never knew it before. You like to make people suffer."

"Well, now I'll put my little whip away for a bit. Anna, did you take any notice of the name of the woman who denounced me to the Salisbury Council?"

"Es war Pip-is-trel," said Anna, pronouncing it as well as she could.

"Yes. Pip-is-trel," repeated Grania, laughing. "Do you remember me telling you about a woman who swept my Andreas, my one man who never had to be humored into loving me, but who loved me perfectly spontaneously—yes, just swept him away from me?"

"Yes."

"That was Pipistrel, too. She had plenty of men, and Andreas never was much to look at, and I'm convinced she did it to annoy me. It was the most frightfully unconventional Council meeting, and poor Vivien didn't know what to do."

"I suppose you thought you might as well show some jealousy at last. Grania, don't you see that—well, you've always had to be rather jealous of other women, haven't you?"

"Yes."

"And yet in large ways you have perfectly good control."

"Yes."

"Don't you see that your whole idea, your life passion, which was at first unconscious and then conscious, may be hatred of women? Because they've so often pulled you down and humiliated you, and you've always had to suppress your anger, you really want to humiliate *them*, the whole lot of them. But you rationalize it by telling yourself men must be free, and the race mature, and other more noble things?"

"Of course I've thought of all that. Why, Anna, every drop of blood in me might be a doubt, a little stinging doubt to torment me by day and by night, over months and years, and then there'd be more doubts yet."

"Then how can you come here and be so certain?"

"I was certain after I walked on the bank of Avon, yesterday. Yesterday. Oh, it seems so long ago. A long time since I was miserable and doubting. Anna, don't get up. Don't go. See, sit here with me by the window and let's talk about other things."

"For a little while, then. But you needn't stay here when I'm gone, unless you want to."

"But where can I go?"

"Anywhere in München."

"I might make revolutionary propaganda with your Germans."

"You must promise me not to do that, nor to make any with Elsa, and you can go where you like, with her, or without her, but you must come back at night."

"Why? Do you think I'm likely to be tempted beyond my strength to make revolutionary propaganda at night?"

"At night you must make it with me, for it is the only free time I have for about a fortnight, except for weekends, and this morning."

"All right. How can I get Elsa if I want her?"

"Use that telephone, and tell the woman who answers to find her and send her to you. She is quite free."

"We can go and bathe. Anna, when can I see Neil?"

"*Then*, but not till then."

"Is it not allowed?"

"No."

"Is it allowed *then?*"

"Not really, but that can be done. Now, you promised, no more whips today."

"No, no. Let's remember things."

When Anna had gone Grania had a meal, with Elsa, and afterwards they went out, first to the Art Gallery and then to the women's bathing place, where they spent hours swimming and sunning.

She felt so happy and at ease, so strong and free and young, that at first she was afraid she was in the grip of a death-hysteria or martyr-complex or something equally shameful and shady. But all at once, when she was lying on her back in the river, seeing fiery colors shine through the drops on her eyelashes, and feeling the cool water round her limbs, she knew that it was not death-hysteria, but the intensification of the life-sense under the menace of death. And this vividness, this ecstasy of life, was made even more sharp by the foreknowledge of victory, not only over Anna, but through her over the evil of the world.

"I shall win," she thought. "The triumph is mine."

Later, when she and Elsa were sitting, pleasantly tired with sun and swimming, in a public garden, Elsa said in a low voice, "Do you know, Grania, that it is here, in this which is now a garden, that Adolf Hitler used to make speeches to his Braunen Battalionen?"

"Jawohl, Elsa. I expect I know as much about Old München as you do."

"Speak English, Grania, or in Latin."

"All right. Are you much interested in Hitler?"

Elsa came closer to her on the seat.

"You know, we of München must be a little rather interested in the Nazism because it started here, in our town. In our town those bad men started their bad things, to make the Fascism for Germany."

"I've sat in this garden many times, Elsa. When I was a young woman at the Art School, and later when I knew your Mother, with her, and alone or with other people, and I've never been here without thinking some of the time I hear that great brassy bull's-bellow of a voice, pouring out male absurdities, and urging Germany on and on, into the deep heart of the blood-and-violence dream. And then later when I knew Anna, marked for rule she was, at only twenty, I'd hear her voice on the other side of me whether she was there or not. A small quiet voice, reasonable and controlled, and a quiet person she was, to rule Germany, and Europe. And I used to think are these two, the female and the male principle, forever at enmity, and forever standing face to face grinning hatred at each other; or are they really back to back and part of the same thing? And could some good be made between them, some better far higher kind of life, or could it never? And then *now,* I think of Hitler, and how he was the most purely male man there ever was perhaps in the world, most monstrously male, and how his fundamental thought was purely emotional and silly; and I think of Anna, who seems to be his exact counterpart, and purely female and reasonable, but I doubt it now, I doubt. Anna is not quite monstrous, and in her there is a saving grace."

Elsa said, "If you talk English so very fast, Grania, I cannot follow it well."

Grania started, and laughed.

"Just as well, Elsa. Why, I had forgotten you, you child."

"I am not a child, nor a girl, but a woman."

"Ah, you'll be a woman some day, and Heinrich will be a man."

"Natürlich," said Elsa. "And he will never know about Adolf Hitler."

But Grania thought he might come to know about Adolf Hitler, and about Jesus of Nazareth, too. But she made no more revolutionary propaganda, not even in absence of mind.

When it began to grow dark they went back to the Women's House. Grania sent Elsa away after they had had a meal, and waited a long time for Anna. She did not come. Grania was exultant and sorrowful. She knew Anna was afraid to come, but then it was sorrowful, because there was only one night left, and little time, no time now to talk of other things. So she went to bed, and slept very well without dreaming, and the next day passed as happily as the one before.

Elsa said, when they parted in the evening, "On Saturday we shall be able to go up to the cottage on Ammer, and you can see Heinrich, and you and I and Mother can sail in the boat all day long."

Grania felt a pang like a forecast of the dissolution of death. Elsa saw a change in her face.

"What is it, Grania? You will come, won't you?"

"I have to go home tomorrow, Elsa."

"To England? So soon? Why, what was the good of coming at all, for only two days?"

"Well, I have seen Anna. And they've been nice days, gemütlich, nicht wahr?"

"Sehr gemütlich!" said Elsa, nodding and grinning. "Then I shall see you before you go tomorrow. Auf wiedersehen, Grania. Good-night. Sleep well."

But Grania said, "Adieu, Elsa."

She went to the window and stood looking out. The pain and dread of death had passed. She felt strong and very calm.

About midnight the door opened and Anna came in. Grania laughed, a large and noisy ringing laugh.

"Ha, Anna, warum bist du gekommen?"

"To see you," said Anna, with perfect composure and coolness.

"But why didn't you come to make revolutionary propaganda last night?"

Anna said nothing. Her determined mouth was set in a thin hard line, and she met Grania's glance steadily. The battle was joined once more.

"You won't answer because you daren't tell me a lie, and you daren't tell me the truth, either. You were shaken, you're afraid of me, and so you didn't come. How did you sleep?"

"Not well," said Anna, shaking her head.

"I slept very well, as well as the dead sleep. And why, when you wouldn't come last night, have you come tonight?"

"From personal weakness, emotionalism and loss of control."

"Ah, you are honest, but that won't save you." Grania went up to her, and taking her by the arms shook her gently back and forth.

"You were shaken, Anna, like this, and you can't stop me shaking you spiritually any more than you can if I choose to shake you physically; but tonight you're not to be shaken only, but cast down, and this house with you, and all the houses like it all over the world. Your fall will pull them all down in the end, and the people must put something better in their place."

"No, Grania. But listen, for this night can't we talk of other things? Not make any revolutionary propaganda?"

"No!" cried Grania. "It's *my* night, my last on earth, not yours. By your cowardice you wasted last night when I would have been nothing but your friend and your love, and tonight I shall be your enemy and your tyrant, and we shall talk of what I want and not of what you want. You can go, or you can stay here and listen to me. Which will you do?"

Anna shrugged her shoulders.

"I shall stay till you put me out."

"Ach, I am nasty to you," Grania said, much more calmly and gently. "I'm all worked up, Anna. I feel so terribly alive and frothing with strength, so that I could murder you for twopence, just because I love you."

"You do still, then?"

"Of course, you fool. Why, you've come to mean Germany for me. This afternoon I remembered Wiltshire, the downs and the little chalk rivers and Stonehenge, and I felt a fearful blood and bones drawing and agony like one feels when one first sees one's Mother lying dead. It's a stirring of something terrible deep down. But this, our Germany, Anna—come to the window here with me and look at what we can see—this is a different drawing. It's like physical sex-love, when you want the thing that is opposite, not the thing that's the same. And so I belong to England, I'm part of England, but I *love* Germany, which is so different, as different as my father and me."

They leaned their elbows on the sill and looked out into the night.

"If we could fly now, Anna, we could go straight over the

mountains nach dem Alt Oesterreich, where all the trouble used to come from. Ah, Germany was born late, but born a giant."

"A stupid cruel bloodthirsty giant."

"Naturally. When the whole of Europe was being stupid, cruel and bloodthirsty, of course Germany would be the stupidest, the most earnest in cruelty, and the most thirsty for blood of them all. It is her spiritual strength, the tremendous power of concentration there is in Germans, the great vitality, that makes them do *every-thing* that is being done about three times as well as other nations can do them. Bad things, or good things, stupid things or terrible things, beautiful things or ugly things—it doesn't matter. All are done with earnestness and conscientiousness and might. In the Big War it took nearly the whole world to beat Germany. In the sexual and moral collapse after the war Germany outdid everyone else. The very finest bloom of that dunghill plant Fascism grew in Germany. And who made the best, the bravest, the most clever and ingenious of all the underground Communists? The German working men. And who started the Last War? Germany, of course. And which nation outside Russia got the child Communism first and most quickly to its feet, in a ruined and disorganized country at that?—Germany. How quiet it is out there, Anna. All Germany is asleep."

Anna shivered.

"Are you cold? It's a warm night, though the moon makes the mountains look cold."

"I must be cold, because I'm shivering. No, let's stay here."

Grania put her arm round Anna.

"That'll be better then, because I'm as hot as the inside of a volcano. There, is that better?"

"Your heart beats like a big dynamo."

"Ah, it is a big dynamo, my heart. Anna, I can see across these last four thousand years, these level flat dull centuries, as plainly as I can see things out of this window, and see the mountains on the other side, like the Bavarian Alps out there. Mountains of diffi-culties, and then the long, long easy safe plain. But it is going *uphill again*, this end. More mountains are coming. More difficulties, less safety. To lead to what, I don't know. I can't see so far. Only the hills coming."

"Nein," said Anna.

"Ja, Anna. But listen, what is a nation? Do we love our countries any the less because we hate no others, and despise no others
for being different, and have given up offering our own blood-
sacrifices? Do I love England and Germany, and you, Germany? I
believe we do. But what *is* a nation? It must be the land itself. This
Germany, the mountains and the rivers and the plains, and the
cold rim of the northern seas, it must be much the same now as it
was in Hermann's time. We—*you* are different. You, Anna, are not
like a woman of Hermann's time, or a woman of the Christian
civilization. But the land itself is the same. The great Mother-body
you come from is the same, and so though you are so different you
must be really the same. You are still German. You have the power
of this land in you, you have the vitality, the tremendous concentration, the spiritual strength and hardness of a German person. You can use it for the safety and stagnation and injustice and
lovelessness of Germany and the world; or you can use it for
courage, Anna, for growth, for change, for love, and for a better
life. But see, how soundly Germany sleeps. Four thousand years of
sleep, and no sign of waking yet. Why, that's too long."

She leaned forward out of the window. She called out, not
loudly, but very roundly and clearly, *"Deutschland, erwache!"*

The cry made Anna's scalp prickle and tingle. She shivered
again.

Grania spoke in a low voice, as if she were listening to something.

"There, you see, it goes all over Germany. Through Alt Oesterreich and back through München, the city lying there so still, and
up through Bayern, and through Silesia and into Prussia, and up to
the far north where the old Polish Corridor used to be, and to the
sea. And along the sea and then all up the Rhine and through the
Harz mountains and the Schwartzwald, and through Baden, and
back to München. There is no one to hear it. No one to take it in. So
it must come back, in here. *Where it will be heard.* And it comes back,
and it finds a place of rest."

Grania touched Anna's two ears, then laid her hand on Anna's
breast.

"Er ist da," she said.

"Nein," said Anna.

"But I say Ja, Anna, and so it will be. I have bound my spell. And so, Auf wiedersehen."

She lifted Anna off the couch, kissed her, and took her gently to the door. She put her outside, shut it and locked it. Then, finding she was in a wringing sweat, she had a bath and went to bed.

Next morning Grania's fires were out. She had no more feeling of life, no strength, no placidity and no courage. She felt half dead already, and yet the fear of death trembled so in her blood and nerves and muscles that she could hardly put her clothes on, and could not eat, nor drink anything but a little water. She could not think of anything but one Latin sentence, where it came from she had no idea, for she was not accustomed to *think* in Latin, so she must have read it somewhere. It went on drearily repeating and repeating itself in her head while she moved about weakly and clumsily, dropping things and picking them up again. *Timor mortis conturbat me.* God, oh God. *Timor mortis conturbat me.*

At last she was dressed and sat down to wait until something happened. She could not stop her hands shaking nor her mouth quivering, nor lumps rising in her throat, nor a sick feeling in her stomach. She who had always had as much power over herself as any other woman was now reduced to the helpless emotional condition of a very frightened, very unhappy little boy.

"This is awful," she thought. "I shall break down there, before all those women, and Anna, and cry, or faint, or be sick. And I simply must *not*, apart from pride, because if Anna could think I was not a real woman it'll hold her back. Where *is* my control? Oh, dear, what *has* happened? I've used up too much of myself the last two days and last night, and there is nothing—nothing at all of Grania but a quaking physical shell. Grania, come back to me quick, or we're both lost."

But nothing got any better, until the door opened and two women she hadn't seen before came in. Under their cool gaze her childhood training miraculously, it seemed, reasserted its power and she became calm. Her mouth and hands stopped quivering, and her legs supported her as they ought to do. She was so relieved that she almost smiled.

She was taken through a great many halls and corridors until they came to a locked door, which one of her guides, or jailers, unlocked.

"Where does this go to?" Grania asked.

"To the men's part."

"Oh," said Grania, trembling again, but only inwardly. Was she to be tried *with* Neil, then? If she saw, before the very worst of this day's business was done, that great dark-bearded man, her son, would she be able to hold on to this control? "That won't be nice, to have Neil there," she thought. "Will Anna know it? She wouldn't like to make anything worse for me, but then her boy is so small and she doesn't know what it feels like, how pathetic it is when they're bigger than you and stronger, and have beards. Will she know? Oh, Anna, dear dear Anna, think quickly, and if Neil is there, turn him out."

Another door was opened and she was ushered into a biggish room. There was no man there. Only the Council sitting round, and Anna in an ordinary office chair by a desk. She looked up as Grania came in, a fleeting glance. She was very white, the faint flush of her cheeks quite gone, very haggard; she looked her full age and more.

"You poor child," thought Grania, touched almost to weeping, and for a moment quite forgetful of what she was there for, or Anna either. "I did murder you, but not for twopence."

Anna briefly informed her Council that the proceedings would be held in German, as the accused, though English, could both speak and understand it. Then she went on in a low, flat, but clear voice, "Grania Carlasdaughter, you have been indicted on a capital charge which is proved upon you by your own confession, signed by you in my presence. Do you object to being sentenced by this, the German Supreme Council, having its headquarters in Münich, Bavaria?"

"No."

"Do you object to any of the members?"

Grania looked round at them. They were all unknown to her.

They sat still, and their faces were quite expressionless, but there was tension in the circle, just the same. There was indeed such a powerful amount of intense German concentration in the room that Grania began to feel like a cork, borne up on a huge dark wave. However, she said she had no objection to them.

"Do you object to me, the Judge?"

Grania forgot the other German women. Their tenseness and concentration seemed to recede. Anna was looking at her now, for the first time since she had come in. Grania's voice went. She longed to tell Anna she did not object to her, but could say nothing at all. She opened her mouth and shut it again.

"Do you object to me, the Judge?" Anna repeated.

"Not at all!" said Grania very loudly, in English.

"In German, please."

"Oh, sorry. Nein."

"Did you know, when you broke the Women's Oath and conspired against World Order, that the penalty on your conviction would be death?"

"Yes."

"Members of the Council, do any of you ask me to exercise my prerogative of mercy?"

But none of them would ask that. Grania was again aware of the huge dark wave under her as she listened to the 'neins' and watched their impassive faces.

"Have you anything you wish to say?" Anna asked her.

"Nichts."

"Then I and this Council now sentence you to death by poison, self-administered, the sentence to be carried out—at once." There was the smallest possible faltering pause between the words. Then Anna said, "Take off your circlet and give it to me."

Grania took it off with a steady hand, untwisting the hair. But as her hair fell forward over her cheeks she felt a quite irrational agony of spiritual dissolution. She thought, "I am shamed." She made no effort to give the circlet to Anna, but stood swinging it on one finger, staring at her.

"Give it to me, please."

Grania's false shame passed away. She went up to Anna and put the circlet on the desk.

"Will you go with these two women by the door, please," Anna said.

"Of course. Anna, where is Neil?" Grania said in a very low voice.

"Up there. Grania, go quickly," Anna whispered.

"Adieu, Anna."

"Adieu."

Grania went to the door without glancing round, and walked out looking very tall and stiff. But when she got outside, from sheer relief that that part was over, her feet wavered in their steps, and she had to put a hand on the arm of one of her jailers. She was taken up some stairs, not noticing anything much, but she did see, on a landing, six very large men, sitting on a bench looking miserable.

"Neil's guards," she thought.

Then she was put into a room, and saw Neil sitting on a sofa. The door slammed, a lock clicked, and she was in Neil's arms. They were so firmly clasped, so much together, that they were like the sea and a wave. Both of them had a little time, or it might have been quite a long time, of the most blessed physical joy and peace.

"Ah, Neil," Grania said at last, down his neck, "I'm your feel-Mother at last, you great lout, nicht wahr?"

"Yes," said Neil. "But don't talk German, for God's sake."

"No, no. My German time is done. Neil, my extraordinary and most amazing baby, have you had a perfectly horrible time?"

"No," said Neil stoutly. "Not at all. Or that is, not after I got your message in Salisbury. Did you see my guards outside here?"

"Yes."

"I think they picked the six biggest men in England to come with me."

"You child! Still so proud of being strong in the body?"

"I must think about something," Neil said. "Well, nothing was very bad except that terrific Judge woman. She's dreadful. So cold and stony, like a piece of ice. That wasn't so good, that part."

"She's not cold, Neil. She's a friend of mine."

"She can't be."

"She is. That is Anna K."

"Oh," said Neil, overawed. "No wonder I thought she was terrible. But then—did she sentence you, too?"

"Yes."

"That must have been awful, Mother."

"It was rather difficult for both of us. But listen, Neil. *We've not failed.*"

"Well, if you say we haven't," said Neil dubiously. "But I *don't* think much of those other men. I don't see how they can get far without us. And they've had such a fright, too, and they know I'm going to be killed."

Grania gave his arm a convulsive squeeze.

"I've killed you, my poor son. I'm an unnatural Mother, and always have been. But listen. We failed in England, but in Germany we haven't failed."

"Do you mean in just this little time you've been here you've been able to—?" Neil stared in amazement.

"In just this little time. Neil, Anna will go on with it. And far better than we could. She's got much more brain, and caution and energy and thoroughness. I was wrong about trouble in Germany. This is where *it is to start.*"

"But then why, if she knows we're right, is she killing us? Mother, you must be making a mistake. No woman would do that."

"She doesn't know she knows. She's got into a perfectly inevitable pychological tangle. She'd rather do anything, but wrong, than have me killed, and so whatever would stop me being killed *is* wrong, and her own weakness and love for me. Do you see?"

"No. But if you say so, it is so."

"Well, it is rather difficult. But I know that when I'm dead, or a few months afterwards, Anna will see straight and know what she really knows now. So, Neil, *I must die,* but if you like to break down that door and knock out your guards if you can, and get away out of here, I give you my full permission and my blessing on your enterprise. But I can't go too, apart from any question of my womanly honor. While I live, Anna will never see straight."

"I won't go without you," Neil said. "I had thought we might possibly do something. But I don't want to go, if you don't. I should be lost, no use."

"Well then, my darling, I think we'd better get on with it. I've been shamed once today, though it was a stupid shame, but anyway I couldn't bear it twice, and I feel someone might come to see why we don't do anything except talk. Where is this dog-poison?"

"Over there," said Neil, pointing.

On a table in the corner of the room stood two glasses, each half full of fluid.

Grania kissed Neil, and then fetched one of the glasses.

"Now, Neil, if you can drink this straight off, without any hesitation or trembling or fear of death, I'll say you're the first man of the new world that's to come after us."

"The first man," repeated Neil. He took the glass and drank the contents. He fell back on the sofa and died instantly, so quickly that Grania was amazed. She could not believe it. She felt his heart. It had stopped.

As she looked at the huge limp body of her son, her bone and her flesh, lying there, she thought she was dead already, and that there was no need to drink anything out of a glass.

"Without Neil, without Andreas, without Anna, I am dead, but someone said to me—somewhere—that we must *die twice*."

She got her glass and raised it towards her lips. She remembered her dream. In a flash she saw it all, from the octopus-thing to the little comfortable grave, and that it was Anna who was there, and told her that dying twice made sure.

"So the end *is* known," she said, and drank her draught.

AFTERWORD

The desire and pursuit of the whole is called love.
                              Plato, The Symposium

I

Katharine Burdekin's *The End of This Day's Business*, now published for the first time more than fifty years after its composition, is a novel written in passion, sadness, and hope: passion to understand human history; sadness at what male domination has made of it; and hope for a different sort of future. Written in the ever-lengthening shadow cast by the rise of Mussolini and Hitler, Burdekin's is one of many anti-fascist novels produced in England during the 1930s.[1] But unlike these other books, it is unique in its understanding of gender as a political issue. Adopting a self-consciously feminist standpoint, Burdekin follows through the revolutionary implications of her vision in a book of great philosophical and historical intensity.

In one of her many startling insights, Burdekin once described the society of her time as one in which the phallus was the guarantor of civic power. If *Swastika Night*, her best-known novel, is a vision of phallocracy gone mad, *The End of This Day's Business* can fairly be said to reverse the genital signifiers, for in the society portrayed in this novel it is women who rule, and women's word that is law.

Set more than four thousand years in the future, in a concordant world in which women have at last come into their own, *The End of This Day's Business* depicts a truly utopian way of life, a global society in which distinct national cultures are preserved but coexist without competitive nationalism, without violence, and without war. In this society, women, characterized as the reasonable sex, care for the earth and all its creatures. Only one price must be paid for this harmony. It is the subjection of men, who, stripped of their history and deprived of any knowledge of women's sacred rites, complacently accept their "natural" inferiority and consequent condition of dependency. Appeased by games and athletic contests, knowing only their mothers but not their fathers, enjoying the freedom of casual sexual liaisons with women who are never jealous or possessive, ignorant of responsibility and indifferent to social status, the men of Burdekin's novel live secure and passive lives in their inconsequential separate sphere. There is no marriage; the ring, former emblem of women's subjection, has become a token of female maturity and power and is worn by women as a circlet in their hair, a mark of their initiation into the bond of sisterhood and a symbol of the esoteric knowledge that accompanies it.

One woman, Grania, an artist and leader, namesake of the greatest of Irish folk heroines, comes to question this way of life, and chooses to betray her oath to her sisters for the sake of a vision of a better world in a future beyond gender inequality. Through the struggles of this protagonist, Burdekin creates a powerful drama that lays bare the destructiveness of the long patriarchal past, but also exposes the moral dilemma inherent in matriarchy. Not knowing where her actions will lead, Grania repeatedly recalls (imperfectly, for the literature of the past now exists only in Latin, women's secret language) the lines that give the novel its name, lines spoken by Brutus, another tragic betrayer, in Shakespeare's *Julius Caesar:*

> . . . O that a man might know
> The end of this day's business, ere it come:

But it sufficeth, that the day will end,
And then the end is known. . . .
                    [Act 5, Scene 1]

Burdekin's political imagination was so far ahead of her time that today, more than fifty years after the novel was written, readers are likely to experience a shock of recognition upon encountering her work. For in the midst of the post-World War One lull in British feminism, Burdekin, like Virginia Woolf and Rebecca West, continued to cast a critical and distinctly feminist eye on her society. But unlike Woolf and West, Burdekin faded from the literary record. This fate may well be related to the very challenge her uncompromising vision posed to her society. There seems to have been no critical standard in Burdekin's own time capable of incorporating her writing. The fate of innovative literature depends upon finding an audience able to see what is in it. Even Virginia Woolf's most strongly feminist texts (such as *Three Guineas*, published in 1938, the year following Burdekin's similar analysis, in *Swastika Night*, of the relationship between fascism and patriarchy) disappeared from view, until recent feminist criticism reestablished them. If Burdekin was an alien presence in her own time, to ours she is a precursor. For Katharine Burdekin approaches the issues of what we now call gender ideology from a perspective, and often in a vocabulary, that it has taken us decades to relearn.

II

Katharine Penelope Cade, later Burdekin, was born in July 1896 in Spondon, the youngest of four children of an upper middle-class Derbyshire family. Her father managed the family estate, hence did not go to university. Her mother's formal education had ceased at the age of thirteen, but she was a voracious reader. Although Burdekin appears to have been closer to her mother, who was described to me as somewhat eccentric, than to her more conventional father, there is no evidence that either of her parents resembled the sometimes idealized parental figures in her fiction, unfailingly supportive and wise as they deal with offspring who can never be at ease in this world.

The family moved to Cheltenham, where the children were

educated at home by a governess until, the girls at age eleven or twelve, the boys earlier, they went to school. The boys entered Cheltenham College as boarders, and the girls went to Cheltenham Ladies' College as day students. Penelope, as she was called, attended the school from 1907 until 1913. During this period, Cheltenham, after nearly fifty years of the pioneering leadership of Dorothea Beale, had passed under the direction of L. M. Faithfull, who, as principal from 1907 to 1922, continued the college's position of leadership among girls' schools. As early as 1910 a Red Cross detachment was formed at the college, and girls were trained to participate in the work of national defense. By the time the war started in 1914, the college's Red Cross Hospital was fully prepared for opening in case of invasion. Two Voluntary Aid Detachments were formed at the school, and by 1914 about four hundred girls had earned certificates in first aid and nursing.[2]

When Penelope Cade completed her secondary education at Cheltenham, she told her parents that she wanted to go to Oxford, like her brothers; but they would not agree. Instead, in May 1915 she married an Australian barrister, Beaufort Burdekin, who had been at Cheltenham College with her older brother. In view of her later criticisms of masculine and feminine norms, including dress codes, the newspaper announcement of the wedding strikes a strange chord, truly belonging to another life, another world: "Lieut. and Mrs. Burdekin are to spend the honeymoon partly in London and partly on a motor tour. The bride's travelling dress was of soft Dreadnought grey covert coating, worn with a very smart hat *en suite*."[3]

While her husband, who had been invalided from France at the time of their marriage, returned to serve in the war, Katharine Burdekin worked as a nurse in a Voluntary Aid Detachment at the army hospital housed on the Cheltenham Racecourse. Out of this experience was to come her sixth novel, the fiercely anti-war and decidedly feminist *Quiet Ways*, published in September 1930. Burdekin's two daughters were born in 1917 and 1920, and in August 1920 she went to Sydney with her husband, the children, and a nanny. It was apparently in Australia that she began writing. Her first novel, *Anna Colquhoun*, was published in London in April 1922; the annotation on the novel's last page, "Sydney, May–June 1921," is the first sign of Burdekin's lifelong habit of rapid and intense composition with little or no revision. A sequel to *Anna Colquhoun,* promised at the end of that novel and indeed written while Burdekin was still in Sydney, was later destroyed by her for reasons I do not know.

By 1922, her marriage was at an end and she returned with her children to Cornwall, where her mother and sister had moved after her father's death. In 1926, she met the woman who was to become her lifelong friend and companion, and who, although she has provided me with invaluable help and information, some of it cited throughout this essay, as well as access to Burdekin's unpublished writings, wishes to remain unnamed. From then on they lived together, raising Burdekin's two daughters and later her companion's child as well.

Burdekin read a great deal, especially in the fields of history, religion, myth, legend, fairy tales, and fiction (including fantasy fiction), and all of these forms found their way into her own writing. In 1927 she wrote her only children's book, specifically for her daughters. Origiinally entitled *St. John's Eve,* it was published in the United States in 1929 with the title *The Children's Country.* A "nonsexist children's book" long before there was such a category, it recounts the adventures of a boy and a girl in a gender-free children's country, and depicts the two children's increasing liberation from their own society's gendered notions of personal identity.

Throughout the 1920s and 1930s, Burdekin wrote in what her companion describes as periods of near possession, producing novel after novel. She rarely talked about a book before actually writing, but it was evident when the composition was about to begin: she would hardly eat for the last few days before setting to work. While she wrote, she "would not really be there for some weeks." She "was not in the accepted sense a *thinker,*" her companion has written to me, "she was a piece of cosmic blotting paper, or sponge, which some power squeezed, and out welled a strange confection! . . . She never, in all the years I knew her, took longer than six weeks in writing any book. While she wrote she was an automaton—this is implicit in the simplicity and tautness of the writing." Burdekin, her friend states, on a day to day basis "really had very little connection with the writer. I know that this may sound quite ridiculous but the writer had very much the character of a visitant" (letter of June 29, 1987). In an earlier letter, her friend wrote that Burdekin's best work, "almost amounted to automatic writing" (September 10, 1984). After finishing a book she descended into the "depths of misery," as if wrenched out of a world where she had control of the incidents and forced to return to a world which we call "reality"—"which is debatable."

Burdekin referred to her first three novels as her "baby books," and considered *The Rebel Passion*, published in April 1929, to mark the transition from her youthful to her mature works. It is the first of her novels to possess the broad historical sweep—across thousands of years, encompassing not only the past but also the future—that Burdekin found so essential for the working out of her ideas. What these books reveal is her ability to project herself beyond the particular constraints of her own time. They show her desire to get out of the present century, but certainly not, as her companion told me, to return to a past one, for they were all dominated by men, and cruelty prevailed.

Intensely responsive to the growing political crisis in Europe, Burdekin was especially prolific during the decade of the 1930s. In addition to the six novels she published during this period, seven other, unpublished, novels survive, of which one is *The End of This Day's Business*.

Burdekin and her companion, though quite capable of putting on a good social appearance when really necessary, lived the private lives of "eccentric country gentlewomen" (letter of December 1, 1984). "We always talked a great deal, read very widely, belonged to no coterie. . . . We knew many writers but as isolated individuals. Indeed we always lived in the country, very rustic and private with sorties to London" (letter of September 10, 1984). Some of these writers had contacted Burdekin in response to one or another of her books. This was the case, for example, with Radclyffe Hall, who wrote to say how much she liked Burdekin's 1927 novel *The Burning Ring*, but whom Burdekin did not meet until about 1930. And H.D. wrote to Burdekin about *Proud Man*, a novel Burdekin published in 1934 under the pseudonym Murray Constantine. H.D. later sent Burdekin several of her own books, inscribed to "Murray Constantine." But of the many writers whom Burdekin and her companion knew—Leonard and Virginia Woolf, Bertrand and Dora Russell—only a few, Margaret Goldsmith, her husband Frederick Voigt, and Norah James, were special friends.

Once she had resettled in England, Burdekin never went abroad again. Holidays were often spent in Cornwall, visiting her mother and sister. Rowena Cade, three years Burdekin's senior, was to become famous as the designer, builder, and director (for more than fifty years) of the Minack Theatre, an open-air amphitheater fashioned out of a granite cliff at Porthcurno, near Land's End, where the Cades used to put on plays in their youth.

In 1934 Burdekin began to use the pseudonym Murray Constantine ("Murray" was chosen because it was a family name, and "Constantine" after a village in Cornwall), and all her subsequent work, both published and unpublished, from then until her death, bears this name. Whatever the intial reasons for the pseudonym, it seemed wise to continue its use, for her novels were becoming increasingly political and overtly anti-fascist. Among their acquaintances outside of London, Burdekin and her companion were almost alone in being anti-Franco: "The Spanish Civil War loomed very large to us," Burdekin's companion told me. Even Margaret Goldsmith (1894–1971), the American journalist and novelist who lived and worked primarily in England, and who, together with her husband Frederick Voigt, the *Manchester Guardian*'s diplomatic correspondent in Berlin in the 1920s and early 1930s, were important sources of Burdekin's knowledge of the rise of fascism, was careful to refer to Burdekin, in a book written during the war, as Murray Constantine. With the cooperation of these and other friends, and of her publishers as well, Burdekin covered the tracks of her real identity quite effectively. As a result, when, in the early 1980s, I grew interested in Murray Constantine, it took considerable effort to learn that she was indeed Katharine Burdekin, whose name was already familiar to me as the author of the engrossing 1929 novel *The Rebel Passion*, which I had read as part of a research project on forgotten utopias by women.

Like many other pacifists of the World War One era, Burdekin abandoned pacifism in the light of the threat represented by Hitler. Able to envision, at least six years before the event, the extermination of the Jews (mentioned in *The End of This Day's Business*, and

more emphatically still in the anti-Hitler dystopia *Swastika Night*),
Burdekin, so her companion has told me, was afraid England
would not to go war, and went through a particular low point at the
time of the Munich Conference in September 1938.

Throughout the second world war Burdekin did not write
fiction. Instead, she spent over two years working in a shoe factory,
until health problems forced her to stop. She never liked living on
unearned income, her companion told me, and this was the one
reason she acknowledged for wanting her books to be a success.
But during the war "she wrote nothing, as she was fully occupied
by warwork . . . or keeping our garden producing vegetables. One
had no time to do other than maintain life!" (letter of June 11, 1988).

Although Burdekin resumed writing after the war, something
had happened meanwhile, and that was Hiroshima and Nagasaki.
There is a marked difference between the passionately political
novels composed in the 1930s and the half-dozen works (all of
which have remained unpublished) that date from the late 1940s
and early 1950s. While not losing their feminism, these later novels
are far more concerned with spiritual problems than with political
ones. Issues relating to religion and mysticism, which appear as
peripheral themes in some of Burdekin's earliest novels as well,
now take center stage in their own right.

In addition to the more than twenty novels that she composed
before she stopped writing in 1956, Burdekin also wrote plays,
short stories, and poems, including a number of reworkings of
Arthurian literature, a favorite subject. In the late 1940s, she was
employed for over a year at a printer's shop, and thereafter in a
flour mill; a manuscript fragment exists that describes the operation
of the mill and the women who work there.

Like so many of her heroines, Burdekin was tall, slim, and
athletic. But she had experienced health problems earlier in her
life—migraines that decreased over the years and bouts of depres-
sion of which the most severe occurred in the autumn of 1938, after
Munich. In an effort to ease Burdekin's distress at the time, her
friend Margaret Goldsmith gave her the extensive research notes
she had been accumulating on Marie Antoinette. Burdekin wrote
up the material and it became the historical novel *Venus in Scorpio*,
published in 1940, with both Goldsmith and Murray Constantine

as its authors. This was to be Burdekin's last published book, the only one not growing out of her own ideas. In 1955 Burdekin nearly died of an aneurysm: "They said she wouldn't live for four days, but she lived for eight years, and we had a lot of fun," said her companion. After four months in the hospital, Burdekin returned to her home in Suffolk in February 1956, and there she remained, bedridden, until her death in August 1963.

In that same house, in the summer of 1986, a trunk was brought down from the attic for me to look through, and it contained more than a dozen typescripts and manuscripts of Burdekin's unpublished novels. In response to my queries about the dates of composition of particular manuscripts, Burdekin's friend states that, owing to a lack of diaries, she simply does not remember, for Burdekin's " 'writing' was not an 'event' and much written work was chucked out!" (letter of June 11, 1988). I have therefore had to infer their dates from the internal evidence of contemporary events that Burdekin alludes to, as well as from the occasional presence of labels indicating Burdekin's addresses, presumably at the time of composition. Some of the manuscripts bear marks of having been sent to her agent, Audrey Heath; upon their return they were evidently packed away. It seems that Burdekin allowed Heath to be the final arbiter of the value or timeliness of a manuscript ("she didn't care, you see," Burdekin's companion told me). Other novels Burdekin apparently made no effort to publish. "She really veered in her keenness to see her work in print" (letter of August 15, 1988). Of this trunkful of material, *The End of This Day's Business* is first to be published.

III

The End of This Day's Business is an important example of a kind of literature known as the sex-role reversal. Working mainly through a process of assimilation and estrangement, such fiction habituates us to new worlds even as it renews our perception of the actual world whose customs, beliefs, and social conventions are not usually the objects of a distanced and critical eye. For there exists in most of us a habit of perceptual and psychic economy (strongly reinforced by ideology) that makes us look at our society through invisible frames that structure both what and how we see. Writers of utopian fiction alter this frame by envisioning new and different structures within which the behavior and attributes of their characters make sense, however farfetched these may seem if viewed through our conventional lens. In some cases, a writer's frame serves to reinforce our conventional ideas and behaviors. More often, however, reversals work to break down old assumptions.[4]

As written by feminists, sex-role reversals typically perform two main functions. They enlist the reader's sympathy in the cause of social change by making glaringly evident the meaning of social structures so much part and parcel of our daily routines that they are not normally amenable to critical scrutiny. Perhaps of equal importance in unfettering the reader's imagination, these texts also present the reader with a kind of social laboratory in which alternative human arrangements are made credible through the imaginative participation of the reader in a time or place different from— and better than—our own.

This was Thomas More's strategy in his *Utopia* (1516), which gave its name to the genre. More shows how "good" behavior can be generated by a social system that makes such behavior seem reasonable. His own society, by contrast, makes predatory and rapacious acts perfectly rational. Later utopian writers developed elaborate metaphors to convey their sense of human potentialities thwarted by erroneous and hypocritical appeals to "nature." Thus Edward Bellamy, for example, whose 1888 bestseller *Looking Backward 2000–1888* argues for the benefits of complete economic equality, likens humanity to a rosebush planted in a bog. Against the commonplace view that the rosebush's failure to flourish is explained by its deficient "nature," Bellamy describes how the rosebush blooms once it is transplanted to a healthy soil.

In this way, writers of positive utopian fiction, an eternally optimistic literary genre, invite readers to perceive clearly their own unutopian societies and contrast them with the better societies that human beings are capable of creating. Except for some religiously oriented utopias, which rest on the assumption that individual character can be changed only through religious commitment or revelation, utopian fiction typically stresses the interaction of individual and society and focuses on defining the kinds of social structures required to bring about the hoped-for change.

Among their deviations from conventional "novelistic" technique, utopian writers typically dislocate the traditional novelist's concentration on individual character in favor of exploration of a broader social landscape. Katharine Burdekin's novels reveal that an author may choose the utopian form precisely in order to be able, in the context of a graphic description of an alternative society, to engage in lengthy discussions of society and history. The characteristic strategies of utopian fiction must be understood as conscious departures from traditional fictional norms for the sake of some other concern of the authors.

But compared even with other utopian writers, Burdekin is much more interested in the history, psychology, and ideology behind the alternative social structures her utopian and dystopian novels set in motion than in conveying detailed descriptions of them. To explore these underlying forces, she makes ample use of explanatory dialogue, historical disquisitions, and didactic discourse, all of which appear in *The End of This Day's Business.* More theoretically inclined than many utopian writers, often impatient with the trappings of fiction, under an intense inner pressure (palpable in the rhythms of her prose) to explain to her readers how things were, are, and could be, she allows us to share, both intellectually and viscerally, her own vision of how people might think, feel, and act in social and political environments so different as to make these alternative modes plausible.

Long before theorists such as Ruth Bleier and Ruth Hubbard articulated the false dichotomy between nature and nurture,[5] Katharine Burdekin was dissolving this neat polarization by showing that the very concepts held of nature and its attributes are cultural products. Adopting what has since become a characteristic feminist strategy, Burdekin exposes the ways in which the gender hierarchy is conventionally construed as part of an unquestioned "natural" order that serves to maintain the power of the dominant class or group over the devalued one. Observing the decline of feminism in England after the first world war—about which she makes some biting comments in this novel—Burdekin probed the interconnections of gender, class, and political conflict. What is most astonishing about the series of remarkable utopian and dystopian novels in which she carries out this exploration is how much sense her ideas (not understood in her own time, as reviews of her novels reveal) make to us today.

Burdekin's works offer the contemporary reader striking insights and stunning formulations. In *Proud Man*, for example, Burdekin's narrator is a genuine *human* from a utopian future, a person who sojourns for two years in the England of Burdekin's time. To this narrator—a brown-skinned, vegetarian, single-sexed, fully conscious, independent, self-fertilizing being capable of mental telepathy, rapid movement, and utter stillness—our world seems filled with "subhumans," whose ways the alien is at a loss to comprehend. Attempting to explain them, the novel's narrator says: "A privilege of class divides a subhuman society horizontally, while a privilege of sex divides it vertically."

In her fiction Burdekin deals with major epistemological questions: how do we know what we know? what justification is there for believing what we believe? could our knowledge be constructed differently? how? with what consequences? In examining these problems, Burdekin not only offers us imaginative depictions of different futures, she also rewrites history, providing her readers with a feminist revisioning of the conventional past. The very estrangement from habitual categories and concepts that we experience when confronted with these techniques causes us to relativize our own history and to start noticing the threads that can be drawn out to form a startling variety of alternative designs. An imaginative leap into the past thus leads directly to the future that is still to unfold. We see that what we shall call "history" later on is, in fact, a range of open possibilities, shaped at each instant by the interplay of individuals and their circumstances.

Sex-role reversals, however, do something of special importance: they cut through the discussion and endless focus on "women's differences" by showing that gender roles are systemic. It makes no sense to look at *one* gender role without focusing simultaneously on the contrasting "other" which, by its very contrast, provides meaning and justification. A very important function of the sex-role reversal is that "masculine" behavior is also deconstructed and reconstructed. The entire "sex-gender system," as Gayle Rubin called it,[6] therefore emerges from the shadowy realm of a "nature" in which "inevitable differences" abound and takes center stage as an interlocking series of beliefs, behaviors, and attributes resting above all on power and its absence.

Among the more than twenty novels, published and unpublished, that she wrote between 1920 and 1956, Katharine Burdekin explored the systemic nature of gender roles with special intensity in works composed between the late 1920s and late 1930s. Two themes dominate her writing, taken as a whole. One is the spiritual evolution of our species, a development that leads us progressively toward a mature and fully human existence. The other is the political dangers and consequences, increasingly evident with the rise of fascism in the 1920s and 1930s, of our age-old commitment to traditional notions of masculinity and femininity. These two themes are intricately linked, as in novel after novel she argues that gender is what keeps us from being human. Furthermore, what is remarkable about Burdekin's work is the intimate connection in her novels, especially those of the 1930s, of historical moment, fictional vision, and the forms within which she was working.

IV

Writing and reading as metaphors of agency and understanding play a key role in Burdekin's fiction. The narrator of *The Rebel Passion* records his visions of past and future. The writing of a book and the author's changing relation to it play an important part in *Quiet Ways*, while *Proud Man*'s futuristic narrator creates a kind of ethnographic report of her/his two-year stay in our subhuman world. In *Swastika Night*, all books are destroyed, along with all other evidence of the past, replaced by a spurious Teutonic mythology that promotes masculine ferocity, arrogance, and hatred of women. But the main character of that novel, Alfred, is given a secret book that supplies him with knowledge of the past and comprehension of his own Hitlerian society.[7] In *The End of This Day's Business*, men are not taught Latin, the lingua franca of all women and the sole language in which books still survive; lacking access to books, isolated by women's silence, rationality, and calm superiority, the men are deprived of history and, thus, of the knowledge of their past achievements and status. In all these works, and in other novels as well, the acts of writing and reading are central: in this sense these are self-referential novels. They do not purport merely to describe our or another world, but to make us consider the role of the word in our construction of reality.

Burdekin's companion insisted to me that Burdekin utterly lacked a sense of "work" about her writing, and she contrasted this attitude with, for example, an episode in which Radclyffe Hall told them that she had spent all morning "putting in a comma" (to which Una Troubridge added: "Yes, and you took it out in the afternoon"). Burdekin, by all accounts, would not "toil at" her writing. Certainly her political novels of the 1930s seem to have been produced in a state of extreme psychological urgency rather than by means of the laborious and self-conscious artistry so prized today. Moreover, Burdekin's novels themselves contain reflections on literature and the power of the word.

In *Quiet Ways*, Burdekin outlines a theory of literature that clearly applies to her own best work. Through Alan, the novelist-protagonist, Burdekin explores the figure of a young and embittered writer whose strength as an artist is his rage. No one wants to publish Alan's first novel, a bitter exposé of the ugliness and stupidity of war, of the concept of "manliness," and of cherished notions of patriotism. But his next novel, about a witchlike woman he knew as a child (the kind of woman Burdekin was to write about later, in several unpublished manuscripts in which midwife-seers appear as admirable and tragic figures), is published and becomes a success. Some years later, Helga (Alan's wife and the novel's central character) reflects on his contentment, for which she is largely responsible, having channelled her own energies into providing a calm domestic life for him. Listlessness and torpor have taken hold of him. While still composing an occasional satire, he is no longer bitter or enraged. "The head of steam was gone. The fires were out." The irony is that only now can he publish his earlier anti-war novel, though it appears exaggerated to him. Helga's own view of war has not changed, but she urges him not to publish the book, as he no longer believes in its passionate critique of war. His ruin would be complete, she feels, were he to betray his earlier vision for the sake merely of another literary coup.

Helga's objections suggest what Burdekin herself valued in

literature, and it is what characterizes her best writing. After the second world war, some of her own fires were out, perhaps from ill health, perhaps from fatigue and inability to maintain the indignation that had sustained her earlier, perhaps simply from having moved into a different stage of life. Her works exploring the theme of reincarnation and spiritual evolution date from this period, as does a curious sequel to Radclyffe Hall's *The Well of Loneliness*, a project Burdekin seems to have toyed with for some years. She did not try to publish any of these later novels.

Because Burdekin read widely and eclectically, it is difficult to begin to sort out the influences on her work. But books dealing with time travel and time warps were among her favorites. Two among these stand out: Ford Maddox [Ford] Hueffer's *Ladies Whose Bright Eyes*, first published in 1911, whose technique closely resembles that of *The Burning Ring* and also that of the unpublished *Children of Jacob*, and Margaret Irwin's 1924 novel *Still She Wished for Company*. Although especially partial to the latter, Burdekin's use of time warps in her own work is considerably at odds with Irwin's. Irwin's aim is to show a merging of time past, present, and future—a seamless texture. But this implies lack of change and development. Burdekin's novels, by contrast, as they range across thousands of years, seek to understand the historical process, to explore how we have come to be what we are. Not identity or the interpenetrability of different moments in time, but the process of development is Burdekin's chief concern. This is evident also in another of her unpublished postwar novels using the time warp device, whose very title, *Father to the Man*, suggests that it is always the past that begets the present.

Practicing an incipient form of feminist literary criticism, keenly sensitive to misogyny in its various historical manifestations and consequences, whether in the writings of the Church fathers or of other novelists and poets, Burdekin was also one of the earliest—perhaps the very earliest—feminist critics of D. H. Lawrence.[8] In a notebook dating from about 1930, a long satirical poem on upper-class women refers to Lawrence:

> I am a very proud and haughty woman
> I make up my face thrice daily with creams,
> And perfumes and powders.

I do not often wash it because that's bad for the skin,
And I might begin to look old.
I am very proud & haughty,
And despise all other women,
And farm labourers and mechanics,
Of course equally or more so despising their wives
Who live uncomfortably and unbeautifully
And have too many babies.
Their passions are ugly to me, coarse and dark,
I have no passions but I read the works
Of Mr D. H. Lawrence,
And discuss them with my friends,
He is so male, don't you think? so attractive,
He despises us so completely.
For though we are all so proud and haughty
We adore to be despised as a sex,
Don't you think so, darling?
And of course as everyone knows
Mr Lawrence was impotent
Which makes his work more attractive
And so cerebral
His masculinity is then so pure & refined
And has nothing alarming about it
Like the odious and terrible masculinity
Of our husbands. . . .

This excerpt also reflects Burdekin's awareness of female self-hatred, a theme that is analyzed at length in *The End of This Day's Business*. It is men who, in this novel, treat one another with jealousy, contempt, and suspicion—the inevitable lot, the book explains, of rearing one sex to despise itself, however unconsciously, while promoting belief in the superiority of the other. And the sex that despises itself will admire those members of the opposite sex who also despise it.

A brief passage in *The End of This Day's Business* returns to D. H. Lawrence, noting his ambiguity (his personal dislike of violence) and then charging him with being "the English prophet of the cult of emotion and blood and instinct which later on, after he was dead, swept over most of the European nations like a disease." In later comments in the novel on the literature of what we today call the post-World War One period, Burdekin excoriates women for imitating, in their own writings, men's sexual sadism. She attributes the antifeminism of many women's writings during this period to their habitual desire to placate men and their lack of self-esteem because they could only give life, not take it in battle. At times sounding like an early Mary Daly, Burdekin perceives this as part of the "death-hysteria" of male rule. But unlike Mary Daly, whenever Burdekin touches on this theme—as she does in novel after novel—it is always with sadness, not with glee at having found men out. Misandry is absent from Burdekin's writing, as is a tone of bitterness and despair.

V

The fundamental social transformations addressed in *The End of This Day's Business* first appear, in brief outline, in Burdekin's pacifist novel *Quiet Ways* (1930). Here, in one long passage, an entire theory of feminism and a vision of its future are adumbrated. Helga, Burdekin's six-foot-tall, 160-pound heroine, is described as self-contained in a way that a conventional misogynist male acquaintance, a man tellingly named Carapace, finds intolerable. The scene is recounted from the man's point of view, and through his reactions the reader is made to see the gender work routinely done by women who in one way or another place men at the center of reality, striving to win their attention, whether through conventional feminine artifices or through debate and argumentation meant to demonstrate women's anxiety to be considered men's "equals." Helga does neither. Burdekin contrasts Carapace's "hominism" to Helga's disturbing "feminism":

> Carapace despised women who aped men, but that at least was flattering. This heavy impenetrability [of Helga's], this self-sufficiency, this almost contemptuous absence of mind when men were speaking was a portent. It was new and dangerous; it threatened, if it became at all general, to upset the world far more than the ordinary type of feminism which concentrates on votes and professions. Carapace was a passionate hominist, and his spiritual home was Greece in the age of Pericles. His sensitive soul was for ever being pricked and scraped by twentieth-century ideas of equality. But Helga did more than prick and scrape him; she lacerated him. For the first time in his life he felt femininity to be not flippant, weak, fundamentally

indecent and contemptible, but a massive, patient, immensely powerful thing. His revolt was tinged with fear. He was deeply afraid that
Helga did not believe herself inferior to Alan [her husband], and if
women like this became common what in God's name was to happen
to the world? Would they not bring up their daughters in their own
calm sense of superiority, a sense, not less dangerous, but rather
more, because it made no noisy assertions? Would they not bring up
their young sons to think themselves of less absolute value than the
girls? Carapace's brain, racing into the future, saw a complete reversal
of the accepted order of things. Son worship abolished, and daughter
worship set up in its place. Women being brought up to thank God
they were not men. Boys brought up to wish they were women.
There was no limit to the horrors that might come if women once
really lost their sense of inferiority. And that it could be completely
missing he had the proof before him. (239–240)

Here Burdekin gives us a glimpse of the female-dominant world
elaborated, later, in *The End of This Day's Business*. It is a habit of
Burdekin's to mention, in passing, ideas that will become crucial
structural elements in future works. In *Quiet Ways*, for example,
Burdekin attributes to Carapace the revision of classical mythology
that will form an essential part of the Hitler-ideology in *Swastika
Night*. Carapace's hatred of women is such that he would have liked
to have been born from the head of a man. The fantasy appears
again in *Swastika Night*, where Hitler, according to the official myth
of his origins, was exploded from the head of Zeus and had never
been in the contaminating presence of a woman. (Readers who find
Burdekin's imagination farfetched on the subject of male fear and
loathing of women are urged to look at the illustrations in Klaus
Theweleit's book *Male Fantasies*.[9]) Helga, for her part, never re-
sponds to Carapace's provocatively malicious comments about
women, with the result that "[t]he unfortunate misogynist felt
himself dismissed as not worth an argument." Her failure even to
be envious of Carapace's friendship with her husband further
unnerves Carapace. "Never before had he been made to feel such a
fool. . . . She was a woman. They were only men."

Hints of a new way of being, however, are not enough for
Burdekin. She wants to demonstrate the power of her angle of
vision for past and future history. Hence her recourse to the utopian novel set in the future—one of the prominent conventions of

which is the disquisition on how things came to be the way they are. Fully utilizing this device, Burdekin applies to thousands of years of history her insights into male dominance. This she accomplishes in a succession of novels in which our entire history is told and retold, all of them written under the political pressure of the rise of fascism in Europe, the key element of which Burdekin identifies as the "cult of masculinity."

Burdekin's perception of fascism in the 1930s sharpened her analysis of the political effects of gender in society. Several novels, in particular, touch on these effects, each of them moving further away from a personal and spiritual toward a more broadly political scenario. Thus, in *The Rebel Passion*, the first of Burdekin's utopian novels, we meet a monk born with the soul of a woman, and through this man's understanding of the straightjacket of gender we explore past and future. In *Proud Man*, probably composed in mid-1933, Burdekin's fully human narrator, sojourning in 1930s England, casts an anthropologist's eye on such bizarre subhuman practices as our rigid commitment to gender roles. There follow several novels that must have been produced in rapid succession. One is the unpublished *No Compromise: A Political Romance*, set in an England of the very near future, with fascism on the rise and communism the sole hope for combatting it. *The End of This Day's Business*, also written at about this time (1935), develops the idea, already noted in *Quiet Ways*, of a complete reversal in gender ideology through a total loss of women's sense of inferiority and the inculcation, in men, of precisely such a sense, accompanied by the suppression of their history. The long central section of this novel retells our history from Burdekin's unusual feminist perspective.

Events, however, overtook Burdekin, and Hitler's increasing hold over European political life perhaps suggested to her the greater likelihood of a dystopian masculinized future. The result of this pessimistic reflection was *Swastika Night*, most likely also written in 1935. *Swastika Night* displays Burdekin's remarkable recognition that Nazi ideology represented a difference in degree, but not in kind, from the traditional masculine values that dominate patriarchal society.

One may hazard a guess as to why *Swastika Night* was published while its mirror image, *The End of This Day's Business*, was, until now, forgotten. It may have been simply the pressure of historical events, which made a far-off feminist future, in which the only major problem is the imposition (however benign) of an inferiorized identity on men, a futile expectation. But Burdekin seems also to have been obsessed at this time with attempting to understand how National Socialism could have arisen. She made yet another effort at explaining this phenomenon, and this is the unpublished novel *Children of Jacob*. Written in the aftermath of the German annexation of Austria in March 1938, this book represents an even greater imaginative leap into the past. Through her protagonist's reincarnations at various moments in history, Burdekin traces the theme of masculine violence from Old Testament times to the present, locating its source in Jacob's theft of Esau's birthright—the original act performed out of a desire for power and in wilful disrespect for their mother, Rebekah, who, enraged at men's disdain of women, condones an everlasting hatred among the races of men until such time as they might learn to love and respect women.

There is a consistent view of history in Burdekin's novels, and it survives her experience of the rise of fascism. Burdekin rejects Hesiod's image of the declining "ages of man"—from gold to iron and adopts instead a teleological, specifically Christian, belief in a progression that must lead to a better world. But she gives this traditional belief a characteristic hue by associating human beings' spiritual improvement with their increasing rejection of a conventional gender dichotomy. In this vision, the painful past must give way to a future devoid of hierarchy and the processes of domination needed to maintain it. This is a statement of faith on Burdekin's part, and *The End of This Day's Business* expresses it clearly in its feminist revision of the Marxist view of history.

Confronted with a key dilemma—what is to prevent history from repeating itself if men are once more restored to human dignity?—Grania, the novel's heroine, ponders the question of how change is possible. She cannot give a final answer. But she does articulate a conviction toward which Burdekin had been moving since the late 1920s: that change does occur, that individuals possessed of a different consciousness are, in their very persons, proof of a change in process. Burdekin does not necessarily attribute "leadership" qualities to these individuals, nor do their ideas become social agents. She is saying that their ideas are an indication of changes already in motion; her misfits and prophets (however few in number) can think as they do because change is occurring, though in barely perceptible forms. Thus Burdekin links individual to society and keeps intact her belief in progress—however difficult to discern and even if at any given moment those who embody these changes are defeated.

When one studies Burdekin's literary production overall, the working out, in ever greater detail, of particular ideas and themes becomes apparent. Thus, in *No Compromise*, Burdekin's characteristic critique of privilege, developed at length in her earlier novel *Proud Man*, takes a political turn, as the heroine's mother—one of Burdekin's many strong females—says: "Unjust things have been done in Russia, and will be done for many years yet I am afraid. But Communism is the gate through which all the world must go if it is ever to get to the society without privilege, which is the only society in which all human beings will be just." Again, as in *Proud Man*, Burdekin writes, in *No Compromise*, of our lack of knowledge of what "women" are or could be.

> None of us know what women are really like at all. Least of all the women themselves. Ever since there have been any women . . . they've always had men sitting on their necks telling them what they must think and believe and say and do. They've never had the chance to do and think what they like, and what appeals to *them* as right and natural, so they've never been *themselves* at all. And I feel that when they're free and can be themselves, they'll be quite different from any women that are alive now. . . . When there've been two or three generations all born free they may not want to do at all what they think they do now. They're consciously straining to show they're as good as men. If they'd been born free for a hundred years they wouldn't bother at all whether they were as good as men or not. They'd just be themselves, whatever that turns out to be, and enjoy it.

Here, as elsewhere, Burdekin hints at a reality she elaborates in detail in *The End of This Day's Business*, where women are indeed reared with no sense of a devalued social and sexual identity. And this provides us with one answer to the question of why she sets this novel in such a far distant future, far beyond the time of *Swastika Night*. Burdekin's vision is a long-range one, looking back as well as forward. The drastic changes she imagines cannot happen in a short time.

In *The End of This Day's Business*, explaining to Neil that "the food of militarism . . . is the admiration of women," Grania describes how the second fascist reaction, in the twenty-first century, was thwarted by women's refusal to admire or (Lysistrata-like) consort with military men. Withdrawing their assent to violence, rejecting the notion that the destruction of human life is heroic or even acceptable, these women, reared in the egalitarian communist society that left some men longing for the past, grew determined that women alone must rule. In some respects the novel resembles Charlotte Perkins Gilman's *Herland*, published in 1915 in *The Forerunner*, the journal Gilman singlehandedly produced. But, despite similarities between the two books (such as the adulation of mothers, and women's psychic control of their fertility), it is improbable that Burdekin could have read *Herland*, which was not available in book form until 1979.

Perhaps it grew clearer to Burdekin by the mid-1930s that men would not readily embrace a truly egalitarian way of life; hence her revision of her earlier belief in a rapid rejection of gender privilege. But her fundamental understanding of fascism and communism as the negative and positive poles of social change persisted. Fascism perpetuates, and communism banishes, murder, cruelty, and injustice, she writes in *The End of This Day's Business*. And, adumbrating the discussion she would undertake in *Swastika Night* of the "cult of masculinity" as the core of fascism, Burdekin draws the conclusion that "nothing could ever prevent war except bringing up all the boys and girls in all the countries in an entirely different way."

The memory of privilege is not easily lost, as revealed by Burdekin's scenario, in *The End of This Day's Business*, of the second fascist reaction, in the twenty-first century. But the memory of oppression lasts even longer, as the remnants of women's fear in the sixty-third century indicates. "After all," says Grania, "what's four thousand years in the history of the whole race? Just nothing. A little breathing-space."

VI

In all Burdekin's novels a tension exists between two views: that gender is socially constructed, and that there are essential non-sexual male and female traits and "soul" types. In giving expression to this tension between contradictory models, Burdekin prefigures much contemporary feminist writing. Nor can our usual neat distinction between "sex" and "gender" explain the enmeshed arguments that typically accompany any extended discussion of why a world run by women might be different. What occurs in such cases—and this is apparent in Burdekin's writings as well—is a kind of seepage of biological arguments into social constructivist positions. There are, however, very good reasons for insisting, as does much radical feminist writing today, on "essentialist" explanations that celebrate femaleness. As dangerous as this order of reasoning has been to women in the past, it is important to recognize that the denial of difference is often a mere consequence of the fact that it is *men* who have power in our world. This is the trap of liberal feminism, in which men are the measure of all things and any progress for women must be framed in the language of sameness. The observation that it is typically women who embrace this language, while men by and large deny it, tells us all we need to know about the sexual politics at work in the entire argument.

Yet despite Burdekin's persistent exposure of the social construction of woman, she is, in fact, a great respecter of biology. Grania is not alone among Burdekin's protagonists in her emphasis on the male's superior physical strength and its implications. And the depiction of men's lives in this novel might in some respects warm the heart of a sociobiologist. For Burdekin clearly assumes a direct connection between male biology and violent behavior—even if, as in this novel, that violence is harmlessly discharged in games and contests of physical prowess. Such assumptions about male biology are complemented in Burdekin's writings by beliefs about femaleness. Burdekin describes and valorizes those "special" characteristics which allow one to speak of a women's way of being even in historical periods characterized by the oppression of women. Yet, like socialist feminists, she discerns in gender stereo-types the workings of capitalist patriarchy, and attempts repeatedly to deconstruct assumptions about the "naturalness" and "inevitability" of the distortions that pass for a normal gender identity for both men and women.

These overtly political analyses of gender notwithstanding, the essentialist strain in Burdekin's writing cannot be denied. Although apparently not acquainted with the writings of Karen Horney (which were available in English in the 1920s), Burdekin understands the male imposition on women of a devalued social identity as an expression of jealousy and fear of women's procreative powers: womb envy, in short. Men's pride, as the narrator of *Proud Man* says, is "not founded on a solid biological fact." In response to his awareness of men's lesser importance, Burdekin's hero in *Quiet Ways* asserts that men's "only hope is to find out how to make satisfactory children in laboratories." Burdekin wrote this several years before Aldous Huxley actually delineated such a project, for quite different reasons, in *Brave New World* (1932). In *The End of This Day's Business*, furthermore, men are described as having weaker brains and less will power than women. But by far the most damaging opposition drawn in this novel is between men's past death-hysteria and emotionalism, and women's reason and discipline. Nor should it be thought that Burdekin is mechanically reversing male and female stereotypes, merely turning the conventional nature/culture associations on their heads, for indeed, as she reviews the history of her time, she makes quite a good case for her characterization of men.

Still another example of the essentialist strain that surfaces in such fascinating ways in Burdekin's writing is her embrace of androgyny, which may seem surprising given her negative characterization of men. Giraldus, for example, in *The Rebel Passion*, is depicted as possessing the "understanding of a man and the soul of a woman." Another novel from about this time, *Two in a Sack*, which I have read in galleys dated 1928 but which, for reasons I have not been able to establish, was never published, has a protagonist who is Giraldus's counterpart: a young woman with a "masculine soul."

Like writers as diverse as Coleridge and Virginia Woolf, Burdekin holds that the artist is inherently androgynous (an entire theory of form in painting and sculpture is developed from this notion in *The End of This Day's Business*). In her treatment of love she calls to mind Plato's *Symposium*, where love is depicted as "the desire and pursuit of the whole."[10] But Plato's myth of the original complete being invokes three distinct types—male, female, and male-female—with each type, once the original wholeness of being is lost, doomed to an eternal search for its lost half. Burdekin, on the other hand, returns again and again to a single model: that of male-female complementarity. By this, it is important to point out, she means a spiritual complementarity, capable of occurring in any two bodies. Her novels repeatedly show same-sex partners whose souls form a perfect whole, as well as male-female couples whose communion and understanding exclude sexual attraction.

Each person's true aim is to achieve completion and, in this completed state, know God—an aspiration, Burdekin is careful to say, not to be thought of in terms of formal religion. Throughout, her writings proclaim a clear ethic: the use of another person to satisfy one's lust or vanity is fundamentally immoral. Burdekin cares not at all whether it is a man so using a woman, a woman using a woman, a man using a man, and so on. She depicts love, any expression of love, as moral and good. She toys with the notion that an individual could possess the body of one sex and the soul of the other. Despite the recurrence of these philosophical ideas in all her fiction, however, during her most political phase her emphasis was increasingly on the analysis of gender identity, how it is systematically produced in men and women, and what its disastrous consequences are.

In all of Burdekin's texts essentialist and social constructivist interpretations of gender exist side by side. Yet Burdekin's arguments from nature are in fact contradicted by her analyses, cited earlier, of the problem, in a patriarchal society, of discerning what "woman" is. To the extent that women have lost their sense of identity—or, as Burdekin argues in *Quiet Ways* and *Swastika Night*, have never acquired one—no one actually knows the meaning of "woman," only what women are in their various distortions. Their complicity with men in their own degradation sustains the male world and its rules, and this, in some of Burdekin's arguments from nature, could never be done by a healthy animal. Women teach their daughters inferiority feelings; they accept, however conflictedly, their status as men's subalterns, and they channel their own energies into men's causes and endeavors. Thousands of years of sublimated female energy and aspirations have gone into the development of civilization. But all this is part of the condition of women under patriarchy.

Since Burdekin also creates heroines who seek their own identity, the question arises: if one's identity is largely a social construct, how can a woman in a patriarchal society ever develop her "own" identity, outside the bounds of conventional society? In *Quiet Ways*, Helga demonstrates one such path, and, in keeping with Burdekin's interest in and knowledge of both Freud and Jung, this path is dependent upon childhood experiences, especially the inculcation of a sense of self-worth in one's youth. As if in illustration of the indissolubility of nature and nurture, Helga, who in the immovable strength of her femininity (cited earlier) provides a good portrait of the essentializing aspect of Burdekin's argument, paradoxically got this sense of self-value from her father. In fact, most of Burdekin's strong female characters have supportive fathers—and only occasionally supportive and unconventional mothers. The logic of this situation may be quickly grasped if one stops to ask oneself what chances the reduced women of *Swastika Night* have of transmitting a sense of personal worth to their daughters.

Early childhood experiences are crucial elements in Burdekin's texts for explaining the psychological development of men and women, as the two alternative models of *Swastika Night* and *The End of This Day's Business* illustrate. Burdekin revised Freud along lines similar to recent feminist critiques. In *Swastika Night*, Hitlerdom has succeeded, with the complicity of conventional demoralized women, ever ready to attempt to please men, in the total "reduction" of most women to the level of animals. In a stunning imaginative leap, Burdekin saw that the male apotheosis of women as mothers was part of an ideology that could also result in their degradation to mere breeding animals—two points on the continuum of women's lives as defined by male obsessions. The women in *Swastika Night* are stripped of knowledge, history, dignity, love. They are deprived even of sexual attractiveness, since this constitutes a potential source of pride and sense of self, for the "right of rejection" enjoyed by women in the old days, as the novel explains, was a permanent affront to the dignity of Nazi masculinity. Lacking the most minimal human rights, these women are kept in caged compounds—an image that makes Margaret Atwood's *Handmaid's Tale* (1985), which in a few respects resembles *Swastika Night*, look pleasant by comparison. In one of the novel's few signs of hope, biology itself protests, and the reduced women no longer produce female babies in numbers sufficient to maintain the population.

The Nazi society Burdekin envisions seven hundred years in the future rests upon two fundamental institutions: the separation of the boy child from his mother at eighteen months, at which time his initiation into the world of men begins; and males' right of rape. Understanding that rape is in its essence an assault on female autonomy, Burdekin articulates its logic in a male supremacist society.

The End of This Day's Business of course institutes its own customs and norms, which, in some respects, resemble those of *Swastika Night*. In both novels marriage is abolished, the sexes live apart, children are separated from one parent, training in gender ideology takes place. But how different are the contexts that give meaning to these structural features! There is nothing in *The End of This Day's Business* like the class society of *Swastika Night*, and hence no need to offer the sop of gender oppression to keep less privileged members of the dominant class in line; there is no mystique of blood and lineage; no cult of violence; no pleasure in domination. Girls develop fully and eventually acquire knowledge of the historical (not mythical) past.

Even with its inferiorization of males, nothing in *The End of This Day's Business* remotely resembles the unfettered gendermania of *Swastika Night*'s dominant sex. And this is an intriguing point. In all the feminist sex-role reversal novels that I have read—even when the author is using the sex-role reversal to argue against any sort of gender oppression—the horror of the hypertrophied masculinity apparent in such novels as *Swastika Night* or *Nineteen Eighty-Four* is totally absent. These novels, in other words, may begin as satires intended to sensitize the reader to women's actual position in patriarchal society, but they quickly turn into earnest efforts to describe a better world.

Gerd Brantenberg's *Egalia's Daughters,* published in Norwegian in 1977 and in English translation in 1985, is a case in point. It is the most thoroughgoing sex-role reversal yet to be published, for it takes the turnabout right into the bedroom, that last bastion of biological thinking. While certainly incorporating (and of course reversing) gender discrimination and even violence against the devalorized sex (Brantenberg's menwim are sexually humiliated, beaten, and raped by the dominant wim), in many respects her fictional society is indeed a utopia. Other, earlier, satirical novels reveal the same tendency on the part of the author to envision a society that is far better than ours, even while it is oppressive to men. Generic literary conventions are strained at the seams in such works—half satire, half genuine utopia.

What is happening here, I believe, is that the mere prospect of a female-run society seduces the imagination of these feminist writers into the creation of a better world. The essentialist-social constructivist conflict reproduces itself in such texts, and, even while arguing for the latter, these writers cannot help but imbue their fictional creations with their apparent conviction that women *are* different, and, if once able to govern on their own behalf, would in many respects do things differently. Thus, again and again one finds female-dominant societies in which, though men are oppressed, and political, professional, domestic, and even sexual roles (not to mention those fascinating details such as dress codes and verbal and body language) are indeed "mere reversals" of our own unjust practices, the society as a whole is, nonetheless, a better one, as is the world of which it is a part. Typically, wars are abolished, ecological considerations are paramount, collective social needs are served in a variety of respects, vegetarianism may even prevail. In other words, female "difference" has been preserved and has produced a better world, although gender inequalities exist.

This is what we see also in *The End of This Day's Business.* Although Burdekin's vision does not lack passion and conflict (unlike, for example, Gilman's *Herland*), Burdekin evidently cannot imagine women, no matter how powerful, behaving like men. In effect, then, in her mind, as in that of so many other writers of feminist utopias and even of sex-role reversal satires, "gender" is not merely social. For indeed—let us be clear about this—*The End of This Day's Business* depicts a society light-years ahead of anything we have ever seen on this planet. It is essentially an *eu*topia, just as *Swastika Night* is a *dys*topia. No wonder, then, that Burdekin projected her good society more than four thousand years into the future. No such long leap was required to relate the Europe of the 1930s to the Hitlerian society of *Swastika Night*. Seven hundred years are long enough to bring about women's complete degradation. But women's elevation, as in *The End of This Day's Business*, requires not hundreds but thousands of years to accomplish.

In the female-dominant society of Burdekin's fertile imagination, though national cultures differ, there is no patriotism and hence no war, no religious oppression and no oppressive theology, no economic or physical violence against the devalued sex. Women are subject to capital punishment for crimes including breaking their word to a man or betraying the women's secret knowledge, while for men treason is the sole capital offense. Grania's betrayal of this society is undertaken out of a view similar to that expressed in *Proud Man:* revolutions that are merely "reversals of privilege," and do not address the fundamental issue of domination, are doomed to failure. Hence Grania's belief that dignity and knowledge must be restored to men, that this path alone represents the hope of the future. And she manages to hold this belief even while describing the differences between males and females in ways that suggest the frightening risk she is taking: "The fundamental object of all purely female governance is to protect the young; but the fundamental object of all purely male rule is to protect male power." But if this is true (and how hard it is to imagine something positive arising out of the combination of these two objectives), her effort to transcend the rules of her own society must be deemed misguided—as, indeed, many readers may conclude.

Through the sex-role reversal, Burdekin exposes the fraudulence and lack of dignity implicit in the standard wisdom of "they're happy in their place"—as her men (unlike the women in *Swastika Night*) by and large are. For it is this that she rejects, as her

Socrates-like heroine undertakes to "corrupt" some young men by revealing to them (despite their nearly total incredulity) something of men's past status and accomplishments. In one of her early discussions with Neil, Grania states that the basic human need is self-esteem. It is this that makes full mental and moral development possible. Neil's lack of self-esteem, his increasing awareness of a sense of shame (there were no terms such as "sexual objectification" when Burdekin described his feeling), lead to his "incomprehensible vague discontent." As Grania says, giving voice to one of the novel's many images of fertility: "The embryo of the dignity of a human being cannot be aborted."

But Burdekin does not pretend that her heroine has all the answers; far from it, which is why Grania's actions are based more upon faith in the process of human evolution, as it gets ever further away from the Childhood Age, than upon an argument that can be clearly articulated. The novel affirms the hope that the species *will* evolve, that the remnants of the Childhood Age, still extracting their due, can and will be transcended. As revealed by Grania's history of the ages of man and her dream of the ages of woman, the long nightmare time of patriarchy gives way to the far better matriarchal society in which women live in dignity and peace. And beyond this lies the good society without sex antagonism and without fear.

Ultimately, then, Burdekin addresses such fierce questions as: what is a human being? what constitutes a worthy life? And her answers are clear: dignity, a sense of self-worth not tied to diminishing the other, equality without identity, cooperation without coercion. In Katharine Burdekin's teleology, nothing short of a life rooted in these qualities will make us, at long last, fully human.

DAPHNE PATAI

NOTES

Previously published works by Katharine Burdekin cited in this essay:

The Rebel Passion. New York: William Morrow, 1929
Quiet Ways. London: Thornton Butterworth, 1930
Proud Man. London: Boriswood, 1934
Swastika Night. Old Westbury, N.Y.: The Feminist Press, 1985. (Originally published: London: Victor Gollancz, 1937)

1. See Andy Croft, "Worlds without End Foisted upon the Future: Some Antecedents of *Nineteen Eighty-Four,*" in Christopher Norris, ed. *Inside the Myth: Orwell, Views from the Left* (London: Lawrence & Wishart, 1984), 183–216; and Nan Bowman Albinski, *Women's Utopias in British and American Fiction* (London: Routledge, 1988).

2. A. K. Clarke, *A History of the Cheltenham Ladies' College 1853–1979* (Great Glemham, Saxmundham, Suffolk: John Catt, 1979), 3rd ed., 95ff; and Elsie M. Lang, *British Women in the Twentieth Century* (London: T. Werner Laurie, 1929).

3. *The [Cheltenham] Looker-On,* May 29, 1915.

4. For a discussion of some early examples, see my "When Women Rule: Defamiliarization in the Sex-Role Reversal Utopia," *Extrapolation* 23:1 (Spring 1982), 56–69.

5. For a brief overview of current scientific research on the nature/nurture controversy, see Sue V. Rosser, "Good Science: Can It Ever Be Gender Free?" *Women's Studies International Forum* 11:1 (1988), 13–19. Expressing a contemporary perspective that obviates much earlier debate, Rosser writes: "I contend that we can never know whether or not there are real biological differences between males and females because we can never separate the biological from the environmental" (17).

6. Gayle Rubin, "The Traffic in Women: Notes on the 'Political Economy' of Sex," in Rayna Reiter, ed., *Toward an Anthropology of Women* (New York: Monthly Review Press, 1975).

7. Even this brief summary suggests the resemblance between *Swastika Night* and George Orwell's *Nineteen Eighty-Four,* published twelve years later. In my introduction to the reprint of *Swastika Night*—to which the reader is referred for a discussion of some of the sources of Burdekin's novel—as well as in my article entitled "Orwell's Despair, Burdekin's Hope: Gender and Power in Dystopia," *Women's Studies International Forum* 7:2 (1984), 85–95, and in my book *The Orwell Mystique: A Study in Male Ideology* (Amherst, MA.: University of Massachusetts Press, 1984), 251–263, I discuss the indebtedness, suggested by many elements, large and

small, of *Nineteen Eighty-Four* to *Swastika Night*, which was first published in 1937 by Victor Gollancz, Orwell's own publisher in the 1930s. I point out that there is no evidence, other than specific textual similarities, that Orwell knew the novel. But Gilbert Bonifas, in *Notes and Queries* 34:1 (March 1987), 59, adds some missing pieces to strengthen the case. Bonifas points to the fact that Geoffrey Gorer, a good friend of Orwell's, published a letter in *Time and Tide* (February 12, 1938, 204), a journal Orwell frequently contributed to and hence probably read, praising *Swastika Night*, which Gorer considered unjustly neglected. Gorer, who guessed that Murray Constantine was a woman, judged the novel to be far "more probable, moving, and better written" than the whole group of prophetic novels circulating at that time, of which *Brave New World* was then the most notorious example. In fact, *Time and Tide* had published a review of *Swastika Night* in its June 26, 1937, issue. In 1984, Gorer wrote to Bonifas on this subject. He affirmed that, though by now he had no specific recollection of *Swastika Night*, it seemed to him that, since he had had high regard for the book at the time of its publication, he was likely to have given or lent a copy of it to Orwell. Bonifas points out that, although we still do not have positive proof, it becomes very plausible that Orwell did indeed read Burdekin's novel. The interesting question then becomes: why, while borrowing many of its elements, did he learn so little from it? I believe the answer lies in Orwell's own androcentrism and the powerful constricting effect it had on his vision, which I discuss in my book *The Orwell Mystique*.

8. Cornelia Nixon, author of *Lawrence's Leadership Politics and the Turn Against Women* (Berkeley: University of California Press, 1986), has told me that she does not know of any earlier feminist critiques of Lawrence.

9. Klaus Theweleit, *Male Fantasies, Volume 1: Women Floods Bodies History*, trans. Stephen Conway (Minneapolis: University of Minnesota Press, 1987).

10. See Carolyn G. Heilbrun, *Toward a Recognition of Androgyny* (New York: Knopf, 1973).

The Feminist Press at The City University of New York offers alternatives in education and in literature. Founded in 1970, this nonprofit, tax-exempt educational and publishing organization works to eliminate sexual stereotypes in books and schools and to provide literature with a broad vision of human potential. The publishing program includes reprints of important works by women, feminist biographies of women, and nonsexist children's books. Curricular materials, bibliographies, directories, and a quarterly journal provide information and support for students and teachers of women's studies. Through publications and projects, The Feminist Press contributes to the rediscovery of the history of women and the emergence of a more humane society.

NEW AND FORTHCOMING BOOKS

Always a Sister: The Feminism of Lillian D. Wald, a biography by Doris Groshen Daniels. $24.95 cloth.

Bamboo Shoots after the Rain: Contemporary Stories by Women Writers of Taiwan, 1945–1985, edited by Ann C. Carver and Sung-Sheng Yvonne Chang. $29.95 cloth, $12.95 paper.

A Brighter Coming Day: A Frances Ellen Watkins Harper Reader, edited by Frances Smith Foster. $29.95 cloth, $13.95 paper.

The Daughters of Danaus, a novel by Mona Caird. Afterword by Margaret Morganroth Gullette. $29.95 cloth, $11.95 paper.

Families in Flux (formerly *Household and Kin*), by Amy Swerdlow, Renate Bridenthal, Joan Kelly, and Phyllis Vine. $9.95 paper.

How I Wrote Jubilee *and Other Essays on Life and Literature*, by Margaret Walker. Edited by Maryemma Graham. $29.95 cloth, $9.95 paper.

Lillian D. Wald: Progressive Activist, a sourcebook edited by Clare Coss. $7.95 paper.

Lone Voyagers: Academic Women in Coeducational Universities, 1870–1937, edited by Geraldine J. Clifford. $29.95 cloth, $12.95 paper.

Not So Quiet: Stepdaughters of War, a novel by Helen Zenna Smith. Afterword by Jane Marcus. $26.95 cloth, $9.95 paper.

Seeds: Supporting Women's Work in the Third World, edited by Ann Leonard. Introduction by Adrienne Germain. Afterwords by Marguerite Berger, Vina Mazumdar, Kathleen Staudt, and Aminata Traore. $29.95 cloth, $12.95 paper.

Sister Gin, a novel by June Arnold. Afterword by Jane Marcus, $8.95 paper.

These Modern Women: Autobiographical Essays from the Twenties, edited and with a revised introduction by Elaine Showalter. $8.95 paper.

Truth Tales: Contemporary Stories by Women Writers of India, selected by Kali for Women. Introduction by Meena Alexander. $22.95 cloth, $8.95 paper.

OTHER TITLES

Antoinette Brown Blackwell: A Biography, by Elizabeth Cazden. $24.95 cloth, $12.95 paper.

All the Women Are White, All the Blacks Are Men, but Some of Us Are Brave: Black Women's Studies, edited by Gloria T. Hull, Patricia Bell Scott, and Barbara Smith. $12.95 paper.

Black Foremothers: Three Lives, 2nd edition, by Dorothy Sterling. $9.95 paper.

Carrie Chapman Catt: A Public Life, by Jacqueline Van Voris. $24.95 cloth.

Cassandra, by Florence Nightingale. Introduction by Myra Stark. Epilogue by Cynthia MacDonald. $4.50 paper.

Competition: A Feminist Taboo? edited by Valerie Miner and Helen E. Longino. Foreword by Nell Irvin Painter. $29.95 cloth, $12.95 paper.

Complaints and Disorders: The Sexual Politics of Sickness, by Barbara Ehrenreich and Deirdre English. $3.95 paper.

The Cross-Cultural Study of Women, edited by Margot I. Duley and Mary I. Edwards. $29.95 cloth, $12.95 paper.

A Day at a Time: The Diary Literature of American Women from 1764 to the Present, edited and with an introduction by Margo Culley. $29.95 cloth, $12.95 paper.

The Defiant Muse: French Feminist Poems from the Middle Ages to the Present, a bilingual anthology edited and with an introduction by Domna C. Stanton. $29.95 cloth, $11.95 paper.

The Defiant Muse: German Feminist Poems from the Middle Ages to the Present, a bilingual anthology edited and with an introduction by Susan L. Cocalis. $29.95 cloth, $11.95 paper.

The Defiant Muse: Hispanis Feminist Poems from the Middle Ages to the Present, a bilingual anthology edited and with an introduction by Angel Flores and Kate Flores. $29.95 cloth, $11.95 paper.

The Defiant Muse: Hispanic Feminist Poems from the Middle Ages to the bilingual anthology edited by Beverly Allen, Muriel Kittel, and Keala Jane Jewell, and with an introduction by Beverly Allen. $29.95 cloth, $11.95 paper.

Feminist Resources for Schools and Colleges: A Guide to Curricular Materials, 3rd edition, compiled and edited by Anne Chapman. $12.95 paper.

Get Smart: A Woman's Guide to Equality on Campus, by Montana Katz and Veronica Vieland. $29.95 cloth, $9.95 paper.

Harem Years: The Memoirs of an Egyptian Feminist, 1879–1924, by Huda Shaarawi. Translated and edited by Margot Badran. $29.95 cloth, $9.95 paper.

How to Get Money for Research, by Mary Rubin and the Business and Professional Women's Foundation. Foreword by Mariam Chamberlain. $6.95 paper.

In Her Own Image: Women Working in the Arts, edited and with an introduction by Elaine Hedges and Ingrid Wendt. $9.95 paper.

Integrating Women's Studies into the Curriculum: A Guide and Bibliography, by Betty Schmitz. $9.95 paper.

Kathe Kollwitz: Woman and Artist, by Martha Kearns, $9.95 paper.

Las Mujeres: Conversations from a Hispanic Community, by Nan Elsasser, Kyle MacKenzie, and Yvonne Tixier y Vigil. $9.95 paper.

Lesbian Studies: Present and Future, edited by Margaret Cruikshank. $9.95 paper.

Library and Information Sources on Women: A Guide to Collections in the Greater New York Area, compiled by the Women's Resources Group of the Greater New York Metropolitan Area Chapter of the Association of College and Research Libraries and the Center for the Study of Women and Society of the Graduate School and University Center of The City University of New York. $12.95 paper.

The Maimie Papers, edited by Ruth Rosen and Sue Davidson. Introduction by Ruth Rosen. $10.95 paper. *Special price for limited time:* $6.00.

Mother to Daughter, Daughter to Mother: A Daybook and Reader, selected and shaped by Tillie Olsen. $9.95 paper.

Moving the Mountain: Women Working for Social Change, by Ellen Cantarow with Susan Gushee O'Malley and Sharon Hartman Strom. $9.95 paper.

Portraits of Chinese Women in Revolution, by Agnes Smedley. Edited and with an introduction by Jan MacKinnon and Steve MacKinnon and an afterword by Florence Howe. $10.95 paper.

Reconstructing American Literature: Courses, Syllabi, Issues, edited by Paul Lauter. $10.95 paper.

Rights and Wrongs: Women's Struggle for Legal Equality, 2nd edition, by Susan Cary Nichols, Alice M. Price, and Rachel Rubin. $7.95 paper.

Salt of the Earth, screenplay by Michael Wilson with historical commentary by Deborah Silverton Rosenfelt. $10.95 paper.

Sultana's Dream and Selections from The Secluded Ones, by Rokeya Sakhawat Hossain. Edited and translated by Roushan Jahan. Afterword by Hanna Papanek. $16.95 cloth, $6.95 paper.

Turning the World Upside Down: The Anti-Slavery Convention of American Women Held in New York City, May 9–12, 1837. Introduction by Dorothy Sterling. $2.95 paper.

We That Were Young, a novel by Irene Rathbone. Introduction by Lynn Knight. Afterword by Jane Marcus. $29.95 cloth, $10.95 paper.

What Did Miss Darrington See? An Anthology of Feminist Supernatural Fiction, edited by Jessica Amanda Salmonson. Introduction by Rosemary Jackson. $29.95 cloth, $12.95 paper.

Women Composers: The Lost Tradition Found, by Diane Peacock Jezic. $29.95 cloth, $12.95 paper.

FICTION CLASSICS

Between Mothers and Daughters: Stories across a Generation, edited by Susan Koppelman. $9.95 paper.

Brown Girl, Brownstones, a novel by Paule Marshall. Afterword by Mary Helen Washington. $8.95 paper.

Call Home the Heart, a novel of the thirties, by Fielding Burke. Introduction by Alice Kessler-Harris and Paul Lauter and afterwords by Sylvia J. Cook and Anna W. Shannon. $9.95 paper.

The Changelings, a novel by Jo Sinclair. Afterwords by Nellie McKay, and Johnnetta B. Cole and Elizabeth H. Oakes; biographical note by Elisabeth Sandberg. $8.95 paper.

The Convert, a novel by Elizabeth Robins. Introduction by Jane Marcus. $8.95 paper.

Daddy Was a Number Runner, a novel by Louise Meriwether. Foreword by James Baldwin and afterword by Nellie McKay. $8.95 paper.

Daughter of Earth, a novel by Agnes Smedley. Foreword by Alice Walker. Afterword by Nancy Hoffman. $8.95 paper.

Daughter of the Hills: A Woman's Part in the Coal Miners' Struggle, a novel of the thirties, by Myra Page. Introduction by Alice Kessler-Harris and Paul Lauter and afterword by Deborah S. Rosenfelt. $8.95 paper.

Doctor Zay, a novel by Elizabeth Stuart Phelps. Afterword by Michael Sartisky. $8.95 paper.

An Estate of Memory, a novel by Ilona Karmel. Afterword by Ruth K. Angress. $11.95 paper.

Guardian Angel and Other Stories, by Margery Latimer. Afterwords by Nancy Loughridge, Meridel Le Sueur, and Louis Kampf. $8.95 paper.

I Love Myself when I Am Laughing . . . And Then Again when I Am Looking Mean and Impressive: A Zora Neale Hurston Reader, edited by Alice Walker. Introduction by Mary Helen Washington. $9.95 paper.

Leaving Home, a novel by Elizabeth Janeway. New foreword by the author. Afterword by Rachel M. Brownstein. $8.95 paper.

Life in the Iron Mills and Other Stories, by Rebecca Harding Davis. Biographical interpretation by Tillie Olsen. $7.95 paper.

The Living Is Easy, a novel by Dorothy West. Afterword by Adelaide M. Cromwell. $9.95 paper.

My Mother Gets Married, a novel by Moa Martinson. Translated and introduced by Margaret S. Lacy. $8.95 paper.

The Other Woman: Stories of Two Women and a Man, edited by Susan Koppelman. $9.95 paper.

The Parish and the Hill, a novel by Mary Doyle Curran. Afterword by Anne Halley. $8.95 paper.

Reena and Other Stories, selected short stories by Paule Marshall. $8.95 paper.

Ripening: Selected Work, 1927–1980, 2nd edition, by Meridel Le Sueur. Edited with an introduction by Elaine Hedges. $9.95 paper.

Rope of Gold, a novel of the thirties, by Josephine Herbst. Introduction by Alice Kessler-Harris and Paul Lauter and afterword by Elinor Langer. $9.95 paper.

The Silent Partner, a novel by Elizabeth Stuart Phelps. Afterword by Mari Jo Buhle and Florence Howe. $8.95 paper.

Swastika Night, a novel by Katharine Burdekin. Introduction by Daphne Patai. $8.95 paper.

This Child's Gonna Live, a novel by Sarah E. Wright. Appreciation by John Oliver Killens. $9.95 paper.

The Unpossessed, a novel of the thirties, by Tess Slesinger. Introduction by Alice Kessler-Harris and Paul Lauter and afterword by Janet Sharistanian. $9.95 paper.

Weeds, a novel by Edith Summers Kelley. Afterword by Charlotte Goodman. $8.95 paper.

The Wide, Wide World, a novel by Susan Warner. Afterword by Jane Tompkins. $29.95 cloth, $11.95 paper.

A Woman of Genius, a novel by Mary Austin. Afterword by Nancy Porter. $9.95 paper.

Women and Appletrees, a novel by Moa Martinson. Translated from the Swedish and with an afterword by Margaret S. Lacy. $8.95 paper.

Women Working: An Anthology of Stories and Poems, edited and with an introduction by Nancy Hoffman and Florence Howe. $9.95 paper.

The Yellow Wallpaper, by Charlotte Perkins Gilman. Afterword by Elaine Hedges. $4.50 paper.

Witches, Midwives, and Nurses: A History of Women Healers, by Barbara Ehrenreich and Deirdre English. $3.95 paper.

With These Hands: Women Working on the Land, edited with an introduction by Joan M. Jensen. $9.95 paper.

With Wings: An Anthology of Literature by and about Women with Disabilities, edited by Marsha Saxton and Florence Howe. $29.95 cloth, $12.95 paper.

The Woman and the Myth: Margaret Fuller's Life and Writings, by Bell Gale Chevigny. $8.95 paper.

Woman's "True" Profession: Voices from the History of Teaching, edited with an introduction by Nancy Hoffman. $9.95 paper.

Women Activists: Challenging the Abuse of Power, by Anne Witte Garland. Introduction by Frances T. Farenthold. Foreword by Ralph Nader. $29.95 cloth, $9.95 paper.

Women Have Always Worked: A Historical Overview, by Alice Kessler-Harris. $9.95 paper.

Writing Red: An Anthology of American Women Writers, 1930–1940, edited by Charlotte Nekola and Paula Rabinowitz. Foreword by Toni Morrison. $29.95 cloth, $12.95 paper.

For a free, complete backlist catalog, write to The Feminist Press at The City University of New York, 311 East 94 Street, New York, NY 10128. Send book orders to The Talman Company, Inc., 150 Fifth Avenue, New York, NY 10011. Please include $1.75 postage and handling for one book, $.75 for each additional.